Peter Benjamin is the pen name of Peter Cunningham, the author of the acclaimed Monument novels published by Harvill. He lives in Ireland.

www.petercunningham.ie

High Ride

Peter Benjamin

POCKET BOOKS

TownHouse

First published in Great Britain and Ireland by
Simon & Schuster/TownHouse, 2003
This edition published by Pocket/TownHouse, 2003
An imprint of Simon & Schuster UK Ltd,
and TownHouse Ltd, Dublin

Simon & Schuster is a Viacom company

1 3 5 7 9 10 8 6 4 2

Simon & Schuster UK Ltd
Africa House
64–78 Kingsway
London WC2B 6AH

Simon & Schuster Australia
Sydney

TownHouse Ltd
Trinity House
Charleston Road
Ranelagh
Dublin 6
Ireland

A CIP catalogue record for this book is available from the
British Library

ISBN 1-903650-25-9

Typeset by SX composing DTP, Rayleigh, Essex
Printed and bound in Great Britain by
Cox & Wyman Ltd, Reading, Berkshire

Acknowledgements

My sincere thanks to the many people who helped me with the research and writing of *High Ride*, including Lucinda Hall for her dedicated research; Dr Declan Gilsenan and Dr Andrew Rynne for their insights into medical matters; Dr Antoin Murphy, who is an expert not only in economics, but also on the layout of the golf course at Saint-Cloud; Mme Melanie Troublé, who is familiar with Rungis; and Bobby Powell for his insight into financial instruments. Also Lee Air Services; Tattersall's, Newmarket; the Savoy Hotel; Claridge's; the San Diego Convention & Visitor's Bureau; and the management of Santa Anita Racecourse. Thank you also Treasa Coady, Carol Cunningham, Jessica Cunningham and Liz Cowen for helping to make the book better.

– Peter Benjamin

Joanna

Prologue

The church bell was beating out four o'clock in the afternoon as he let himself into his house. He wiped his feet on the doormat, walked straight to the kitchen, put down his rucksack on the counter and hit the switch on the electric kettle. Then he went to the phone and checked his messages. These actions were all known, later. They were all set down in a typed report on sheets of A-4 paper and stapled to a cheap manila folder.

The house was in Ringsend, one of a long terrace that had for a hundred and fifty years housed the families of the men and women who had worked in the factories around there, but which had now been renovated and sold under the tag 'artisan'. He had lived during his fifty years in a number of houses, many of them far grander than this one; and he had lived too – if it could be called 'living' – under the stone arches of viaducts and the steel frames of railway bridges. These last memories were part of his dark side now. Sometimes they stirred in the deepest recesses of his consciousness, like vermin, reminding him of how far down he had once gone, of how near he had come. The vermin made him shudder. But he would never forget they were always there – like sentinels of the pit from which he had escaped.

The kettle boiled and he put two round tea bags into a pot then, as they soaked, opened the refrigerator. He had spent the morning doing what he knew best: down on the Curragh, looking at two-year-olds working. Evaluating each individual, the way they strode out, the way some didn't, the balanced stride, the carriage of the head, the whole, almost indefinable business of movement. Elegance incarnate. The gods had been bountiful when they had created the thoroughbred horse.

He searched for the jug of milk, frowned when he couldn't find it, for he could have sworn he put it back in that morning when he had finished what he called breakfast. Ten hours ago, and in the meantime he had eaten just a salad roll. Another legacy. Instinctively, now that he was well at last, he liked to keep his weight below a hundred and fifty pounds. Not that he would ever again ride professionally, but it was the discipline, a matter of pride to be slim and trim. And diet kept him sharp as well, kept his mind alert. He would sit down with his mug of tea and he would write up his notes on the young horses he had seen, each pen picture as accurate as a photograph.

If he could find the milk!

'Any idea where the . . .?'

He began the question, then realized that she wasn't here this evening, that she would not be back home for another twenty-four hours. He smiled as he thought of her. Then he saw a half-litre carton, already open, on the lower shelf of the fridge door. If it had been there this morning he must not have noticed it. He took it out and whitened his tea.

He was excited. Not just because he had spent a day doing what he loved most, but because of the way the other project was developing. What a story! He'd spent five months of grinding, patient work putting the details in place. Now he was nearly there. Sure, it would upset a lot of people – had they not tried to buy him off? But what a story! It would turn the racing world upside down. And his byline would be there at the head of it.

He smiled as he sipped the warm tea and took out his notebook from the rucksack. All his life he had strived on excitement. When, as a seventeen-year-old apprentice he had ridden more winners in one season than the legendary Morny Wing, the excitement had seized him. He had gone on, with hands of silk, to steer down Tattenham Hill in Epsom a colt so fragile of temperament that it had only once ever before been on a racecourse; but that day, as if born for the moment, it had surged through the tired horses, taken the famous Tattenham Corner as if on oiled tracks and strode majestically up the straight to win the Derby by three lengths. The excitement had nearly overwhelmed him. And it was excitement beyond words to have ridden to victory the favourite in the Prix de l'Arc de Triomphe. He remembered the battle over the last furlong against a filly with seven pounds less weight on her back. She had come to his boot. Her open nostrils, pink, each one anatomical perfection. He could hear, if he listened, her jockey's guttural rasps of breath as he urged her to win. The race he had then sat down and ridden had been referred to as a masterpiece in strength and tenacity. But it was when they had passed the post that he remembered best: he had let his horse run on past the stands as he stood high in the irons, one clenched fist aloft, and then, past the windmill, gently pulled the colt up and taken the congratulations of the other jockeys. There were over ten thousand people back in the stands, every one of them tingling from the victory they had just witnessed. Been part of. And he came back down the track last, alone. And every one of those people got to their feet and sent up such a tumult of noise that the colt had begun to skitter sideways on its aristocratic feet, and he just leaned forward and patted its withers, and said, 'That's a good lad, it's all right.'

He cut the memories there. He didn't want to remember what had invariably been the next part. The downside. As if what had been so perfect and beautiful then had to be destroyed. A demon had possessed him. Sometimes, when he had come in from a big victory, it seemed as if alcohol was the only way to take the unbearable shine away. He had had to do it. Each time that he had scaled the heights he had then plumbed the depths, as if he had had no choice.

He yawned as he wrote up his notes and refilled his mug. He wondered if the milk was off. He estimated it would take another two weeks before all the remaining pieces of the project fell into place. The last corroborating items of evidence. The last people to go on record. Then he would write it. He was looking forward to doing that. The same way he had looked forward to riding a good horse in a big race. He was still proud of what he'd once been: strong, with perfect balance, immaculate hands, an inbuilt Swiss clock in his head and brave as they come.

He looked at his notes made earlier that day and as he did so they began to swim out of focus. He finished the tea, stood up, blinked, sat down again. He was suddenly so tired. And lightheaded. Sinking his head down on his forearms, he closed his eyes and slipped into the zone that runs along the border of sleep.

The two men who entered the house by the front door both wore white overalls: one was small, powerful and rotund; the other a thin, tall man of sallow complexion. Both carried attaché cases. In the kitchen they put on latex gloves. The sallow-faced one went straight to the milk carton, emptied its contents down the sink, placed the empty carton in a plastic bag and put it in his attaché case. He took out from the case a fresh carton, opened it, poured half its contents down the sink and put it on the counter where the original carton had stood. The groggy figure at the counter might have been surprised by the uninvited presence in his house of two strangers but, if so, he didn't show it.

'All right, here we go then,' said the smaller man, who had taken off his jacket and rolled up his sleeves to reveal tattoos on his forearms. He had once been in an army where he had served seven years and during that time trained as a paramedic.

He caught up the light figure and transferred him easily to the kitchen table. The other man put his hand gently beneath the chin and tilted the head back. Standing at the patient's head, the paramedic dampened the end of a three-foot-long, three-millimetre naso-gastric tube and fed it up through the right nostril. When only nine inches of the tube remained he took a stethoscope from his bag, put it on, then blew air into the top of the tube whilst at the same time listening through the stethoscope to the patient's stomach.

'We're in,' he nodded, removing the stethoscope.

Their patient felt dizzy, helpless, although something insisted he should not be. He had drunk nothing – or had he? Sometimes, in the old days, he could not even remember starting. This was like the old days. He felt so relaxed.

The neck of the transparent tube was upturned and slightly splayed. The sallow-faced man fitted a miniature plastic funnel, also white and opaque, to the head of the tube. Reaching into his attaché case, he took out a bottle of rum, unscrewed the cap and with great care poured the equivalent of a double measure into the funnel.

'You'll like this, believe me,' purred the paramedic with practised smoothness.

From his supine position all the patient could bring himself to concentrate on was the man's hands. Short but strong. Pudgy, almost. His own hands, now hanging at his sides, had been what people had remarked most on in the great days. 'The best pair of hands in racing,' they had said, 'the lightest hands on God's earth.' What they had meant – and what he knew innately without having to be told – was that a conduit of meaning had flowed from his hands into the understanding of the horse. Rare at the best of times, but at the level to which he had brought it, unique. He suddenly smelled the rum.

'Be *still* – or I'll be cross!' scolded the paramedic as the patient made to struggle.

'Do not hit him!' said the other man sharply. 'No marks!'

It was, of all the drinks, the one he had done most damage with. Its smell haunted him like the perfume of a former lover. He had both adored and hated rum. It had come to be known in racing circles as *his* drink. No one else he knew could stand the stuff. And now – again. After so long. How long? He felt a stab of panic. *How long?* He couldn't think. He tried to shout out. *Lou!*

The sallow-faced man looked at his watch. He walked around the kitchen until he came to a sound system on a shelf. He peered along the row of CDs.

'Verdi?' he asked.

'*Trav,*' the paramedic said.

'You're in luck,' said the thin man.

The music filled the small room. To the chorus of 'Libiamo! Libiamo!' both men sang lustily, swaying with the tempo. Occasionally the sallow man looked at his watch and then came over and carefully fed another measure into the funnel. 'Libiamo!'

The patient heard the music as if he were inside it. Opera was something he had discovered late in life, something *else*. But he enjoyed it. 'Libiamo!'

The two men standing were enjoying the music.

'D'you like rum?' the paramedic asked his companion, whom he had met for the first time that morning in the arrivals lounge at Dublin airport.

'I don't drink,' the other man said.

'It's a funny drink, rum,' said the paramedic, one professional eye on his patient. 'Lovely in a warm place, you know, the West Indies and the like.' He threw his eyes to heaven. 'But how anyone drinks it over here is beyond me.'

The patient had been drunk so often that all the stages of the process were graven in his mind. So he knew now that he was very drunk and that very shortly he would reach oblivion.

At least an hour went by. The sallow man who had left the kitchen, now came back in the room. In the interim period he had been upstairs in the patient's workroom, carefully assembling the relevant documents and downloading the key files from the computer. Now his hand was steady as he steered the last of the bottle into the mouth of the funnel.

'Have you got everything?' the paramedic asked.

'I think so, although it may have hidden back-ups,' replied the sallow man.

The paramedic watched the last of the dark liquid slide down the transparent walls. Then he gently withdrew the tube.

'How long more?' asked the taller man.

The paramedic pursed his lips, looked at his watch. 'In another ten minutes his blood will think it's Christmas Day in Jamaica,' he said.

Something wrong was happening, but he was powerless to stop it. He could barely see now, let alone stand, or raise his arms or speak. If only Lou were here. *Lou!* He had a sense of being surrounded by people, but he could not work out how that had come to be. He wanted more rum. He craved it. Simultaneously, as so many times before, the craving brought with it a sense of deep and bitter remorse. Once more he had gone down. Down so often, he had eventually been unable to climb back up. Only Lou had

been able to get him up the last time. And now this. *Lou!*
He tried to work his mouth and ask for more.

'See?' The paramedic was smiling with the quiet
satisfaction of professional accomplishment. 'He wants
more. He's pissed as an owl.'

It was good down here, he had always known, down
here you could hide and be yourself without anyone
making demands of you. Oblivion. Non-existence. Limbo.
The music surrounded him. Even the guilt would be gone
soon. The promises. Lou's declaration that there was no
going back. He could cope with that. He was the best.

'Right, now for the tricky bit.'

That word made him fasten on it, as if he had heard
something important. With the sudden, unexpected focus
returned the unwelcome impression that something was
very wrong.

'Just hold your head still!' snapped the paramedic,
speaking above the music.

He had taken a laryngoscope, a long and thin stainless-
steel instrument ending in a flat blade with an inbuilt light.
Softly humming with the opera, standing again at the head
of his patient, he inserted the instrument into the very back
of his patient's throat. He began to lift the base of the
tongue forward. He had done this before. Sometimes this
needed force, as now. He levered. The handle of the
laryngoscope struck the front lower teeth.

'Shit!' the paramedic hissed.

He levered again and this time the epiglottis, the valve
at the back of the throat, folded neatly over the blade of the
instrument. Guided by the light of the laryngoscope and
taking great care not to tear or mark the mucosal lining of
the pharynx, the paramedic now fed the transparent tube
he had recently used down between the two vocal cords
and into the trachea.

'Ready?' he murmured, smiling as one of his favourite arias filled the room.

'How much?' asked the other man, who had opened a second bottle of rum.

'A nice full glass would be fine, thanks very much,' the paramedic replied.

As if an electrical circuit in his brain had suddenly surged alive and in the process delivered horrifying but vital information, the patient understood what was being done to him.

'Christ, hold him!' the thin man cried above the music.

The patient was trying to twist away his head, but the paramedic's strong arms held him as if in a vice.

'Do hurry up.'

'I am trying!' the thin man said and poured.

He realized that when they said there comes a point when your whole life passes before you they were right. The soprano's voice filled his head. He could see the tilt of the bottle and the rum being poured in. He began to choke. He saw a stable yard, clean and swept, and heard hooves, and smelled hay. He saw a stable hand pushing a wheelbarrow of hay with a small child sitting on top of it. Himself. No air, all of a sudden. And something happening inside his head. He heard people cheering, felt the exhilaration of a ton of thoroughbred muscle and blood beneath him. Adda boy. *Yes!*

'That's it.'

The paramedic withdrew the tube, then stepped back. The face of the man on the table was puce. He tried to draw a breath. Coughed weakly. His whole chest seemed to be involved. He rolled sideways and fell to the floor, doubled, gasping. Then there was a huge and involuntary stiffening of the jaw and his whole body quivered. The eyes looked directly at the paramedic for just a moment. Then his pupils appeared to roll back in his head and his eyes slowly closed.

The two men spent just another five minutes in the house. They left the rum bottles, one of them empty the other mostly full, and a glass on the counter. They packed their equipment, clicked shut their attaché cases, then, having removed the CD and turned off the sound system, went out by the front door just as the church bell was dealing out the Angelus. They crossed the Liffey by way of the East Link toll bridge and drove up through the North Strand. Thirty minutes later in Dublin airport's departure area, they shook hands. The sallow-faced man was getting a flight to London, the paramedic to Amsterdam.

'Nice working with you,' the paramedic said.

'My pleasure,' said the other man and walked through the gate.

In the waiting area, on a huge screen, Leeds was playing AC Milan. The paramedic sat down and watched it for fifteen minutes. He almost missed his flight.

Part One

1

I looked out of the plane window and saw the brown starkness of mainland China plunging into the blueness of the China Sea. I was miserable. In another ten hours I would be in Sydney.

I could tell you that what pissed me off most in being on a first-class flight to the other end of the world was having to leave behind three deals that were just coming to the boil very nicely, thank you, for Grace Equity, the company of which I was chairman; or that in mid-August I got jumpy if I wasn't west of Galway with a fly rod in my hand; or that flying long distances, even first-class, held no appeal for me any longer – and all these things would be partly true. Neither would I be exaggerating if I told you that whenever I let my heart rule my head, as was the case here, I invariably ended up knee-deep in what Hannelore called *shize*, and thus I had this very bad *shize* feeling about what had started out as a favour for a business colleague, but had now evolved into something far deeper and more serious. But to be absolutely honest what was most on my mind as we tunnelled down through the ever-depleting ozone layer towards Antarctica that first week of August was the feeling that I had fucked up with Hanny.

When people describe a woman as being too young for the man she's seeing/screwing/married to, they're not being kind. What they're really saying is: Hello there, we're watching you, and boy are we looking forward to seeing you fall flat on your smug face when she walks, as inevitably she will. You can tell yourself all you like that the bastards are jealous of the fact that you're with this five-foot-ten goddess, any of whose limbs they'd do jail for ten exclusive minutes with, but they've laid a guilt rap on you all the same so that when the problems begin to pop – and boy, do they ever! – you begin, or I begin, to wonder, maybe I *am* too old for her, maybe *that's* the problem here!

I'd already drunk most of one bottle of Bollinger, which fact alone put me in the category of Very Low IQ, since consuming high quantities of alcohol on long-haul flights was only something morons did, according to Hanny. But I'm stubborn and I like Bollinger, so if that makes me a moron, I thought, raising my glass and toasting the sky outside the window, so be it. Hanny is thirty and I'm not yet forty-seven, which may sound to you like splitting hairs, but at thirty-nine-thousand feet and going into the abyss, so to speak, it was suddenly relevant. She worked for a German media outfit and was now based in a flat in Jervis Street with a psychotic budgerigar. I lived in Howth. Much of the time when Hanny was in town she brought her budgie out and stayed with me and so I got my daily ration of Teutonic beauty, blue eyes that I associated with Nordic forests, skin like honey, legs that went on for ever – you get the picture. We had been through a lot together, good times and bad, and had at last, we thought, found each other; but then we kept losing each other again, it seemed. Not just careless – stupid at the high end of the moron scale as far as I was concerned. Had I done enough to keep her? The very use of the word 'enough' made me cringe, for I could just hear her saying, 'Joe, I want more than just *enough*!' That would be followed, most likely, by something airborne coming my way. Women. That was the problem. It always is the problem, it seems. High finance is a doddle compared to women.

She had gone to Germany for three weeks to 'work it out', which meant that, despite what we might have said, neither of us in reality was sure of the way ahead. Part of

her, the German part that you find in camper vans in all the
world's most inaccessible places, that part of Hanny loved
Ireland's wild unpredictability, which, I think, included me;
but the cool central European part of her, the part I had
sometimes unwisely reminded her should be on top of a
Panzer tank gunning for Moscow, that part had reservations. And I began to question my wisdom in having a
relationship with a woman of Hanny's age.

When Hanny had been two weeks in Munich, during
which we had spoken by phone at least once a day, what
had always happened then happened: we began to miss
each other to a degree that exceeded our mutual circum-
spection. Hanny spoke about coming back. I told her this
time we'd make it permanent. Plans were laid, including a
week in Renvyle, lazy days in boats fishing for brown
trout, long mornings in bed. She arrived back on a
Monday evening and on the Tuesday morning I left for
Sydney. That's what I mean by fucking up. When it came
down to it, I was the greatest all-time Olympian gold-
medal fucker-upper to compete in that highly competitive
and ever-crowded sport.

2

The basis for this latest dislocation to my life had been laid almost three months before. I'd got a call one morning in early May from Sam Landy. He was one of my chief investors, a man I'd actually met only once, an old guy in his late sixties who lived in New South Wales, Australia. When I say 'one of my investors', I should explain that Grace Equity, the company I started some years back and modestly called after myself, is a sort of respectable financial predator, an outfit that lives in the swamps and jungles of the world of high finance keeping its eyes peeled for any supple young impalas of the business community that may wander innocently into the clearing, where-upon Grace Equity leaps out and, having shagged them, then devours them. That's a joke, of course – or almost completely untrue. We invest in other companies, which by definition means that those companies need our invest-ment. We pick and choose, a bit like vultures, depending on your point of view. I started off with a hundred grand in cash and nowadays we never look at anything less than a $5 million deal. And, of course, I always use other people's money, which is one of the cardinal rules of investing. And that is how I became involved with Sam Landy – or, to be accurate, with the investment company he had used in the States to make his investment in Grace.

Landy's wealth was second generation. His father had been a friend of Winston Churchill, Beaverbrook, you name them – the old man had been a fixer, tough as nails. Developed land in Australia, lived six months of the year there. Bought property by the street in London. Sam, his son, was a modern businessman whose reputation was for being ultra tough but fair. Which translated means he'd eat you alive without salt, but that's business. He had married an English society heiress, an elegant woman by her photographs, Mrs Elizabeth Landy. She had died of cancer a couple of years before. Landy's great wealth came from property and shrewd investments, particularly in the computer industry. And from horses. His stud farms in Kentucky and in Slow Creek, New South Wales, stood some of the world's top stallions, by all accounts. Epic money was involved. Bloodstock, I had learned when I did my checks, occupied the central place in Sam Lundy's life.

As far as Grace Equity was concerned, at that point in time Landy was a pivotal investor: in January we had pitched a $50 million rights issue to our shareholders and by early May all of them, Landy included, had agreed to run with it. Timing was everything since we had a number of choice investments lined up, which was why we needed the money in the first place. Translated into cash, Landy would now be shelling out a further $20 million in addition to the $10 million he had already invested. He was, not to labour the point, important to me.

'Joe, I need a favour,' he said that day when he rang and, of course, I said fire right ahead. People like this normally ring me when they want tickets for Lansdowne Road or a table in Patrick Guilbaud's or some other such seeming impossibility, although Landy had never come to Ireland since I'd started dealing with him. Apparently years ago he'd made the trip every November when he used to host a major charity bash at a pheasant shoot in County Wicklow.

'A friend of mine has been screwed,' Landy said.

Just because someone pitches in big to your company doesn't mean you have to nanny him and his friends; but then there was the question of the rights issue so, let's face it, everyone needs a shoulder to cry on.

'I'm sorry to hear that, Sam,' I said, going into nanny mode. 'What's the problem?'

'His name is Ito,' Landy said. 'Tom Ito. We do a lot of business together in Asia. It seems Tom made some horse investments in Ireland with a man called Guy Steer.'

Now, I had heard of Guy Steer. He was one of those businessmen, like Marc Rich, who were somewhat notorious. But notorious for what, I was unclear. A Canadian, I now remembered, a miner's son. Owned a lot of racehorses, of that I was aware too, but not owning a racecourse, after staying out of jail, had always been high on the list of my ambitions. I liked horses and as a kid I'd learned to ride and been good at it. I'd also liked the whole bit that comes from hanging around with horses, but the people attached to thoroughbred racing had always seemed to me to be idiots wearing stupid hats whose accents made my neck hair stand up.

'I've heard of Steer,' I said. 'A tough customer, by all accounts.'

'I've heard that too,' Landy said, 'but this is outrageous.'

It now appeared that a couple of years before Tom Ito, Landy's buddy, had trusted Steer to buy him some expensive yearlings in Ireland. A partnership deal, Landy told me. Ito had never been to Ireland and knew no one there, so when the investment went badly wrong, as it just had, Tom Ito turned to his pal, Sam Landy, to see what could be done.

'How much is involved?' I asked.

'Three million US,' Landy said. 'Look, I've seen all the correspondence and it's as plain as day to anyone who knows anything about horses that this man Steer screwed Tom Ito blind.'

'Why doesn't Ito just sue Steer?'

'He will – when he gets all the evidence. That's why I'm calling you. I want you to bring the documentation to a man in Dublin and ask him to investigate the case. He's the best when it comes to horses. Just tell him you're acting on behalf of Ito.'

It didn't seem too arduous a task to perform for my biggest investor.

'That's all?' I asked.

'That's all,' Sam Landy said.

I said, 'Fine. Send the stuff on. Who's the man?'

Sam Landy said, 'Tricky Dawson.'

3

'Could you repeat that?' I said.

'Dawson,' Landy said. 'Tricky Dawson.'

I had thought that's what he had said. I felt suddenly as if someone had slipped me a non-alcoholic drink.

'Sam,' I said, 'that's difficult. There's a personal connection.'

'I'm aware of that,' he said.

I didn't like that either. 'Then you'll understand if I decline.'

'I'm not asking a lot here, Joe,' said Landy and his voice rose. 'Just that you brief the fellow.'

'Problem is, the fellow in question is sort of like family.'

'You're not asking him to do anything wrong.'

'It's still difficult, Sam.'

'Joe, I wouldn't ask you if I didn't need this. Tom Ito has done me big favours in his day.'

'Why don't you ask Dawson yourself?'

'Because Tricky Dawson wouldn't do this for me. He and I don't see eye to eye any more. Look, we used to be close, like brothers, but that was years ago. But he's the best man in Ireland to find out this information. Tom Ito is willing to pay Tricky. Ten thousand down and a further twenty when he delivers. This is important to me, Joe.'

Well, that left me in little doubt as to my options – that's if I wanted Sam to stay on side for the rights issue. So I said, 'I need to think about this, Sam.'

'I'm going to Tokyo in three days to meet Tom Ito,' Landy said firmly. 'I'd like your answer before I leave.'

He hung up and I was left looking out the window at two seagulls fighting over the remains of a dead cat.

Tricky Dawson had been a top-class, international jockey, then a trainer, but his career had ended abruptly – in the gutter. Dawson was a lush. The boozer in him had eventually conquered and killed the world-class athlete. His marriage broke up, he lost everything. For the best part of a decade he had vanished into the vapours of the Stygian world of drink and drugs, emerging only in the last four years as a reformed man: on the dry, a freelance turf writer and living in Ringsend in a new relationship. The woman who had changed his life was a freelance sports photographer named Lou Halpin. The reason I knew all this was because Lou Halpin was my sister.

Families, after women, are one of life's most impenetrable mysteries. I have one brother, John, whom I adore and who lives in New York; and two sisters, Bess, who is married and lives in South Africa, and Lou. There's nothing rational or reasonable about the way in which some people in families don't get on. From the start Lou and I fell into this irrational category. She was younger than me by a few years. Whenever we sat down together as a family for a meal, she and I could not be put together. I'd end up teasing her, she'd end up in tears. She could always get under my skin, yet I'd have killed anyone who laid a finger on her. Why? That's the mystery, I suppose. I found Lou neurotic, she found me selfish – I could trade insults with Lou until one of us simply fainted from exhaustion. So we grew up and I went away to the States and when I came back, although we had both matured and could behave like civilized adult siblings, I discovered that deep down we both still regarded each other with the same mutual suspicion. We had a lot of work to do, but for my part, above all, I wanted to get on with this pretty, bright girl. I loved her as my sister. I was dismayed when she got married to a bum called Halpin, who treated her appallingly, but the one time I tried to talk to her about it she told me, thanks, it was none of my business. So I didn't ask again. Then she left Halpin and made a career for herself as a sports photographer, a very good one too, and the next thing I heard she was living with this man twenty years older than her, the once famous Tricky Dawson. I'd never met him and I'd not set eyes on Lou since we'd both met at an aunt's funeral some years before. An absence I regretted, but that's the way it goes. Now my principal investor wanted me to front an approach to her live-in boyfriend. You can imagine why I didn't want to get involved.

I was going through a period of relative equilibrium with Hanny, insofar as she and I were living in my house and I was ministering to her every need and she was responding with warmth and enthusiasm, so much so that it left me wondering how I could ever have imagined that women might be complex. I lived near Howth in a nice Edwardian house whose bedroom windows overlooked the sea. I'd bought it from the executor of an old lady who'd lived there for nearly a hundred years; I'd retained all the old windows and fireplaces and done as little tarting up as possible. A local lady, Stella, came in three times a week and kept order. Every morning before breakfast Hanny and I walked down the garden and out on to the beach and when there was a low tide we dug cockles and brought them in and boiled them up and ate them in bed, looking out at Ireland's Eye. Tough life.

Grace Equity had moved from Temple Bar into the Irish Financial Services Centre a while back, and at the same time I had withdrawn from the day-to-day running of the firm, delegating much of it to Tim Tully, who had started out with me as financial point man. The arrangement was working fine. I went into Dublin two or three days a week and left Tim to get on with the nuts and bolts. This was meant to leave me free to pursue the more dimensional aspects of my life and in the process to work out the answers to such questions as 'Who Am I?' and 'Where Am I Going?' I sometimes thought, however, that only people with too much money wallowed in such self-indulgent crap, and that the net result in my case was that instead of getting on with making even more money, I frequently found myself up to my neck in issues that any sane observer would have told me to avoid.

In this case I hoped that Landy might have the decency to reflect on my obvious reservations around Tricky Dawson and my sister. I hoped that, in the few days after we spoke, some other aberration would rear its ugly head and distract him, like the varnish on the deck of his yacht, or the next type of jet he was thinking of buying, or maybe a project to buy the island of Tasmania. Money is a pain, that's for sure – and the more you have, the bigger the pain. Not that anyone's complaining, of course.

But the reality was that people like Sam Landy never just melt away – in fact obstinacy is one of the prerequisites for being rich. This I knew. I was both rich and obstinate. So I called Mick Davitt and suggested lunch.

4

Mick Davitt and myself and another friend called Harry Quinlan, who according to himself ran the Department of Foreign Affairs, played golf now and then or sat around drinking pints and talking about playing golf. We had known each other for a long time. Mick was both a cop and a barrister. Nowadays he worked exclusively for the CAB, the Criminal Assets Bureau. In his early forties, a big man with a baby's face and hair like black squid, Mick had preserved from his younger days a kind of smoked salmon socialism, but socialism nonetheless. With drink taken, he was a fierce advocate of the underprivileged. He was also a lunatic horse punter, which was why, following Landy's request, he was the first person I thought of. We sat at a banquette table in the Unicorn, a restaurant to which Mick made the journey up from the CAB at least twice a week. Mick caught the girl's eye and we both ordered *penne* followed by sole. He sniffed and sipped the Piedmont white, nodded assent and munched a long stick of Italian crispbread.

'How's that nice girl?' he asked.

Mick was crazy about Hanny. I knew the next question, so I headed him off.

'And no, we haven't yet agreed to give you all a big day out. Sorry, but there it is for the moment.'

Mick shook his head. 'You're a complete eegit, you know that, don't you?'

'I know that.'

We talked about the state of the nation and the state of the roads and whatever the latest political scandals were. Mick knew everything that was moving in Dublin: every couple of months we met like this and I topped up on the low life. When we had finished the *penne*, I told him that I had been asked by someone to approach Tricky Dawson to investigate a possible horse fraud.

'The brother-in-law, so to speak,' Mick said and his eyes became inscrutable.

'I hear she's happy,' I said.

Mick was well aware of my non-relationship with Lou; during her difficult marriage I had confided in him my worries for her safety and he had advised me to mind my own business. He'd been right.

'Tricky Dawson was some jockey,' Mick said. 'Arguably the greatest Ireland has ever produced. Writes some good stuff too. He was the first to write in detail about that Landy horse disqualification in France.'

I felt an unpleasant sensation tap-dance its way through my digestive system.

'What Landy disqualification?' I asked.

'Sam Landy is a big horse owner from the old school,' Mick began.

'I know. He's also an investor in Grace Equity. He's the person who has asked me to approach Tricky.'

Mick made a face. 'Landy's been losing all the big races to new money in recent times,' he said, 'but a few years ago a horse of his won the French Prix Lupin – only to be disqualified afterwards when a prohibited substance, a drug, in other words, was found in the horse's piss. Landy went ballistic, said he knew nothing about it. Withdrew all his horses from training in France.'

'And Tricky Dawson wrote about this?' I said.

'Yes, about the likelihood of whether or not Landy really knew – you see, he'd known Landy well from the old days; he rode for Landy, then trained for him – but there's certainly no love lost between them now. Tricky

savaged Landy in his piece. Said the likelihood was that
Landy knew about the doping. It was a real hatchet job,
if I remember. Not that it mattered a shite, of course,
since Landy's horse had had the race taken off him
anyway.'

I wondered why Landy would choose, of all people,
someone who had savaged him to investigate such a
sensitive matter as the alleged fraud on Tom Ito; but then,
I reasoned, people like Landy have necks as tough as a
jockey's bollocks. As a portable table was put beside us and
a deft waitress began relieving two large sole of their
bones, I explained to Mick everything Landy had told me
about Tom Ito and Guy Steer.

'Landy's smart,' Mick said when I had finished. 'Tricky
is just the sort of person who'd find out the low-down on
who screwed who in a horse deal here in Ireland.'

We ate our sole and salads and finely cut, crisply fried
potatoes.

'Who exactly is Guy Steer?' I asked.

Mick sat back thoughtfully. 'An Anglicized Canadian,
his father was some kind of a claim jumper out in the
boondocks, left his only son a bundle of worthless deeds –
worthless until Steer found, literally, a gold mine on one of
the claims. That was twenty years ago. The story is hazy.
Was it really his claim or did it belong to a neighbour? Steer
sold out for a fortune to one of the big mineral companies,
moved to London, became a trader in commodities, made
ten fortunes. Then sometime in the late-eighties he
discovered horses. Since then he has become the dominant
player in the market.'

Mick drained his glass then described a global, com-
mercial, thoroughbred breeding operation with tentacles in
every corner of racing. Steer employed the best judges of
horseflesh, the best agents. His top managers had become

millionaires themselves through their participation in the shares of various stallions.

'He's received like royalty wherever he goes in the racing world,' Mick said. 'Keeps permanent suites in half a dozen top hotels in different countries. He's got a yacht the length of Grafton Street, a jet, he's married to a top model. He's apparently got this aura about him that makes people want to die for him.'

'Sounds like someone to avoid,' I remarked.

'There have been rumours,' Mick said, 'some of them not a million miles from what your man Landy is alleging.' He shrugged. 'But the horse business is like a nightclub – everyone there is trying to screw someone else, so who gives a fuck if one multi-millionaire is being shafted by another? Boo-fucking-hoo.'

'I'll drink to that,' I said.

'In that case we need another bottle,' Mick said and made signals to the effect. He continued, 'Apart from Landy, Steer's main opposition nowadays comes from the Sultan of Tamil. We're talking despot there. Money comes out of holes in the ground somewhere in the Far East. Flies around the world in his own 747, has absolutely no concept of the value of money – which makes him the wildest of wild cards when it comes to buying horseflesh. Steer and he go head to head at the sales for all the most expensive yearlings. You know, see your five million and raise you two.'

The wine always loosened Mick up. He put a flame to a long cheroot and blew a zephyr of smoke over my head.

'I've always avoided the horse business,' I said.

Mick gave me a long, cool look. 'I'm a punter,' he said, 'so I understand that racing is largely unregulated. I mean, most people wouldn't recognize a good horse if it was giving them a blow job. So, in that respect, the horse business is still a bit like the Wild West.'

I felt exactly the same misgivings about approaching Tricky Dawson as I had when Landy had first asked me to, except that now, following Mick's description of Guy Steer, I felt them tenfold. And yet, if I was going to refuse Landy, I was going to have to do so without putting our rights issue at risk. I now shared these problems with Mick.

'Landy's even authorized me to pay Tricky ten grand up front and to promise another twenty on delivery of the information,' I said in conclusion.

'A lot of money,' Mick said. 'And I'm sure Tricky Dawson could do with it. Maybe you should talk to him and let him make up his own mind.'

I thought of Lou and as always got the shivers. 'I don't want to walk him into something,' I said.

'Look, if there's one man who knows the horse business inside out and can take care of himself, then that person is Tricky Dawson,' Mick said. 'I saw him in action in the Phoenix Park when I was thirteen. He was riding a filly in a one-mile handicap. Sixteen runners. I had a pound on him – on the nose at twelve-to-one.'

Mick sat back, glowing nicely and drooling blue smoke.

'I've never seen a ride like it. He was everywhere on that filly – out over her ears one moment, the next back over her tail. He won by a short head. Three strides past the post, he wasn't in the first six.' Mick chuckled again. 'Anyone who can do that can look after himself with these rich wankers who think they know everything about racing but in fact know fuck all.'

I thought of having to go into the IFSC and tell Tim Tully that Sam Landy was pulling out of our rights issue.

'There's a difference between riding a race and

investigating high-level fraud,' I said. 'He was once a jockey, but now he's just another hack.'

Mick shook his head. 'Another hack my arse. He was like a throwback to the Celts. He was part horse. Rode them bareback as a child, slept with them, talked to them, lifted up their feet, opened their mouths and put his fingers in, squeezed their udders, washed their tails. A hack? What hack has mucked out stables since he was ten and tacked up horses beyond counting? What hack knows what it's like to ride winners for millionaires? Or writes as an insider? Get out of here! When Tricky was up there, boy, turning into the straight, he was a genius! He was fucking Cúchulainn!'

Mick warbled on about horses until it was too late for either of us to bother going back to the office. I took a cab home and sobered up over scrambled eggs and a glass of Pinot Noir. Then at nine, on cue, Landy rang.

'Have you thought about that, Joe?' he asked.

'I've thought about it.'

'And . . .?'

'Sam, is Guy Steer dangerous?' I asked, without fully understanding why I had asked.

'Dangerous?' Landy laughed, or coughed, I wasn't clear which. 'He's devious, I believe – but hardly dangerous. He's not Mafia, Joe.'

So I told Landy somewhat curtly, yes, I'd be his messenger boy and to send on the stuff. And two days later the Fedex van pulled up and the man brought in the box which, if it had been any bigger might well have contained a fucking horse. That evening I had a quick flick through the contents – it was all sales catalogues and photocopies of bank statements. And then I rang Lou.

5

When I was eight and Lou was an awkward girl of five, I was asked one day to go and bring her home from a birthday party. I walked from our house the best part of a mile to where her friend lived. I remember the day well: it was in May, the cherry blossom was everywhere on the street, the sun, which had been hiding for six months, was suddenly drenching down. I pushed through the gate of the house in which the party was taking place and rang the doorbell.

My mother had asked me to fetch Lou because I was standing there doing nothing; she probably had forgotten the fact that a week before Lou had reported to my father that I smoked and that the subsequent raid on my bedroom and the thrashing that followed – the old man was a physical education instructor; tobacco was the ultimate evil – were still festering in my mind. Lou emerged from the house. We set out for home, Lou skipping ahead in a paper hat, her face flushed from eating sweets and cake.

Kids of eight and five don't have worked-out relationships for disliking one another, but in our case it seemed it had always been a case of opposing personalities. Perhaps I resented her place in the family's affections – who knows? Perhaps she saw me as an obstacle to her being the conqueror of all affection in our house.

The kerb edge at the end of the road was deep and sharp. One of the reasons I had been sent in the first place was that my mother feared that Lou would fall from the footpath and hurt herself.

'Make sure you hold her hand when you cross the road,' I was told. 'She's always falling.'

I saw the end of the road loom up and saw her skipping on. I knew exactly what was going to happen. I also knew that by hanging back and not actively restraining her, I was indulging a baser side of my nature. Lou came to the end of the footpath, took one skip too many and tumbled face first on to the road.

She skinned both her knees and her nose; but if there had been a car coming she could well have been killed. Instantly, I regretted what I had done, or had not done. More, I felt a surge of affection I would not have thought possible for this now wailing little girl. I picked her up and brought her home, bleeding, and didn't hear the end of it for two weeks; but that wasn't the worst part. What hurt me most was the realization that I had failed in my duty, than in wishing to see Lou suffer I had taken a horrendous risk and that my own sense of self-esteem had been badly lamed. And, in the way that children can sense the centre of good, Lou too realized that something ignoble had taken place at her expense. But she saw my regret too, I believe, and in time rose above her own feelings to join in a sort of truce. I never teased her again. We understood each other better from that time, as if seeing each other through the lens of what had happened.

It was amazing now how thirty-nine years later I still remembered that old incident. But even after thirty-nine years, I was pretty certain that Lou still did not yet fully trust me.

A few days later I found myself in Ringsend, a traditional working-class residential area on the south shores of the River Liffey, only a couple of miles from the centre of Dublin. Ringsend grew up at first around the fishing and boat cargo business and then developed in the early and mid-twentieth century when glass-bottle and other

industries were established there. Nowadays all the
industries have gone and the artisan houses of Ringsend's
workers find themselves side by side with blocks of
modern flats with underground car parks accessed by
electronic entrance gates.

Tricky Dawson's house was one of the old, two-storey
dwellings, a hundred yards from the church. I parked my
car, rang the bell and the door was opened by a woman
who, for a moment, I did not recognize.

'Lou?'

'Well, well. Joe,' she said.

I kissed her cheeks. I'd forgotten how pretty she was,
but I had not been prepared for her prettiness to have
become so weather-beaten or for the fact that the little
sister I remembered had sort of shrivelled up into a still
pretty, but nonetheless wizened, middle-aged woman.

She said, 'This is certainly a surprise. After you called I
asked myself, does he want to buy Ringsend? Or maybe,
just this street.'

We laughed, but it was extraordinary how she could
conjure up all the old vapours as if from nowhere.

'None of the things you mention, actually,' I said,
managing to grin and taking her remarks as just old sibling
banter.

'Come on in, Joe,' Lou said. She stood back and smiled.
'I'm really glad to see you.'

I stepped into the short hall and then into the living
room overlooking the street.

'Not what you're used to, from what I hear,' she said
quietly.

'Never believe what you hear,' I said.

The two chairs and the sofa were worn and shabby. A
couple of faded pictures on the wall showed someone
riding a racehorse. The wallpaper had been put up in a

previous era and even the most judicious use of throw rugs could not disguise the fact that the carpet was threadbare.

'We're getting it together,' she said, 'but it takes time. Cup of tea?'

'That'd be great, thanks.'

'I'll tell Tricky you're here,' she said. 'He works from a room upstairs.'

'Lou.'

She looked at me.

I said, 'Look, I just want you to know that I'm sorry we don't know each other better. Maybe one of us should have lifted the phone – who knows? Whatever happened in the past, let's put it behind us and get to know each other before it's too late.'

She closed her eyes and leaned against the jamb of the door. Her brown hair was going grey; she wore it long and tied in a ponytail. She had on a shirt that was several sizes too big for her and blue jeans.

'Why do you want to see Tricky?' she asked.

'Because there's a job he might be interested in.'

'And that's it?'

'That's it.'

'I agree with what you say, it's silly to carry on the past,' she said. 'It'll take time, but I'm willing to give it a try if you are.'

'I'm willing.'

She stuck her hand out and I took and shook it. Then I put my arm around her neck and kissed her on the cheek, just as a man with the most piercing blue eyes I had ever seen materialized in front of me.

'I turn my back on her for a moment,' he said, 'and she's off with another man.'

'I'm Joe,' I said and we shook.

'Tricky.' All the other aspects of him, so to speak, such

as the fact that his face was worn and scuffed like old leather or that he was tiny in size, were subsidiary to his eyes. 'Would you like some tea?'

'I was going to bring some in,' Lou said.

'The kettle is on in the kitchen,' Tricky said.

I said, 'The kitchen is just fine.'

I walked in behind him along the short hall. There's something about athletes that's intrinsic: the way they move, or glide, an easiness and economy of the physical. This man had it and the result was to make his size seem irrelevant. We went back into a small kitchen. All the wall space was taken up with shelves stuffed with books about horses and horse sales catalogues. On a peg beside a steep staircase, cameras hung from straps. Tricky spooned tea into a pot and Lou put out milk and three mugs.

'You don't take sugar – right?' she said.

'Good memory. No sugar,' I said.

'I've heard a lot about you from Lou,' Tricky said, perching on a stool.

'Not as much as I've heard about you.'

He waved his hand dismissively. 'That's all over and gone, it's the past. This is what I live for now.' He reached over and gathered Lou by her waist into him. 'I don't know if you realize it, Joe, but this sister of yours is a real professional.'

'Stop it,' she said.

'I won't stop it,' he said and held her tighter. 'You'll find her in every weather, curled up inside the rails near the winning post, looking for – and mostly getting – that unique and never-to-be-repeated frame in the closing stages which sums everything up. Right?'

'It's nothing like as professional as the people I'm photographing,' Lou said.

'Oh, I don't know,' Tricky said. 'I always thought it was

the horses were the real stars and that's the truth. It's intelligence that makes the best of them great.'

Lou leaned over and kissed him.

'What can I do for you, Joe?' Tricky asked and they both looked at me.

So I gave Tricky a line of spoof about someone I didn't know called Ito, and how he had been screwed by someone I didn't know called Steer in a business I knew little about, namely horse racing; and the deeper I went the less I liked it, which is what happens when you dig yourself a hole.

'Tom Ito has given me a load of stuff,' I said. 'He wants to expose Steer. I couldn't think of anyone better to become involved than someone who writes about racing for a living.'

Tricky scratched his head. 'I don't know,' he said. 'It sounds like you want me to become involved in a personal vendetta. I mean, I understand the way Steer operates, but this is a game for big boys, you know.'

'Ito's willing to pay a fee,' I said. 'Ten grand up front. Twenty on delivery. I have all the documentation out in the car.'

Tricky winced. 'What's your interest?'

'Tom Ito and I are connected through business,' I said, sticking for all my worth to the technical truth.

Tricky poured himself more tea. 'Racing's not a sport any more,' he observed. 'Maybe it never was, but nowadays there's too much fucking money washing around.' He spoke with an edge of bitterness, as if he felt some of the money should have washed his way. 'Colts that win classics become stallions with multi-million pound price tags. It's still called the sport of kings – which makes me laugh when you think about you've just told me. If this is what kings get up to, then I'm glad I'm a commoner.'

As we chatted, Tricky came across as a man who had

been badly injured by life and who was still licking his
wounds. I kind of liked him, though. And although what I
knew about racing could be written on the back of a beer
mat, I found myself regretting that I'd never seen him in
action. Lou never took her eyes from me.

'What's in it for you, Joe?' she asked suddenly.

'I'm doing someone important a favour,' I said quietly,
'that's what business is all about. However, it's completely
up to Tricky whether he wants to run with this or not.
There may be a big story here, I have no idea. I'm just the
messenger boy.'

'That was never your style, Joe,' Lou said. 'As I
remember it, you were the one who had messengers
running around for him.'

We'd come as far as we were going to. I stood up. 'It's
up to you,' I said to Tricky.

He looked at me curiously, and for a moment all the
failures of his life were there on his wizened but still
somehow youthful face, and he looked sad.

He said, 'How about you leave me the box, I have a
look at it and then decide?' He shrugged. 'I'd love to see
some of these big bastards crash.'

So that's exactly what I did. We went out together to my
car, I opened the boot, Tricky Dawson lifted out the Fedex
box, which contained, in addition to the documents that
had come in it, an envelope with a banker's draft for
$10,000. We shook hands. Lou was standing just outside
the hall door. It was, I decided, chemical: she and I were
just not meant to get on as human beings, and never had
been.

''Bye Lou.'

'Joe.'

We kissed goodbye, then at the last moment, she hugged
me close.

'I've always wanted to get to know my big brother a lot better,' she whispered.

'This is where we start,' I said.

The last I saw of them was Tricky backing in through the door of his house, the box in his hands, and Lou closing the door behind them. I was glowing. We had turned back the past.

6

A couple of weeks went by and other things more important than horses and ex-jockeys took up my time and my mind. Then one afternoon in the IFSC I picked up the phone.

'It's your sister,' said the girl on the switchboard.

I had to think. I had all but forgotten my trip to Ringsend and about Sam Landy's problems.

'Lou?'

'Look Joe,' Lou said in her very direct way, 'whatever you've involved Tricky in, I want you to get him out of it immediately.'

I asked, 'What's going on?'

She let out an exasperated sigh. 'I'm sure you know far more about what's going on that I do.'

'I suggest you tell me.'

'I'm worried. Tricky's under a lot of pressure and I have a fair idea it all stems from whatever it is you walked him into.'

'I offered him a job,' I protested. 'He took it. He got paid ten grand.'

'He won't talk to me about it,' Lou said. 'He's awake at night. This thing is eating him.'

'What do you want me to do?' I asked, feeling myself sink into the old guilt like quicksand.

'I want you to terminate the job. I want you to tell him that Ito or whoever he is has changed his mind. That the final payment of twenty thousand is not going to happen. I don't care what you tell him, but I want this thing you started stopped.'

Despite myself, I asked, 'Why?'

'Why?' Lou's laugh was more like a cry of pain. 'Jesus do you have to have chapter and verse? Tricky is not up for this kind of pressure. Is that enough reason?'

'What pressure? Tell me?'

'He's out late, meeting lowlife types who sell information. He's getting calls at two in the morning. He's poked his nose into something on your behalf and now I want you to pull him out.'

'Give me his mobile number,' I said.

'You'll do it?'

'Yes. Give me his number.' I wrote it down. 'Let's meet,' I said, remembering the promise with which our last meeting had ended.

'We'll meet when this is over,' she said and hung up.

And I did call the number, but got Tricky's voicemail and left a message. And then events took over. The next morning at six I flew to Rome for a two-day round of meetings. There was big money involved and I get focused in these situations. On the second day my mobile phone rang. I normally diverted it when I travelled, but in this case we also had a deal in the final stages of due diligence back home and I was anxious enough to want to stay in touch. I was standing outside the Hassler Hotel at the top of the Spanish Steps when the phone rang.

'No names,' a man said.

I recognized the voice, but couldn't place it.

'We met in Ringsend. I got your message.'

Then I knew. But why this 'no names' routine? My guilt and misgiving surged.

I said, 'Good. Look, I wanted to tell you: this deal is off, ok? I want you to back off.'

'I can't do that now.'

'You've got to. Look, I'm away, but I want to meet you and explain,' I said.

There was a beat of silence.

'OK,' he said, 'but ring me when you get back.'

I caught something in his voice.

I asked, 'Is everything all right?'

He said, 'This thing is getting very hot.'

That was it. Rome went to three days, we signed the papers and became the proud owners of 20 per cent of a company that did something very clever with the inner workings of air-traffic-control systems. I came home late. Hanny was in New York, but next morning her budgie, Salman, was kicking up his usual racket in the kitchen when Mick Davitt rang.

'Have you read this morning's paper?' he asked, his voice strange.

I hadn't. I'd been out jogging on the beach and was still only halfway through a kipper.

'What's in it?' I asked.

'Did you ever get in touch with Tricky Dawson?' Mick asked.

A bad, bad feeling kicked me – hard. 'Maybe,' I said. 'Why?'

'Because he's dead,' Mick said.

7

I popped in and out of sleep on the plane. I dreamed of Hanny riding a white horse along a beach and of Lou taking photographs of her. Suddenly I was chest deep in the sea, trying but failing to come ashore. I felt a fool. With each step forward, the tide caught me and pulled me further back. Neither Hanny nor Lou could see or hear me. I tried to shout louder, but the roar of the sea drowned my voice. Mick said, 'You're some eegit!' I began to lose my footing. The white horse blurred as water slopped between me and the shore. I went under, heard the drone of the undertow.

I fought the undertow, then sat up, sweating. The plane's engines had changed tone as it began to nose down for the approach to Sydney.

It had not been a big funeral. A few racing types, some members of the press. Lou, surrounded by her friends, was on one side at the top of the church and on the other were Tricky's ex-wife and two men in their late twenties, his kids. Most of the newspapers had carried an obituary in their sports sections that morning and *Sportsday*, the paper he wrote most for, had a half-page including pictures of his greatest triumphs. Despite everything Mick had told me, I hadn't quite appreciated just how successful Tricky Dawson had once been. Now he was dead, the result of 'natural causes' according to all the newspaper reports. The truth was more harsh. Lou had gone away for a few days to cover a race meeting down the country and Tricky had gone on the booze. The neighbours found him on the floor in his kitchen. He'd been dead for nearly two days.

Cardiac arrest. I remembered our last conversation. *This is getting very hot.* A thought floated into my mind as the coffin was rolled down the aisle, the kind of thought that should be strangled at birth. I strangled it.

Out in Deansgrange cemetery I tried to talk to Lou, but her eyes were glassy and I got the impression she was sedated. I knew absolutely no one else there. Lou was shepherded to a car and driven off. I drove back across Dublin and out to Howth, pretty sure that I would never see my younger sister again.

I had called Sam Landy and told him what had happened. 'Oh, my God!' he said. 'I am so sorry.' He said he'd have to call me back – which he did, about an hour later. 'He and I went back a long way,' he said. 'He rode first for my father, then for me. He was the best, but he couldn't kick the drink. I sent him horses to train, but he couldn't operate when he was off the wagon. I personally wrote the cheque for him to go into the Betty Ford, but he checked out after three days and drank his way across America.'

'He shouldn't have been asked to look into the Steer business,' I said.

'Why ever not?' asked Landy.

'He called me up and told me he was feeling the heat,' I replied. 'I think the pressure got to him.'

'Look, I know this is difficult to accept,' Landy said, 'but I think Tricky was always going to end up as he did. He had a death wish, I saw it a hundred times. What I proposed and what you brought to him was just a business proposition – no more or less. He cashed the cheque, right? But it didn't mean he had to then go and drink himself to death.'

We left it at that, but as far as I was concerned, one thought wouldn't go away. I'd lied to the man. OK, technically I'd not told him untruths, but I'd concealed Landy's involvement and pretended that I was acting for Tom Ito, when the reality was otherwise. That left me feeling bad. It left me thinking that I'd put a business decision before my own inner judgement. Now a man was dead and a life, my sister's, was in ruins. That kept me awake at night, wondering how I could rectify the unrectifiable.

Hanny was in Germany the week following Tricky's funeral. I was going to be needed in the office for the next few weeks – we'd got all our rights-issue money in and the deals we'd set up in the States were brewing nicely. I got up one morning, walked in the rain by the sea, came back and cooked my breakfast. The doorbell rang. I wondered who it could be, since Stella, the cleaning lady wasn't due till noon and anyway she had her own key. I wasn't in the mood for a door-stepping sales pitch either, as I yanked open the front door.

'Fuck you, Joe,' said Lou.

8

I said, 'Come in.'

'I'm not coming in. I just want to say this: we were happy until you showed up in Ringsend. Why did you do it? Are you satisfied now, Joe? I've no one. The man I love is dead. Why? Because my own brother whose only god is money got the man I love mixed up in his own, sordid business. Isn't that the truth, Joe? Isn't that what you did? And are you happy at last?'

The rain was running down her face so it was difficult to tell between rain and tears.

'Jesus Christ, Lou,' I said, 'what you're saying is off the wall.'

Her knees went for a moment, but I managed to catch her and get her inside the door. I put her on a chair in the hall and went for a glass of water. When I came back, she was on her feet again.

She said, 'The coroner will conclude from the post-mortem that Tricky died of misadventure. But I don't go with that. I know Tricky was an alcoholic when I met him, but then he dried out and started to write. And although he told me that never a day went by when he didn't, at some point, have an overpowering craving to go out and drink, he also told me that he wasn't ever going to do that again, that if he did he'd hate himself so much it wouldn't be worth it. He often wondered why he hadn't found what he called the best two things in his life thirty years before – me and his new work. We were more important to him than drink.'

I looked at her. She waved away my offer of water.

She said, 'So, we had what we called a fall-back deal. He

could get drunk again if he wanted, but first he had to tell me. That was the deal. He didn't tell me. That's why I don't believe them when they say he drank himself to death.'

Her words tumbled out like a child's. Yet she made me think back to the church on the day of the funeral and to the thought that had buzzed across my mind.

I said, 'Was he – I don't know – in a lot of physical pain, for example? Might he have used drink to try and deal with that?'

'That won't work, Joe,' said Lou bitterly. 'As a jockey, Tricky had broken bones on more than a hundred occasions. He had had at least four major surgical procedures. Head injuries, spleen injuries. Horses that reared up and went over backwards. Horses that put him out over the running rail or that just went down like they were shot dead. He had screws in both shoulders, both wrists and one knee. He suffered a lot.' Lou smiled sadly. 'But although I remember him saying to me that he always knew when it was going to rain, he never complained.'

I didn't know what to say. I said, 'I'm sorry.'

'I was away for only three days, yet this seems to be something they've pounced on. That he was alone, that maybe this was the pattern when I went away and this time it just went horribly wrong. I don't accept that. I'd have heard. He was dry for nearly four years. People in Ringsend would know if a man like that was a secret binge drinker. I would have known, if not at the time, then after his death. It would have come out.'

All I could think of were a hundred other confrontations we'd had like this when we'd faced each other down; except that, unlike this one, none of them had been about anything remotely serious.

Lou was saying, 'I've spoken to the doctor who did the post-mortem. I've spoken to Father Nolan, our local parish priest who knew Tricky before I ever did. They all say the same thing in effect – he was an alcoholic, so what do you expect? I'm the woman he lived with, so of course they all expect me to defend him beyond the grave.'

'What are you saying?'

'Tricky didn't break out is what I'm saying. Tricky was killed because he knew too much.'

I had known it was coming, but the force of what she said still punched the wind out of me.

'What did he know?' I asked.

She looked at me, her face suddenly sly. 'Do you think I'm going to tell you?' she whispered.

'So you do know what he found out.'

'If I do, you're the last person I'm going to tell, believe me.'

'Lou, I want to help!' I cried.

'Too late for that,' she said. 'Far too late.'

'Then what the hell do you want me to do?' I shouted, knowing I shouldn't have, but unable to control my ancient exasperation.

She looked at me with a mixture of naked hostility and despair. 'I suppose I thought that if you had a shred of decency in your body you'd admit what you did was wrong,' she said, opening the front door and stepping out into the rain. 'I should never have let him see you or take your money. That was my mistake, Joe. To think that anything had changed and that I could trust you.'

I stood at the door and watched her walk down the path, a diminutive figure. I went back inside and did something I hadn't done in a while at breakfast: I poured myself a drink.

9

I rang Tim and cancelled all my meetings. I'm not much into hyperbole, but it would not be too much to say that Lou's visit had left me gutted. Something visceral. I realized I was grieving for her loss and the thought that I had somehow set Tricky up to be murdered – for nothing less was being inferred here – made me sick. But I'm not much good at being sick either, I'm the sort who has to either walk away from something or get into it up to my armpits. I called *SportsDay* and arranged to meet the editor, whose name was Brendan Power. He was the person who had spotted Tricky's talent and given him his break. He knew all about Lou and said he'd be happy to meet me.

The traffic was, as usual, a disaster. I rarely came further than the IFSC, leaving trips into central Dublin for the evenings when Hanny and I went to a play or a movie. It was noon. The pub that had been designated was off O'Connell Street, a watering hole that had been used by hacks for generations. Brendan Power was a man with bleary eyes, white hair and the kind of paunch that comes with forty years of late-night copy deadlines followed by pints of Guinness.

'Tricky was a natural,' he said, watching the turbulent gases in his glass of stout. 'Pity is that he didn't find his calling twenty years before.'

'Did you meet him much?'

Power shook his head. 'He filed by email or by telephone from the tracks. He only came in here about once a month. He'd drop by the office and we'd come in here, sit right down in this corner. I'd have a pint, he'd have Ballygowan.'

'What kind of stories was he working on?'

'Do you mind me asking what your interest is?'

'I gave him a lead a couple of months ago,' I said and told him about the Guy Steer story.

Power looked at me narrowly. 'So that was you?'

I nodded.

'Yes, he did tell me about that story,' Power said. 'Seems this Mr Steer is a specialist in ripping people off, from what Tricky said.'

'How do you mean, "a specialist"?'

'Well, Tricky reckoned that an Australian millionaire called Sam Landy took a major hit a few years back when Steer and he were partners.'

'*What?*'

Power blinked. 'Have I said something I shouldn't?'

I felt my breath caught. 'Did Tricky tell you that?' I asked. 'Are you absolutely certain?'

'I tend to be certain of my facts,' said the editor coolly. 'Comes with the job.'

'What else did Tricky say?'

'Why do you want to know this?' asked Power suspiciously as if I might be a closet hack from another paper.

'My sister has asked me to find out,' I said. 'She's in a bad way over all this.'

Power seemed to relax. 'I'm sorry, I understand. Look, Tricky had ridden for Landy, so he was intrigued by the story. But then, a week or so later, he called me up and told me that he'd spoken to people in the industry and had found out a disturbing fact: that when Landy sued Steer to try and get his money back, Steer threatened to kill him. Landy believed him. He backed off. The case never went ahead.'

I closed my eyes. *This thing is getting very hot.* 'Go on,' I said.

'Tricky told me he didn't think he'd take the story any further.'

'Oh Jesus,' I said.

'Are you all right?'

I excused myself and stood up.

'Thanks,' I said and shook his hand.

'Hope I've told you something useful,' said Power, concerned.

'More than I ever needed to know,' I said.

'If you do find out more, let me know, I'll run it,' Power said. 'It could be Tricky's last testament.'

I drove straight home and made myself walk on the beach for twenty minutes. But even had I walked into the cold sea, I don't think my anger would have cooled. Landy had duped me. He and Steer had been partners and he hadn't told me. He'd used the fact that I needed his money for the rights issue in order to get Tricky involved. And Landy knew better than anyone that Steer was dangerous – he'd threatened to kill Sam Landy. Yet despite all that, Landy had exposed Tricky to that danger. Now Lou's suspicion that Tricky had been murdered jumped to the head of the list. And if Lou was right, where did that leave me? In a very unpleasant and lonely place, was the answer.

I walked back home and sat the whole afternoon, waiting for the sun to go down. And then when the same sun was just about rising over Australia, I rang Sam Landy.

'Tell him Joe Grace wants to speak to him,' I replied to the question.

I held for nearly a minute. 'I'm sorry, Mr Grace, but Mr Landy is unavailable at the moment,' the person said.

I left a message for Landy to call me back urgently. Then I knocked some eggs together, opened a bottle of Fleurie and spent the evening flicking through the TV stations and hugging the phone. But Landy never called.

10

I don't know how many times I went through the argument, but each time the logic kept forcing me back to the same place: when all the emotion was stripped away from what had happened, the core truth remained that Tricky had died from an overdose of alcohol. Now the fact that Landy had lied to me or that Tricky might have cracked under pressure was one thing – and although I would not feel good about having involved him in something I shouldn't have, nevertheless there was an element of truth in what Sam Landy had said. *Tricky was always going to end up like he did. He had a death wish, I saw it a hundred times*. But if Lou was right, if Tricky's death had been set up – if he'd been murdered, in other words – then the issues were clearly different. If he'd been murdered, someone was guilty of that murder. *If* he'd been murdered.

The doctor who had done the post-mortem worked from Irishtown, a couple of miles from Ringsend. I sat in his waiting room and felt my anger at Sam Landy rise anew. I'd called him half a dozen times. He'd refused to speak to me. My anger had formed into something cold and hard. I'd thought about ringing Mick and telling him about everything, but I decided I'd try and get all the facts together first.

Dr Marsh had sounded gruff and busy on the phone. I anticipated that he mightn't want to speak to me, so I'd introduced myself as Lou's brother. Now I was shown directly into his office. I was surprised to see that he was ten years younger than me.

'Not the happiest mission you've ever been on,' he said

as he squinted at my card, then tucked it into a folder. 'I've met your sister. She is understandably upset.'

I explained that Lou had asked me to try and find out exactly what had happened.

'Mr Dawson suffered a subdural haematoma. In other words he inhaled vomit, which occurred as a result of drinking a massive dose of alcohol. He choked on his own vomit.'

'Would you mind explaining to me in idiot-proof terms how you can be certain of that?' I said.

Dr Marsh leaned back as if dealing with idiots was something he was used to.

'I was called to the house by the guards,' he began. 'The deceased was lying on the floor of the kitchen in a pool of vomit. There was an empty bottle of rum on the counter and another two-thirds full. There was a strong smell of rum.'

Behind the doctor, outside the house in a garden, children were playing. I suddenly longed to be with them.

'The deceased was removed to St Vincent's, where I performed the post-mortem. We began by taking blood and urine samples, then we took the front of his chest off. The poor chap stank of rum. His lungs were swollen and what we called "wet". Classical, if you like. We removed the lungs and his heart. He had suffered heart failure as a result of his lungs being flooded. It's like drowning. Then we went to the abdomen and took out and saved the contents. There was over one-fifth of a litre of rum still in his stomach. Two days later the blood and urine came back. His blood showed three hundred and fifty mils per cent of alcohol.' The doctor spread his hands. 'You don't need to be Sherlock Holmes to work out what had taken place.'

It was a shock to hear the man I'd drunk tea with described in such terms, but it wasn't the doctor's fault.

I asked, 'Were there any signs of violence?'

Dr Marsh frowned. 'None whatsoever, apart from what was self-inflicted.'

'No signs that he'd been held down or the like? No bruising?'

'He'd broken one of his front teeth when he collapsed. Otherwise, apart from the mess inside, he was clean.' He looked at me. 'Do you mind me asking what the point of all this is?'

'The problem is', I said, 'that here was a man who by all accounts had completely reformed. Hadn't taken a drink for nearly four years. If, for example, there had been a pattern of his breaking out, I think what happened would be much easier for my sister to accept. There'd be a precedent. She could rationalize it. This is so out of pattern. Out of the blue. Out of everything.'

'What I'm going to say now shouldn't be taken personally,' the doctor said, 'but I come across alcoholics every day of the week. They are, without doubt, the most charming people you could meet. They'd talk the birds out of the trees. Unfortunately, they are ultra devious. Their true intentions are so well disguised that not even the people closest to them know what's in their minds. They can be drinking for years on the sly and no one knows about it.'

Hardly rum, I thought to myself. You could smell a drunken sailor a block away.

'No evidence to support such a theory has emerged,' I said.

'Look, I see it day in, day out. When something like this happens, everyone is genuinely surprised. But the sad facts are as I've said. So maybe he wasn't tippling at home, maybe he was like another patient of mine who every day got on the DART and went to Bray. His family thought he

liked country walks, but all he really liked was vodka. I'm
sorry, Mr Grace, I really am.'

I was sorry too – for Lou and for Tricky. We got up and
Dr Marsh showed me to the door. Some unused part of my
analytical function must have kicked in. I turned to him.

'What other tests did you do, do you mind me asking?'

He shrugged. 'The usual. We took tissue samples of all
his organs – heart, lungs, liver.'

'Liver?'

'Yes.'

'Don't heavy drinkers usually have bad livers?' I asked.

'Yes, they normally have cirrhosis, or at least a build-up
of fatty tissue.'

'So did Tricky? I mean, you're suggesting he was
tippling away on the sly for the four years everyone
thought he was dry. How was his liver?'

The doctor showed his first signs of impatience. He put
on glasses and stepped back into his office, where he went
to the file. Outside the children laughed and shrieked.

Dr Marsh looked back at me and bit his lip thoughtfully.

'Now that you mention it,' he said, 'his liver was fine.'

11

On an impulse I drove the short distance to Ringsend. Lou had mentioned their parish priest. The church was a big granite structure. As I walked towards it, an overweight priest with crow-black hair was coming out the main door. I recognized him from the funeral.

'Father Nolan?'

I told him who I was.

'Ah, yes, yes, Tricky Dawson. Poor Tricky,' he said. 'How is Lou getting on at all?'

I said she was very upset.

'Why don't we go around here and have a chat,' Father Nolan said, leading the way down a side path.

Where the transept of the church stood out from the main wall, a little suntrap had been formed and a wooden seat set down.

'Tricky wasn't an easy man, but he wasn't the worst either,' the priest said. 'Drink drains a man and it had drained him, to an extent. Men who go on the dry have big trouble in filling up the empty space – but he was doing OK. He had Lou.' Father Nolan smiled, as if Lou would always make men smile. 'She was his salvation.'

'But she didn't save him.'

'Nobody can save us but ourselves and that's part of the truth. I'd add, of course, ourselves and the man above, but maybe that doesn't hold much water with you.'

'I'm not a great one for religion,' I agreed.

'Neither was Tricky. But he was a good man – even if he only found that out in recent years.'

'Did he . . . were you his . . . confessor?'

The priest shook his head. 'Not Tricky's. I doubt anyone

was. We had chats, though. He believed in God. He'd never had an opportunity beforehand to examine such things. You don't if you drink. He was hungry for discussion. I'm not sure I was his type. I'm a busy parish priest, I'm run off my feet most of the time. I suggested he go on retreat if he wanted that sort of space and time for reflection.'

'So he wasn't depressed, that you know of?'

'No. I mean, I might see Tricky once every six weeks and I'd say, "any tips?" and we'd have a laugh and a chat. No, I wasn't aware that Tricky had any problems – other than the overriding problem that someone in his position always has.'

'That's what Lou finds so difficult to understand. This assumption that things follow a certain, inevitable course. Was he suicidal? No. Depressed? No. Then why in Christ's name did he go and drink himself to death?'

The priest looked at me. 'It is sometimes better just to accept it and get on with life,' he said quietly.

'Did Tricky ever mention that he had enemies, for example?'

Father Nolan shook his dark head. 'Never.' He smiled faintly. 'If you don't mind me saying so, he wasn't the sort of man who was afraid of anything – or anyone. I remember him riding, you know. He was fearless. He made heroes of ordinary horses.'

We sat there by the side of the church as the sun eased in behind the spire.

'It's confusing, Father,' I said.

'Addiction is confusing,' he said slowly. 'My view is that it's often caused by pain suffered in childhood. Tricky was brought up on a small farm in County Tipperary and was expected to be a jockey from the day he was born. And yet, as we now know, he had a strong, artistic streak. That artistic side would have been there as a child – yet it was taken for granted that he would be a jockey. That must have been very painful.'

'So he spent his life drinking, trying to drown the pain?'

'Something like that.'

'On the other hand, he and Lou had a deal,' I said. 'Their deal was that, if he wanted to go on the piss, then he could, but first he had to tell her he was going to do it. That didn't happen.'

'She was away.'

'Still. A deal's a deal.'

'So – what are you saying, son?' asked Father Nolan.

'Everything I hear tells me that what he went and did is totally out of character. It leads me to conclude that something else must have happened. Something we don't know about.'

'I do hope you're wrong,' the priest said. 'I really do.'

We shook hands and I watched him walk down the road, rolling slightly from side to side. Inside the church, an automatic timing mechanism began to deal out the Angelus.

12

That night I met Mick.

'Legally, it's a sieve,' he said. 'Possible murder by persons unknown, motives unknown.'

I told him about the way Landy had set me up in the first place and how now he was refusing to take my calls.

'You don't get rich unless you're a tough and devious bastard,' Mick said, 'but maybe you know that already.'

I wasn't expecting sympathy. I said, 'Tricky was on a hot story, he told me so three days before he died. I think Steer may well have had a motive to kill him.'

'What about Landy?' Mick asked.

'I've thought about that too,' I said.

Landy might well have wanted to get even with Tricky for writing the damning piece about the doped horse. If so, he'd succeeded.

Mick said, 'I accept the whole coincidence thing and what it's doing to your head. You give the poor bastard a job and six weeks later he croaks – possibly under suspicious circumstances. But no one's going to run with it. Who killed him?'

'Maybe Steer. Maybe Landy – I don't know. Shit – I don't know what may have been going on!'

'No policeman or prosecutor is going to devote valuable time trying to pin the alcohol-related death of an alcoholic on a non-national who was probably a million miles away on the night of the death – and who by your own admission has no motive for such a killing.'

Mick was right, of course, but I was an obstinate bastard.

'What, in an ideal world, would I need for a prosecutor to become interested?' I asked.

'How about a signed confession?'

'Is that all?' I asked dryly.

'It would do for a start,' said Mick. 'Piece of advice?'

'Go on.'

'Go away and buy yourself another company,' Mick said. 'Buy three companies, if that's better. Get laid or get drunk. But keep your dick out of this sort of nonsense. Believe me, I know. It's a sad, sad scene at the end of the day and you need it like you need the itch.'

13

Hanny came home that weekend and we went to Mayo, to a renovated castle set in a thousand acres, with its own lakes and mountains and a resident chef who attracted Michelin stars like moths. We went down on Friday and on Saturday awoke to the sound of bees in honeysuckle.

I hadn't mentioned the Tricky Dawson business to Hanny yet and, to be honest, I was hoping that, in the same way the yearning for pints wears off if you leave it long enough, so would my preoccupation with his death. I'd file it away in the ugly and unfortunate category.

The castle in Mayo had begun life seven centuries ago as the family seat of a tribal chieftain, had been taken forfeit by English planters, withstood centuries of local pillaging and unrest, survived the War of Independence, had been purchased by a moneyed member of the new Irish middle class and then sold by his descendants to a chain of luxury hotels. In pleasant sunshine, we rode down a winding avenue, a wicker picnic basket strapped to the carrier of my bicycle. Where the avenue climbed left through rhododendrons, we parked the bikes and crossed a wooden stile into a meadow. After some moments a stone-built, slated boathouse appeared, semi-sunken. I opened the door. Two long punts bobbed side by side, like a pair of tethered greyhounds. We boarded one and, untying the painter, glided out into the stillness.

Our relationship was like that of two passengers on the same slippery deck of a storm-tossed ship, if such a thought is permitted on board a punt: although there was an element of co-dependence, still we kept crashing painfully into one another, again and again. I knew that Hanny saw me as evasive, non-committal, whereas I saw her as a woman with a dark, brooding side, which I reckoned I would never know and which, to be honest, at times scared me. We both had pasts. I had once fled from mine to another continent. In Hanny's case, she had suffered nervous breakdowns for which she had been hospitalized. I yearned to be admitted to that side of her life, which she mostly kept in cold shadow – just as she said at heated moments that she was fed up with the basically uncommitted nature of my personality.

'What's on your mind?' she asked, because there was never a time I could successfully keep anything from her.

I pulled on the oars and told her about Tricky and Lou and how I felt guilty that possibly I had contributed to Tricky's death.

'During all the years we were growing up together, I was always sure that Lou was wrong and I was right,' I said. 'About everything. I saw her as a problem, always complaining about me, always the first to find fault. Now I suddenly wonder if I was mistaken all that time. I'm asking myself, what if she's right about what happened to Tricky? And, if she is, where does that leave me with myself?'

'What are you going to do about it?' Hanny asked when I had finished.

'I'm not sure there's anything I can do,' I said.

'I've heard that before,' Hanny said and gave her face, eyes closed, to the sun.

I felt the heat on the back of my neck. In another life, I had been in the US Marines, Intel section, and had, back then, learned how to handle myself in a tight spot. Occasionally, very occasionally, I missed the action – because nothing gets the adrenalin going more than danger and nothing is more seductive than adrenalin.

The lake was far more extensive than had appeared at

first sight: it swung, via a narrow neck, into a much more impressive body of water, which seemed to go all the way to the foot of a purple mountain. The base of the mountain turned out to be an island. We put in, the bottom grating lightly on shingle. The island, no more than half an acre, had an old ruin on raised ground in its centre.

'Monks lived somewhere around these parts over a thousand years ago,' Hanny said, looking at the book she'd been given back in the castle. 'They built a small chapel out here in about 1100 AD. When one of them died, they brought him out here, wrapped like a mummy, and laid him in the vault.'

One gable alone remained and set within it was the granite mullion of an east-facing window. The other walls were now grassy rubble, but still visible within the rectangle was a three-foot gaping slit in the earth. I looked down. For a moment I thought the mound of white spheres was huge mushrooms until I realized they were skulls. Hanny was unpacking the basket and taking out apples and cheese and from a frozen flask a bottle of white wine – Chevalier de Stérimberg, 1997.

We had had our problems, this lovely woman and I, but always, when it appeared as if our mutual regard would sink under the weight of mutual vituperation, miraculously it would resurface.

'The dead are remarkably peaceful,' Hanny said and took off her T-shirt to reveal a bikini top that appeared to be made from cling film. 'Maybe we should try and leave them in peace.'

I kicked off my shoes and felt the comforting probe of warm grit between my toes. Then I lay back and watched swallows high in the sky.

'I'd like us to give it another go,' I said.

We had often come to this place together, this emotional

fork in the road; neither of us knew what lay beyond it. I
saw it as an uncharted desert, someplace I'd go into gladly
on my own, but not with the responsibility of another
person. Hanny caught my hand and pulled me into her. I
could feel the deep muscles of her back, the type of
conditioning that came from daily swimming and aerobics.
I kissed her and she lay back and unbuckled the belt of my
jeans. I unhooked her and circled each of her firm nipples
with my tongue. I entered her and she locked her legs
around my back. She was the most beautiful woman I had
ever been with and I wanted nothing more than for us to
go on like this for ever.

That weekend we decided that we couldn't continue like
this any more. That we'd either try to make a permanent
go of it or cut loose. That's the trouble with weekends
away: whereas things seem to go along just fine on
weekdays, on weekends you've nothing better to do than
make these kind of decisions. So Hanny returned to
Germany to have a final think about things and I promised
to do the same. And the result was that a few days later we
spoke by phone, and she said if I wanted it then so did she.
And I said, great, and for some reason undertook not to
undertake any major trips for a couple of months so that
our new relationship could be allowed to settle down.

   'Permanently,' I said.

   'Every time you and I use such words, we have trouble,'
Hanny had said.

Two days later, on a Thursday morning, I was reading the
newspaper at breakfast when I got a phone call.

   'Joe Grace?'

   'Yes?'

   'This is Dr Marsh, we met two weeks ago.'

I can hear trouble a mile off. 'Yes, Doctor.'

'Look, I was thinking about our conversation, so I asked the state laboratory to run the Dawson blood sample again, this time for a drug screen. They came back to me yesterday.'

I could hear Tricky's words then, actually hear them: *This thing is getting very hot.*

'Yes, Doctor.'

'There's over three hundred mils per cent of Rohypnol coming up. That's a huge dose. Yet it seems there's no suggestion that he was on this drug.'

'So?'

'I just thought you should know.'

'Thank you, Doctor,' I said and put down the phone.

14

The pier in Howth is a much more intimate affair than its more famous relative across the bay in Dun Laoghaire. In Howth the purpose of the pier seems to be much more readily apparent, the way it embraces its clutches of sailing boats and trawlers, the gentle wing of a mother duck between its loved ones and the raging sea.

The wind whipped at Tim Tully's long hair and beard. People sometimes mistook Tim for the night watchman. He looked like a cross between Billy Connolly and Moses, but I doubt if either gentleman ever had Tim's financial acumen. Or common sense. He ran the day-to-day end of Grace Equity and I could not remember when I'd made a decision in my recent life, either business or personal, without first consulting him.

'What does Mick Davitt think?' Tim asked.

'He says that, despite the Rohypnol, no coroner is going to suggest murder on such circumstantial evidence.'

'Then, rationally, should you not be following the same standard?' Tim suggested gently.

'Yes, rationally,' I agreed.

I stood by the sea wall and drank in the view and air I so much relished and which I was now preparing to leave.

'Sam Landy did something very wrong,' I said. 'And he got me to do something very wrong. I want to know why he did it. The man is one of our major shareholders and he refuses to take my calls. Do you think I can live with this situation?'

Tim spread out his hands like a priest at Mass.

I asked, 'Have you got me in?'

'I told Landy's accountancy people there are vital

documents regarding a takeover target that I must get to the man himself. They told me to send them to Mount Landy by special delivery.' Tim winced. 'We're playing fast and loose with one of our biggest shareholders here, Joe.'

'Fuck that. Landy played fast and loose with me and with Tricky Dawson,' I said. 'The bastard refuses to take my calls. What option do I have?'

'You could forget the whole thing.'

I said, 'Landy concealed the fact that he and Steer had been business partners. He lied to me about Steer, he inferred that he didn't know him. Steer once threatened to kill him, for Christ's sake, yet Landy when I asked him told me that Steer, in his opinion, wasn't dangerous. Landy manipulated me, using his position as a shareholder in Grace and my position as Lou's brother. He got me to involve Tricky Dawson in Steer's dirty work, knowing full well the danger of doing that. Now Tricky is dead, possibly murdered, and my sister holds me responsible for ruining her life. And you want me to forget the whole thing?'

Tim looked resigned. 'When are you leaving?'

'First thing in the morning.'

We got back to the cars and Tim handed me a file. 'You asked for information about Tricky Dawson,' he said. 'I put a couple of our new guys on to it. It was a bit different from researching investment opportunities; nonetheless, I'm quite impressed.'

I took the file. I said, 'By the way, Hanny is going to be here. She's coming in tomorrow morning.'

Tim sighed. 'Does she know you're going to Sydney?'

'Not really . . .'

'You mean, no.'

'Yes.'

'Oh, boy,' Tim said.

The way I figured it was like this: I could settle down

with the world's most beautiful woman, but then I'd feel like a shit for the rest of my life for not having followed my instinct. And what beautiful woman wanted to spend the rest of her life with a shit?

15

I liked Sydney, the gigantic scale of the harbour, the people, the food. I took a cab into town and checked into the Regent, which is right beside Circular Quay. Eleven in the morning, raining – typical weather for August. They put me in a room on the twenty-third floor. I crashed for five hours and when I got up in the mid-afternoon, the sun was shining.

I didn't want to confront Sam Landy dying from a cocktail of jet-lag, champagne and personal guilt; before I met him there was a lot I needed to sort out in my head. I went for a walk along the Quay and out towards the Opera House. It had been two years: I had been in Hong Kong on business and Hanny had been with me. We'd come down here to watch Sonia O'Sullivan running for Ireland in the Olympics. Now I sat by a waterside café and ordered oysters and wine as the sun slipped down.

Tim's research department had come up with a lot of information on Tricky and Landy – information I should have asked for before I had ever agreed to become involved. The relationship between them went back over thirty years. Tricky had ridden for Sam and his father. There was a sheaf of newspaper cuttings, many of them with headlines such as 'TRICKY SPARKLES' or 'HAT-TRICKY!' Half a dozen photographs of a young, grinning Tricky standing beside Landy, holding aloft cups, vases, plates. When Tricky retired from riding and began training horses, his main owner had been Sam Landy. That arrangement seemed to have lasted for ten years before they bust up. And the bust up was documented too: at the time it had been big news in the world of horse racing. There was one

piece which quoted Tricky after Landy had left him: 'You
don't expect your friends to do this.' It was after Landy
pulled his horses out of training that Tricky really went
downhill. Six months later he had disappeared.

And there were also some pieces from racing newspapers, a few years old, mentioning the new racing alliance
between Sam Landy and Guy Steer – a marriage of the old
school with the new, as one writer put it. I cursed myself
for not having done my homework. If I'd made even the
most cursory checks, I would have discovered what was
now in front of me and realized Landy hadn't been telling
me the whole truth.

I wondered what kind of person Landy was to have
done what he did. The whole Ito story was clearly an
excuse – to get even. But even with whom? Steer or Tricky?
Maybe Landy had seen the play as a win-win bet: put
Tricky against Steer and one of them was going to lose, big
time. He'd been right.

I watched a cruise liner pulling out from the far side of
the Quay and thought of Hanny. She had been terse, to say
the least, when I had called her.

'Joe, it seems there's always a better reason than me,'
she said when I had explained why I wasn't in Dublin.

'You know that's not true.'

'Well then, why are you not here like you promised?'

'This couldn't wait,' I said lamely.

She hung up. I had no idea whether she intended to
return to Germany.

I walked slowly back to the Regent. The air was cool
and more rain was on the way. My plan when I met Landy
was about as sophisticated as boiling cabbage. I was just
going to confront him with everything that had happened
and watch his reaction. I wasn't going to walk until I had
learned the truth. That's a failing of mine, the inability to

go along with a whole load of crap, especially when the truth hurts. And this had gone beyond hurting as far as Tricky Dawson was concerned.

I got back up to the twenty-third floor of the Regent, where my room had two windows – one overlooking the bridge, the other the Opera House – and saw my message light flashing.

'It's me,' said Hanny's voice. 'I just wanted to say, sorry. You're crazy, but I love you. Sweet dreams.'

I went to bed with a big grin on my face. If ever there was a good omen, I reckoned, that was it. And I needed it, too, before setting out the next morning. I went to sleep blissfully, without a care in the world. This would all work out for the best was my last thought.

So much for omens.

I rented a Mercedes coupé and left the city at seven a.m. It was going to take me the best part of a day to get up to Slow Creek, the nearest town in northern New South Wales to Mount Landy. I could have gone by small plane, but the pace of driving better suited my mood. I stopped for coffee outside Lithgow and again, because I liked the name, at Running Stream, a tiny village where half the buildings seemed to be churches and where white-caped cockatoos screeched and fought with one another in a giant eucalyptus.

I liked the near-Irish countryside, complete with rolling hills and stud railing, set down here at the other end of the world. The difference was the climate, of course. In summer around here heat was so intense that there was a virtual curfew every day between twelve and three. And in winter the deep, scorching frosts needed to impale the hearts of good vines and die them back wrapped Slow Creek in their embrace for two months. Now winter was

all but over, the sun was climbing ever higher and the fields
were greening up. I drove north all day. The climate
became perceptibly milder with each further mile. It was
five before I reached Slow Creek, a place of wide streets set
down in a grid. Twenty minutes later I was driving through
bare-topped, rolling hills, some of them stud railed, not
dissimilar to parts of County Wicklow.

Mount Landy's website gave clear directions to those
bringing mares at this time of year. The Internet had
spewed out pictures of manicured paddocks with grazing
mares and foals, and pictures of two of Landy's best
stallions, Valleyman and The Hunter, and a couple of long
shots of an immense residence sheltered by groves of
eucalyptus. I breasted a hill and pulled in. Below me lay a
luscious valley with a river running through it. Paddocks,
divided by miles of stud fencing, shone a deeper, healthier
green than any of the countryside I had come through since
leaving Slow Creek. There was the sound of an engine
behind me; a jeep and trailer trundled past. I watched them
sink down in the valley and disappear. Moments later they
came into view again, like a miniature reincarnation, and
pulled up by tall gates. As the gates swung inward, a man
in uniform holding a clipboard walked from a gatehouse
and checked the registration of the jeep, then inspected the
trailer. The visitors were waved in. August was a busy time
of year in horse farms in the southern hemisphere. Another
mare was being delivered to Mount Landy.

16

I drove downhill beside wire fencing, where big-fringed merino ewes were nuzzling their lambs. It was five-thirty and the shadows were lengthening. I parked the car and walked into the gatehouse.

'I have some documents for delivery to Mr Landy,' I said and waved the dossier Tim had given me at one of the two uniformed security men.

'Just leave it here,' he said handing me the pen to sign for it.

'I've got to deliver it to him personally, sorry.'

The man pulled a face, then picked up the phone and turned his back to me as he spoke to someone. I filled out a chit in the name of Seamus MacGreana, which is Joe Grace in Irish, and was given a clip-tag which I was told to pin on. Minutes later a big four-by-four Mitsubishi pulled up and a tall man in his early thirties swung out of it. He was a good-looking, well-made bloke with sparkling, even teeth and wore a hat like the guy in the Marlboro ad.

'Hi, I'm Mr Landy's personal assistant,' he said. 'You've got some documents for the boss?'

I showed him the folder.

'You want to give them to me?'

'Thanks, but my instructions are to hand them to Mr Landy.'

He looked me up and down. 'OK,' he said at last, 'but then we need to check you for security purposes, all right?'

I shrugged. 'Fine.'

One of the men came out from the stall. 'Just hold out your arms, please.'

He frisked me with professional thoroughness, including

my crotch, armpits and shirt collar. Then he told me to put
the folder on the belt of a miniature X-ray machine.

'The security people will bring your car up,' said the
personal assistant. 'So if you'd like to jump into my
wagon? I'm Sean, by the way.'

'Seamus.'

We shook. I reluctantly handed the security guard my
car keys and got into the jeep. Sprinklers every fifty yards
shot out fans of fine spray on both sides of the road. The
grounds were closer to those of a classy golf course or
country club than a farm.

'Where have you come from?'

'Sydney,' I said. 'This is a fine property.'

'We run the best stallions in the southern hemisphere,
maybe in the world here,' Sean said as we drove. 'You've
heard of The Hunter?'

'Sorry, no.'

'Now there's a stallion!' Sean said as the road plunged
and ran under a bridge, then rose steeply again. 'The
Hunter has created a whole dynasty, colts and fillies that
run on every continent of the world. Most of them born
right here. I've rubbed life into their bodies on cold
mornings. Just think of it – they're babies when I see them
first, but in a couple of years they'll have ten thousand
people on their feet, screaming them home.'

We had driven round a tall grove of bluey green
eucalyptus, and emerged on a plateau: below us, astonish-
ing because it was so unexpected, lay a large lake, a
fountain on an island at its centre hurling skywards great
jets of water, and beyond the lake lay Mount Landy. The
sheer scope of it made me stare. The residence, whose
lawns ran down to the shore of the lake, was as big as
Leinster House. There was a handsome central porch with
pillars, then two wings, two floors each, either side. The

windows were long and generous. The evening sun had just come around the hills to my left and had picked out the pad.

'Some place,' I had to say.

'Everyone here is so proud of what Mr Landy has created,' Sean said.

'Does he ever get into partnership deals with other horse owners?' I asked.

'Very rarely,' Sean said. 'Mount Landy sees itself more than anything as the maternity ward and nursery where Mr Landy's future winners are born and raised.'

'So you wouldn't remember Guy Steer being involved here,' I said mildly.

The man drew up the jeep and turned to me slowly. 'No, I wouldn't,' he said and turned off the engine. He looked at my identification badge. 'Now, Seamus, if you'd care to follow me.'

He led the way to an entrance around the side where a servant in a white jacket was holding open the door. Reminded me of home. We entered the massive house. The butler or whatever he was walked ahead of us through a courtyard area and on into an inner terrace, where the dying sun was reflected on the surface of an oval-shaped swimming pool. I felt all at once as if a brick were lying in the bed of my stomach, a feeling I used to get before going into combat. The white-coated bod stood aside and held open another door. I hated all this scraping and bowing, but when I stepped into the central hall of Mount Landy, I had to gasp. It was so big that a house could have been built in it. The flunkey padded on past us like a well-trained Labrador. We were now being ushered into a room off the hall, a study with a wall of bookshelves, a desk and photos of horses, and teak filing cabinets. One wall was taken up with the portrait in oils of a beautiful woman.

Blonde hair cascaded from beneath her wide-brimmed hat. She had been about thirty-five when she sat for the artist. I sank into one of the gigantic leather chairs while the man called Sean remained at the back of the study.

I heard a voice ask, 'Is he here?' and a deeper voice reply, 'Yes, sir.'

A door opened in the bookshelves and a man walked into the room. It had been some time since I had seen Sam Landy. He was small sized, trim and almost completely bald. He wore a dark blue blazer, a white polo-neck, dark blue slacks and gleaming patent leather shoes.

'Must be a matter of life and death that you have to hand this stuff to me personally,' he said, coming across the room and putting on spectacles.

'You could put it that way, Sam,' I said.

He looked at me sharply.

'What . . .?'

I said, 'So which of them did you want out of the way? Guy Steer or Tricky Dawson?'

Sam Landy's head went back and he began to hyperventilate.

'How . . . the hell . . .?' he gasped, staring at me. He collapsed.

'You fucking bastard!' said the man behind me.

I heard his blow whistling in and almost managed to avoid it; but almost is no good against someone fit and weighing one-sixty. He caught me on the neck with a round-house punch and I went spinning across the room. Sean came at me. I feinted left, which worked, then tried to bring my foot up between his legs, which didn't. He caught my foot and swung. Strong bastard, I thought as I left the ground. When I landed again it was on a coffee table which may or may not have been an antique. The question became somewhat irrelevant as it splintered beneath me. Sean had grabbed an elegant glass ashtray and flung it at my head. It missed and crashed into the marble fireplace. All the time, I was aware of Landy lying on a sofa, feet stuck out, his face going blue. I faced Sean, jabbed with my left hand and when he tried to grab it, caught him under the chin with an uppercut that straightened him six inches higher than he stood in his socks. As he sank, I heard the door behind me open.

'Put your hands over your head or I swear to God I'll blow your fucking head off!' said a female voice.

I turned. One of the most beautiful women I had ever seen was pointing a shotgun at my top half. She looked as if she knew how to shoot. Beside her stood a towering flunkey in a green jacket. He was breathing hard. The woman took one look at Landy, then nodded urgently to the guy in green, who hurried to the desk, yanked open a drawer and came back, upending a pill bottle into his hand. He cupped his hand to Landy's mouth and got him to swallow. Sam Landy seemed to get immediate relief.

'Call the cops, Jacquimo,' the woman said.

Sam Landy was shaking his head. 'No cops,' he said weakly. 'And please put that gun away, Silken.'

I was sitting in one of the big chairs, Landy was still on the sofa with the woman beside him. Sean, Landy's assistant, had limped out, holding his jaw and telling me with his eyes that next time it would be different. The big butler in the green jacket now materialized at my elbow with a silver tea tray.

'Tea, sir?' he intoned. 'Or something stronger?'

He was strongly built and looked about as cheerful as a career mortician. My tongue was hanging out for a belt of whisky, but this, I understood, was not the time to indulge the baser side of my nature.

'Tea is fine,' I said. I turned to Sam. 'Is the guy who tried to take me out just now the same one you sent to deal with Tricky?'

Landy shook his head as if explanation was beyond him. 'Sean's my right arm around here,' he said, 'a wonderful young man. He wouldn't harm a fly.' He turned to the butler, who was standing at his elbow. 'Thank you, Jacquimo,' he said and the butler poured him tea.

The woman was about thirty, tall, with ink black hair. Her tea-coloured eyes were upswept – almost oriental. She was dressed in a skirt that stopped three inches above her knees. The shotgun lay on the ground beside her. She kept her arm around Landy's shoulders, but it was obvious from her attitude towards me that she was holding me to account for her boss's/boyfriend's nasty turn. 'Are you OK,

Sam?' she asked. She shot me a withering look. 'My father has a heart condition.'

'Your – father?'

'I'm all right, I'm fine, darling.' Landy had composed himself and his breath was coming easily now. He sat up and shook his head. I wondered briefly what Tim Tully would think if I had actually managed to precipitate the death of one of our principal investors. 'This is my daughter, Silken.'

'Pleased to meet you,' I said.

She ignored me.

'I'm not going to die,' Landy said and drank some more tea. 'It just appears that way.' He shot me a look. 'Do you normally call in on people like this?'

'Only when I've been dropped in the shit,' I said.

'OK,' Landy said and closed his eyes, 'OK, OK. I know you've been trying to call me and I can guess what it was about.'

'I never had you down as slow, Sam,' I said. 'You saw a way to get some dirt on your former partner, Steer, so you decided Tricky was expendable – right? Tricky shafted you in his piece about the horse doping and you wanted to get even with him – am I getting warm?'

Landy's face up close was a tapestry of lines and creases.

'Tricky Dawson was my friend,' he said slowly. 'No matter what he wrote, he was still my friend.'

'You have a funny way of treating your friends,' I said.

'You have no idea what that bastard Steer did to me,' Landy said. 'If you'd been in my position you'd have done no different.'

'You mean, I'd have walked a totally innocent man in to dig up dirt on someone I knew might well have him killed? I don't think so.'

'It's not as simple as that.'

'You weren't straight with me, Sam. A man is dead. Now I think it's time you told me what's going on.'

Sam Landy closed his eyes. 'I need a drink,' he said wearily.

'Sam . . .' Silken said.

'I need a drink,' he said with finality.

And so say all of us, I thought. As if by magic, the peon in the green hose called Jacquimo appeared like the Grim Reaper with a tray and a bottle and three Waterford brandy goblets. The bottle was Armagnac. It appeared to be the house tipple, for there was no discussion on the lines of 'Would you care for?' or 'Would you like a splash of Coke?' Jacquimo poured three triple fingers, served Silken, me and Sam in that order, then vanished.

Sam picked up the glass and drank from it. 'OK,' he said heavily. 'I did wrong. God forgive me, but I did wrong.'

18

'It all began five years ago,' Sam Landy said. 'At every horse sale I was coming up against oil money and losing – notably against the Sultan of Tamil. I was simply being outbid. The good mares were being sent to his stallions. Then one day at Keeneland I met Guy Steer. We got talking. Steer was feeling the heat from the Sultan too. He suggested that, if we got together, maybe between us we could block the Sultan's advance.'

Landy made it sound like Gulf War II.

'It was agreed initially that Steer's organization would front the buying of horses identified by both of us as being desirable purchases. I wrote him a cheque for five million dollars.

'And for six months it went fine,' Landy went on. 'We became friends. All in all we invested over twenty million dollars buying horses which, had we competed against one another, might have cost us twice that. In Slow Creek at Christmas my wife and I lifted our glasses and we toasted Guy Steer.'

I saw Silken following every word as her father spoke.

'That was our last Christmas together in Slow Creek,' Sam said quietly. 'Elizabeth became ill in the second week in January. I took her down to Sydney. Ten days after that she was diagnosed with cancer.'

When Guy Steer heard the news he appeared to be devastated. He and Landy agreed that they would together invest $30 million in new bloodstock in the coming year – with one crucial difference: this time, because of his personal situation, Landy would delegate the entire decision-making process to Steer. Landy's financial people

would monitor the details, but Steer had Landy's complete
trust in the matter of picking horses.

'Then one day the following September I got a call from
my accountant,' Landy said. 'He's a man who knows the
horse business inside out. He said, "Mr Landy, I thought
you should know we've just paid half of one point two
million dollars for a filly foal out of a Danzig mare that's
owned by Mr Steer."

'In other words, I had paid six hundred thousand
dollars for a half-share in a foal that was already owned by
my partner. I didn't believe it. But my accountant was
adamant.'

Sam Landy reluctantly called up Steer and asked him
straight out about the transaction. Steer was taken aback.
His explanation was that yes, he had indeed bought the
mare two years ago, but when her first colt had shown
dismal promise, he had then sold her privately. That sale,
he now told Landy, was a matter of regret, for his spotters
had come to him a month ago and informed him that the
mare's latest offspring, a leggy, filly foal by Roberto, was a
foal to die for. Steer bought the foal for the partnership.
End of story.

'I ended up apologizing to him,' Landy said. 'I actually
told the bastard to go ahead and buy whatever he thought
fit. And I told my accountant not to bother me with such
details again, that Steer was my trusted partner and to give
him what he wanted, when he wanted it.'

Sam moved down to the Landy townhouse in Sydney to
be near his wife. Time became a blur. When Mrs Landy
eventually died in August the following year, Landy was
relieved for her but personally drained and devastated.

But he did begin to function again, turning his energies
to his business. What he found in his horse empire was
shocking.

'He had bled me dry,' said Landy in a wavering voice. 'He had essentially used all my money over a two-year period to take out all his weak investments. My accountant had been right. I was now a partner in several dozen useless horses. My money paid at auction had gone straight into Steer's pocket by a variety of routes. He'd robbed me. Worse, he'd robbed me as my wife lay dying and I'd given him my complete trust. I can't think of a worse indictment of a man.'

19

Silken opened the French windows and a little breeze tugged at the curtains.

Sam said, 'I was devastated when I heard Tricky had died, but I wanted to believe it was from natural causes. I kept putting off talking to you because I dreaded hearing what you were going to say. That was wrong of me too.'

'It's emerged he was drugged,' I said. 'Although at this stage they can't say he didn't take the drugs himself, the possibility is that someone then dosed him with alcohol and made it look like he'd gone on his last bender.'

Landy's cheeks puffed out. 'Jesus Christ,' he said and took a drink.

If anyone was stop-watching the speed with which we were drinking, Sam Landy was assured the gold medal position.

He said, 'Let me explain why I called you and asked you to make the approach to Tricky. Tricky Dawson was my *hero*. He was, to me, on his day, the greatest jockey of his generation. As good as Piggott or Saint-Martin. Better than Eddery. A mile ahead of the rest. I loved him and so did my wife. My father looked upon him as his second son. Stepping Tricky down from riding our horses was one of the hardest decisions of my life. Then we gave him the pick of our European yearlings to train.' Landy spread his hands in a gesture of helplessness. 'We had at least half a dozen showdowns. Tricky was a bad alcoholic. It was hopeless. It nearly broke my father's heart.'

As Landy spoke Silken was nodding her head, as if this was a story she had heard many times.

'Then Tricky disappeared. A number of years went by.

My father died. Life went on. When anyone asked me what had become of Tricky Dawson, my answer was that it was a tragedy no one seemed capable of averting. It was a damn shame. To be quite honest, during this time I assumed that Tricky was dead.'

Landy stood up, went to the mantelpiece and from a silver box took out a small cigar and chopped off its tip.

Silken said, 'Sam –'

'To hell with it,' Landy said and lit up. He looked at me through blue smoke. 'As you may know, I won a big race in France three years ago. My horse failed a urine test and was disqualified – but what really incensed me was the suggestion that I'd given the nod to the trainer. I wouldn't dope a horse if my last dollar depended on it. I took my horses out of France. I wanted to show that there was a principle at stake.'

I hate it when people start talking about principles – it normally means they've ripped someone off. I observed Jacquimo hanging around in the shadows at the back of the room. I'd seen him earlier picking up the heavy, laden tray with one hand. I wondered when he found the time to work out.

'You did the right thing,' Silken said with vigour as Jacquimo now came back and splashed booze into Sam's glass and mine.

'I was in London at the end of that year when I was informed that a request for an interview had come through from an Irish journalist called Tricky Dawson. I honestly didn't believe it was him – I really thought Tricky was dead and this was a grotesque coincidence. And so, although I never give interviews, my curiosity got the better of me and I returned the call. I nearly cried when I heard Tricky's voice and that's the truth.'

Silken reached for her father's hand.

'He flew in from Dublin two days later. I didn't know what to expect. Tricky drank tea and told me all about himself and his new career. And about Lou. I was so happy for him.' Landy scratched his forehead. 'But I have to say, that he had changed too. He was – and this is difficult for me to say – he was bitter. It's not that I thought he was blaming me for all the bad luck that had befallen him, but he wasn't absolving me either. He'd suffered a lot.'

'Drink twists people,' Silken said, although how someone as young as her could know this was a mystery.

'So we had the interview. A couple of times I asked him if we could talk off the record and he said OK. When the interview was over, we shook hands and Tricky left.' Landy shrugged. 'A month later he wrote a piece that was brilliantly informed, highly insightful, but as far as I was concerned it was vindictive. He'd honoured none of our agreements and implied heavily that I knew about the doping.'

'It was disgraceful,' Silken said and let me have the full wattage of her amber eyes.

'Then late last year I came across a man called Ito, someone I knew from business here in Australia. It seemed he too had been shafted by Steer, this time in a mare and foals deal in Ireland. Steer had flushed my money through so many different transactions that proof of fraud was impossible. But Ito's case seemed to be cut and dried – that's if you knew racing. But I needed someone to get the inside track in Ireland. Who better than Tricky Dawson? But how could I approach him after what had happened between us? I made some enquiries and found that Lou was your sister. I called you.'

I was exhausted. We'd been talking for over five hours.

'Let me ask you a penultimate question,' I said. 'If Tricky was about to expose Steer as having ripped off Tom Ito, would Steer have been capable of having Tricky killed?'

Sam closed his eyes. 'Guy Steer is living on the side of a financial volcano,' he said quietly. 'He has huge borrowings. He rips off people like me and Tom Ito because he has to. He needs the cash. An exposé like the one Tricky was writing could have been dynamite – Steer's banks might have foreclosed if they read something really negative.'

'That's what you were hoping for, wasn't it?' I said. 'You wanted to ruin him.'

Sam Landy nodded. 'Yes.'

I said, 'So answer my question.'

Landy joined his hands and his head sank. 'I swear to God I didn't think it would come to this,' he said, almost in a whisper. 'But yes, now that you ask, the answer is, yes, yes he would kill to stay afloat. God forgive me, but the answer is yes.'

'Which leads us to the final question,' I said. 'Did you see Tricky as expendable? Was this your way of getting even with him?'

Landy's eyes were almost lost in deep creases of flesh. 'I made a mistake,' he answered quietly. 'I hate being beaten. I'm old and I'm selfish. But I'd put a gun in my own mouth and pull the trigger before I'd harm a hair of Tricky Dawson's head.'

Jacquimo led me to a bedroom with a bed in which two people would have needed cell-phones to keep in touch. He had all the charm of a serial killer with halitosis. I noticed his hands: big-veined and powerful, they hung by his sides like flesh-covered claws. It was two in the morning. I was exhausted. Everything I had heard sank me deeper into the pit of despair. A rich old man had been blinded so thoroughly by his own lust for revenge that he had caused an innocent man's death.

But it was too late in this endless day to think about what the next step might be. I was numb. Sleep crept over me. I drifted off into a deep, deep place thinking of Hanny, but several times during the night I awoke and Silken was the woman in my mind.

20

Morning sunlight poured through twelve-foot-high white curtains. The malachite headboard of the bed had been carved into a soaring eagle. I stood five minutes under a power shower, dressed and pulled open the curtains. It was seven-thirty. Silken was sitting on a terrace, six feet away, reading a newspaper.

'The coffee's fresh.'

I sat down at the table and she handed me a cup. I felt the sun hot on my face.

She said, 'That was quite a night.'

'I didn't know your father had a heart condition.'

'He's been like that for some time, since his wife died.'

I looked at her, now dressed in jeans tight as an onion skin, and at the shape of her face. I wasn't really up to these trips any more.

'I dug out an old video which I thought you should see,' Silken was saying. 'It's interesting.'

A television sat in the shade near the door. She pressed a remote and it came on.

The paddocks and lakes of Mount Landy floated into view.

'This was made over twenty years ago for Australian television,' Silken said.

The camera zoomed in on a paddock in which a very muscular, almost black horse cantered.

'*You see – there's lovely scope to him. And he moves easy. That's The Hunter's secret, I think, or Blackie, as we all called him, his economy of movement, how effortlessly he does it all – and in the process, puts such little pressure on his limbs.*'

The voice was Tricky Dawson's. The camera pulled back and there was Tricky and a much younger Sam Landy, standing in their shirtsleeves in The Hunter's paddock. Tricky now walked right up to the horse, stood in beside him, talked to him, rubbed one hand down the animal's foreleg and then patted The Hunter's neck.

'*What else strikes you about him, Tricky?*' asked Sam.

'*He has a good, big eye, Mr Landy. Don't ever mind the way he rolls it at you now and then, that just means he's impatient – impatient to run, and that's good. No, look at the size of the eye. I've never known a good horse who has a mean eye.*'

The Hunter raised his head and looked at us from large, doleful eyes. I refilled my cup with coffee.

'*A great horse always looks big, even though he may really be quite small,*' Tricky was saying to the camera as The Hunter trotted away in a wary arc. '*It's intelligence that makes the best of them great. I've never ridden a great horse that hasn't listened when I've spoken to him.*'

I felt a jolt of recognition, because Tricky had used almost those exact words in Ringsend when he and Lou had been discussing horses. Now he was elaborating, as if for Sam Landy's benefit.

'*I rode Blackie to win in both Epsom and Paris, then we went to Chicago for the Arlington Million. But the crowd in Chicago made him sweat something awful in the preliminaries. The result: no one touched him in the betting, he drifted out to ten to one.*'

The camera switched to Sam's unlined face; he was smiling and listening attentively.

'*Now I know I shouldn't have done this, but I said in the parade ring to the trainer, "Go out there and have a grand on me," and the trainer said, "You're mad, Blackie's in a bog of sweat," but I said, "It's OK, I'll talk to him."*'

*And as soon as I got the leg-up, I started talking to Blackie.
You know something? By the time we went in the gate,
there wasn't a fleck of sweat on him. Not a fleck. He went
in the stalls like a little lamb.'*

Tricky had paused and savoured the memory. The
camera switched to the great horse, who at that moment
appeared to be listening to the jockey. And now the film
changed from Mount Landy to the footage of the race that
was being discussed.

'He came out like a rocket.'

The Hunter had left the stalls at speed, but then Tricky
dropped him way back off the pace.

*'He needed to be settled and reassured. Spoken to. His
speed would look after everything else.'*

Then came the commentator's voice: *'And tail-l-ed off,
The Hunter!'*

The leaders reached the end of the back straight and
Tricky took up the story again.

*'I said to him, "We better earn our bread and butter
now, Blackie – so if you're ready, so am I."'*

The film showed the horse at the rear of the field begin
what looked like a long, hopeless odyssey up the wide
outside of the tightly bunched leaders. The Hunter seemed
to be paddling – his momentum wasn't of the same,
attacking configuration as the rest of them. Then, at the
furthest point of the bend, when Tricky and his horse were
more distant than anyone in Arlington from the winning
post, something happened.

'I said, "Go for it!"'

There on the terrace in New South Wales, over twenty
years later, I could sense the excitement.

The film showed the wide outside horse, The Hunter,
literally propelling forward at a different speed from
everything else. Still, because of his position, you saw the

leading bunch of four on the rails, the distance between them and the winning post shrinking with every stride; but far out to the left and at the bottom of the picture, here were Blackie and Tricky. Devouring the ground. They were going so fast that each frame represented a further, dramatic improvement in their position, until inside the last two hundred yards you suddenly realized they were going to win.

So they did, by one and a half lengths – a margin that left every commentator flabbergasted.

But the story had a kicker. The camera panned back to Tricky again.

'I liked to kid him, you know, so after I'd given him a big pat and told him how good he was – and he was the best – we were jogging back down the track to come in and the crowd were all on their feet, a standing ovation, and I leaned forward so he'd hear me and I said to him, "By the way, Blackie, just to let you know, I had a grand on us today." And d'you know something? Swear to God, Mr Landy, he gave a half buck there and then, as if to say, "Christ, Tricky, if you'd told me that, I don't think my nerves could have taken it!"'

And Tricky gave a little buck to the camera.

'Swear to God. He nearly had me on the carpet, there in front of all those people. I shouldn't have opened my big mouth!'

The next shot was of Sam Landy and Tricky, Sam's arm around the diminutive man's shoulders. Sam spoke directly to camera.

'This man is not just my hero,' he said, 'he's like my brother.'

Then they walked out of the paddock.

Silken killed the picture.

'It was used as a promotional video for The Hunter,' she

said. 'My father was intensely proud of Tricky Dawson. Do you still think he could have had him murdered over a newspaper article?'

'Someone had him murdered.'

'I hear you're good with money, Joe. Strikes me you should stick to what you're good at.'

'What are you good at, Silken?'

'Quite a few things. One of them is recognizing assholes. I can spot them at a distance, even on a bad day.'

21

It would take me five hours at the most to get back down to Sydney and catch an evening flight heading home. I felt that at least by coming here I had resolved something: I now believed Sam Landy – more, although it went against the grain, I felt sorry for him. Steer had shafted him as his wife lay dying; and when the opportunity to shaft Steer had presented itself Sam had seen nothing else but an opportunity for revenge. And I felt that Sam was now suffering too because of what had happened to Tricky. I called Tim's mobile and found him in a restaurant in Dalkey; we chatted for a few minutes about business, not that much had changed in the few days since I'd left home. It rarely does. I told him I was coming home.

'How's your – project going?' Tim asked.

'It's finished,' I told him.

'Good,' he said and we said goodnight. Then I tried to call Hanny, but got her voicemail. I told her I loved her, then walked out on the terrace, which was drenched in morning sunshine.

I was going home, but I was unhappy. The circumstances around Tricky's death remained unchanged and the fact that Sam Landy had allowed his enmity for Guy Steer to cloud his better judgement did nothing to redress the howling injustice of the situation. And yet, knowing what I did, there was nothing further I could do.

'You see the problem?'

I whirled around. Sam Landy had emerged from the house and was standing directly behind me. He looked even older and more haggard than he had the night before.

He said, 'You're trying to figure what can be done now

– right? But you realize that someone like Steer is out of reach.'

I nodded.

He said, 'Well, I've spent the last five years trying to figure out the same thing: how do I nail Guy Steer? So when I saw a way, I grabbed it. Shouldn't have. God, I shouldn't have, but I did. Now you're in the same position as me. You're trying to figure out a way forward. Steer had Tricky killed. "How do I nail Guy Steer?" you're thinking. Problem is, if he did have Tricky killed, I'd bet any money that whoever did the job has no idea who they were working for.'

'So – that's the end of it?' I asked.

'It's a shame,' said Sam, 'but sometimes you just have to swallow hard. That's what I should have done instead of calling you.'

'I hate swallowing hard.'

Sam Landy looked at me and his eyes were small and pained. 'I accept that there's evil in the world and no matter what you or I do there always will be. Look, if there was a way of nailing this bastard – and I really mean this – I'd be first up to do my bit. But the reality is that such an opportunity may not present itself. So . . .' He shrugged. 'I'm an old man and I'm nearly beat. But I'm also incredibly lucky! I've got this place, I've got enough wealth to look after me if I live to be a thousand. And I have Silken to carry on. I'm blessed. So maybe it's time I forgot Guy Steer and concentrated on all the good things in life.'

He had a point. We sat down.

'What are your plans?' he asked.

I told him I was flying home that evening and needed to leave Slow Creek around noon.

'We haven't spent even thirty seconds discussing business and I've got thirty million dollars invested with

you,' Sam said. 'How about this? Stay here for lunch, we
discuss business and I'll have you flown down to Sydney in
my chopper.'

It sounded like a good idea: there would always be
another rights issue.

'I'll have Silken show you the farm,' he said. 'Do you
ride?'

'Sure,' I said and heard someone clearing his throat
behind me.

'Mr Landy?'

Sean Free was standing there, his jaw crimson and
swollen. 'I just thought I'd let you know, sir, that The
Hunter's about to go into action with Seashell.'

'Thanks, Sean,' Sam said. He looked at his assistant's
jaw, then at me. He grinned. 'Seems like you better learn to
duck quicker, Sean.'

I held out my hand. 'I'm sorry about last night,' I said.
'It wasn't personal.'

He looked at me, then he took my hand. 'I must learn
how you did that,' he said and tried to smile. 'Ouch!'

Sam laughed. 'You ever seen a mare being covered by a
horse that won the Derby, Joe?'

'Not that I can remember.'

'If you had, you'd remember,' Sam said. 'I've got
some telephone calls I must make but Sean will bring you
over.'

I followed Sean around the house and along a shaded
pathway until we came to the business end of Mount
Landy. There were rows of stables, barns, a small office
block and teams of people in green overalls going about
their work. The covering box was a large concrete-floored
shed with an elevated, glass-fronted office overlooking it.
Sean took me up to the office, then went down to the floor.

Silken was standing there, looking out. She turned as I came in and launched a withering look in my direction.

'Sam said I shouldn't miss this,' I said by way of explaining my presence.

'I know. He's just called me,' she said, her voice with a rim of ice. 'Well, let me tell you about the participants. The Hunter as you may by now have gathered is twenty-three years old, so he's like a very randy great-grandfather. You probably know the feeling. What's so wonderful in The Hunter's case is that he can still transmit all the ability of his youth to a horse that, as we speak, does not exist. It's like magic.'

'You mean – as in tricks?'

'I don't know tricks,' she said.

A small mare was led into the covering box.

'She's called Seashell,' Silken sighed. 'Sam bred and raced her. She's five now and she's just had her foal by another stallion, so she's fretting a little about having left her foal behind in the box in order to come here on this date. Sure you can take all this family trauma?'

'I'm an expert in family trauma,' I said.

The mare had begun to sweat and was neighing and looking around her. A groom stroked her neck and made comforting noises and massaged the little hollow at the base of her ears.

'She's small,' I said.

'In her day she was able to run faster over one mile than any other horse of her generation,' Silken said.

Below us Sean had brought over a wide, well-padded bolster-like collar which he laid on Seashell's back and then fastened around her belly. There sounded a shrill neighing in a different register. A diminutive pony was led in through the rear doors of the shed. As soon as it came near Seashell, the pony began to roll its eyes. It penis quivered beneath it like a length of thick hosepipe. The minder brought the tiny horse right over behind Seashell, who, now shining with sweat, splayed her hind legs. The pony, whose head came not even as high as the small mare's hocks, made a comical effort to mount her, the tip of his probing organ a good two feet short of her displayed vulva. I looked along my eyes. I could see the outline of Silken's body. She stood, absorbed, sucking the tip of a pen.

Sean looked up in our direction and I caught a look pass between himself and Silken. 'OK, OK,' he called out, 'she's ready.'

Like an indignant midget, the frustrated teaser was led away, dancing, the whites of his eyes pleading his case. Seashell was in a white lather, her hind legs apart, nature out of its box. I was somehow put in mind of a live sex show that I'd been to in Bangkok, except that this one involved animals too. Then the large, double doors at the back of the shed opened and a very big Aboriginal man came in leading the star of the show.

The Hunter was still a magnificent beast, almost true black in colour, and although now well bowed in the back, shining with the same physical prowess that had won him his place in history twenty years before. The stallion's front legs and hooves were already fitted with long, padded sheaths. He saw the mare and his lips curled back from his teeth. He began to lunge. Sean was beside him with a bucket of sterile water. The stallion's member was hanging like a long sausage between his back legs. A girl groom came alongside Seashell, lifted her tail and gently lubricated her vulva. Sean began to wash the stallion's penis with his plastic-gloved, moistened hand, from scrotum to tip, long, unhurried caresses.

'Attaboy. That's the big, big boy.'

I felt my mouth dry out as The Hunter's organ filled and lengthened. Seashell began to throw back her head in impatience and stood her hind legs apart even wider. Sean still worked the stallion. I became intensely aware of Silken, all the more so because I could feel that she was aware of me. The Hunter was going crazy for the mare, he was trying to whip his head around to take a bite from Sean, but the big groom held him firm and shucked down heavily on the chain of his head collar.

'Let's go! Hold her steady!' Sean called.

The girl groom stood in and lifted Seashell's tail so her vulva lay waiting, red and unprotected. I could, from the corner of my eye, see Silken's bare arm and the fine nap of hairs that lay there. The black groom led The Hunter in. The stallion's rigid phallus now reached almost between his front legs. The horse reared and mounted the little mare and I could feel the force of the mount. It rocked Seashell. The sweat ran down my face. The Hunter sank into her, squealing. Seashell, ears back, eyes wide, held her ground. The Hunter thrust and, as he did so, in the maelstrom of his pleasure, he began to chew Seashell's back, or where the padded collar protected it. The horse thrust and howled. Silken shifted her weight so that her elbow touched mine. All at once The Hunter shuddered mightily and squealed so loud that my ears hurt. Then the horse's eyes rolled and he slithered off the mare. The girl groom lowered Seashell's tail. Silken looked at me and smiled lazily.

'Men,' she said.

22

Back in my room, I pulled on a pair of jeans. Jacquimo produced jodhpur boots and a pair of half-chaps, then he led me down through the garden to where there was a private stable yard. Silken was there watching as a groom led out a pair of tacked-up horses.

'Have you had a ride recently?' she asked.

'You'll have to define the word,' I said. 'I mean "recently".'

She looked at me, then burst out laughing. 'Look, I'm sorry about what I said earlier. It was ill mannered.'

'Forget it. I've been insulted by experts.'

'I can understand how you feel about Tricky, especially since your sister is involved. My father should never have asked you to do that.'

'I just needed to hear him say that to my face.'

'No hard feelings?'

'It depends what you mean.'

She laughed again. 'OK. Let's go see Mount Landy.'

The horses were rangy half-breeds with more than a bit of spirit to them. We rode out into the countryside. The morning contained a sudden, seasonal heat, like a foretaste of the coming summer. Two miles from the house, away from the mares and foals and the stud-railed paddocks, heavy railway sleepers had been incorporated at chest height into the fencing.

'See you later,' Silken said and kicked her heels behind the girth.

Her horse surged forward, took the jump a full eight feet out. I felt my ears tingle in the warm air. I faced my horse and in two strides he'd the measure of it. As he sailed from the ground, I guided my hands up his neck and felt an old symmetry. Silken was fifty yards ahead already.

The countryside was rolling sage-brush terrain, the original landscape from which Mount Landy had been created. I could see Silken, flat out now, hands and heels flapping at her mount. I sat into my horse, clicked my tongue at his pricked ears, felt him go on the bit. I wanted her, I knew, and my want was strengthened by the fact that I knew she was on for it. And yet I was determined not to give in to myself, because the last thing I needed at this point in my relationship with Hanny was an impromptu affair, albeit at the other end of the world.

The land had levelled out into a flat plain without horizons. I was within twenty yards of Silken – and gaining. I came up level. Excitement shone in her face. Her eyes were alive and fixed ahead. I wondered where we were going. At the penultimate moment, I felt my horse check. Then all I was aware of was space, and whistling air, and the sickening feeling of going down.

We hit the surface of the river together. The cold sucked my breath away. Instinctively, I threw myself to one side in order to get clear of the horse. I came up spitting, and grabbed the reins floating by me.

'You're a fucking lunatic,' I gasped.

'You too old for this?' she asked.

We kicked for the shore, swimming the horses with the current. We came into a beach of white shingles. The horses stood and shook massively. Silken untacked them, then took head-collars and lead ropes from their saddle-bags and tied the horses to a bush. Then she took off her shirt and jeans and laid them out: underneath she had on a bikini. Dressed, her figure had been unforgettable, but in a bikini the fullness and firmness of her body was hypnotic.

I took my shirt off and watched as she produced an apple, sliced it in two, handed me half.

'Did you grow up here?' I asked.

Her camomile eyes surveyed me. She shook her head.

'Mrs Landy wasn't my mother.'

In my sleep, this girl's beautiful face and that of the blonde woman in the portrait had defied my reconciling.

'My mother came here as a secretary in the mid-Seventies. She was American, her father had fought in Korea, which is where her mother was from. I met my granny once. She was a kung fu expert, taught my mother. My mother taught me.'

Silken stood up, swung her glorious right leg in a killing arc over my head, then her left. She sat down.

'My mother was doing her great world tour when she got a job here for three months. She stayed two years.' Silken smoothed her hair back with both hands and squeezed it out. 'Things weren't always so smooth for my father and his wife. Mrs Landy had had several miscarriages and was paranoid about having another. Sam badly wanted a child.' Silken shrugged. 'I was born in LA. We never wanted for anything. He came and saw us every couple of months.'

'Your mother must have resented that.'

She looked at me as if I'd said something intelligent. 'My mother loved Sam, but I guess there must have been a kind of Eastern acceptance in her when it came to such things.'

'Did Mrs Landy know about you?'

'I was never spoken of, but I'm sure she knew that Sam had a love child whom he had called after one of his mares.' She smiled. 'Oh yes. Silken won everything, including the Melbourne Cup when she was six. A real star, by all accounts.'

I said, 'You like this business?'

'I think so. A few years ago Sam asked me to keep an eye on his horse interests in the States, which is how I got into horses. It's like any business – everyone's trying to screw everyone else.' She shrugged. 'Then Mrs Landy died.'

She scratched her shoulder, its texture looked good enough to eat.

'Sam came to LA. He was devastated. He'd always told me that I'd never have anything to worry about moneywise – but now he put a proposition to me: come to Mount Landy and work as his assistant for two years. Then, if I liked it, take over.' Silken drew her heel up onto her knee and fiddled with her big toe. 'I thought about it for nearly a year. I made my mind up three months ago. What's your story?'

'A long one too,' I said, envying her big toe.

I told her a little about myself. The sun's heat was now extravagant – I manoeuvred myself into the shade of a bush. She came into the shade beside me. For a moment the mutual awareness that had surged in the stallion shed now crystallized again. I was aware of her skin. I turned my head and saw her lips, just inches away. Then something rare happened; I decided it wasn't a good idea. Why, I wasn't sure. She was available, yet she was also distant. The moment died.

'So what will you do now?' she asked.

'Go back home. Try and forget this episode. Try and make it up somehow to my sister.'

'Forgetting what happened is probably for the best,' she said. 'Sam should have forgotten about Guy Steer and put his losses down to experience.' She gazed into the middle distance. She said, 'I've never before heard Sam admit to anyone that he was wrong. It's hard for him to let go once he's got hold of something.'

'I'd say he holds on pretty hard,' I observed.

'He was hurt,' she said. 'At first it was like a whirlwind romance – they were inseparable, he and Guy. Went to all the horse sales together. Hunted together. Drank together. Probably chased women together, although I wouldn't have been told. It was incredible to see since one would have assumed they had so little in common. Of course what was driving it was Guy's need for cash. He would have done anything for Sam during that period. Whatever Sam wanted was his.'

I was aware of her standing up and pulling on her jeans – but I wasn't thinking of her. Instead my mind was fizzing with the details of a perfectly co-ordinated plan to entrap Guy Steer. It was all there and it had been prompted by what Silken had just said.

'What is it?' she asked.

'Nothing really,' I said.

'You look as if you've seen an apparition.'

She was right, in a way: I'd seen how to do it. But then the risks involved were of such a scale that only a madman would take them. And I thought of Sam's words of a few hours before. *You see, Joe, there's evil in the world and no matter what you or I do there always will be.*

I shrugged. 'One moment you see it, the next it's gone.'

'You're a strange one,' she said.

There was an engine sound from the bush behind us. A quad loomed into view, roared up and stopped. Sean Free swung out of it. I could see him taking in the situation: the horses, our wet clothes. A look passed for a moment between him and Silken, the kind of look that put me very much in my place.

'Everything all right, folks?'

'Just fine,' she said and looked away from him.

'Mr Landy said to tell you not to forget lunch,' he said to me.

'It's time I got back,' I said.

Sean revved up the quad. We remounted the horses and made our way back in the ever-warming day.

23

It was just Sam and myself for lunch. Jacquimo had served a lobster mousse and an Eden Valley Semillon from Henschke. The main course was cold cuts and salad. I outlined the strategies being followed by Grace Equity. Sam was an attentive listener. We discussed takeover targets, funding requirements and economic templates. Once during lunch the idea that had seized me earlier by the river came into my mind; but I binned it. It was a mischievous fantasy, nothing to do with the real world. The real world was the one that Sam and I were discussing, a place of gross yields, dividends and price-earnings ratios. Now Jacquimo was pouring coffee from an antique silver pot.

'You know, it took a lot of guts to do what you did, to fly out here and face me down,' Sam said. 'We know each other now. If there's anything I can ever do . . .'

We shook. I could imagine how, when I got home and reported all this to Tim he'd be grinning like a cat on Prozac. Sam himself drove me in a quad to a paddock, where the blades of a big Sikorsky were already turning. Jacquimo was there with my bag; Sam was going to have someone drive my car back to the rental company. I'd hoped to have one last double-eyeful of Silken, but she hadn't appeared.

'Say goodbye to Silken for me,' I said.

'She likes you,' Sam said and looked at me curiously. 'I can tell.'

'Joe.'

Sean had been standing at the other side of the chopper; now he came forward.

'Have a good flight home.'

I shook hands with them all, even Jacquimo. Then they were no more than a little bunch in a green field and I was going home.

The images of that homeward trip are engraved for ever on my retina. The first-class lounge in Sydney's Kingsford Smith airport, the flight to Singapore, the fact that I drank and ate very little, that I slept a lot and awoke just as we touched down wishing deeply that I was home. I left the plane in Singapore for two hours. In the transit lounge reserved for front-of-the-plane, I drank a pint of fresh orange juice; and as I put the glass down on the table, I saw two, what looked like airline executives standing by the door, looking at me. I knew it was me they were looking at because when I saw them, they turned away. That was the first taste of it. The second was when we boarded a fresh aircraft and the captain opened his cockpit door and had a good look at me. I regretted then that I'd not called Tim from Singapore, regardless of the fact that I'd have been waking him; but now we were hurtling down the runway and climbing into the west.

I slept, I dreamed. From nowhere came the words of an old prayer. *Gentle Jesus, meek and mild ...* The connection through Heathrow was flawless; I walked off the plane in Dublin at five in the afternoon. Blue skies, temperature twenty-two, they said. Welcome to Dublin. I wanted to stay in the air for ever. I didn't want the ground.

'Joe.'

How had I known that this was going to happen – since I didn't even know what 'this' was?

'What are you doing here, Mick?'

He took me into a little room. A man in a suit made a discreet exit.

'What's going on?' I asked. My legs were giving out.

Mick said, 'I'm very sorry, but there's no easy way to do this, old friend.'

'Who?' I asked.

'Lou,' Mick said.

Part Two

Part Two

24

Hanny was superb. No way could I have got through that time without her. As I was leaving Sydney, Mick had called her and given her the news; she had flown in from Germany and was waiting in Howth when Mick drove me home.

Racked by guilt, engulfed by grief, I ceased to function. Lou's funeral was a blur, a sea of concerned faces, people from the past, my brother John, who came home from New York, and my sister Bess from Canada. Why? The eternal question of grief. I thought I knew, but to have voiced the thought even to myself would have finished me. My family were a lot more dignified than I was. I wanted to see no one. The image of Lou's body in the wreckage of her car, which had been found imbedded in a wall at the end of a hill in County Kerry haunted me. And then three days after her funeral, at ten one morning, my front-door bell rang and when I opened it Mick was standing there. I just stared at him.

'Can I come in?' he said.

I knew that a social call by Mick to Howth at ten on a midweek morning was highly unlikely. He shuffled in and accepted coffee, then ran his fingers through his black curls. This was a business call.

'You look shagged,' he said without preamble.

I said, 'Thanks.'

Hanny came in and sat down and Mick's face brightened up. He said, 'Are you looking after this fellow at all for us?'

'He won't eat,' Hanny said.

I said, 'Are you lost or something?'

'Am I not allowed drop in to say hello?'

I looked at him. 'Hello. Now, what is it?'

He fiddled with the handle of his coffee mug and eventually got his eyes to meet mine and stay met. 'Well, I thought you should know what's been going on,' he said and chewed his lip.

'And . . .?'

'There's been a bit of an investigation,' he began. 'It's not my area, as you know, but I've been keeping tabs on it all the same. They put a couple of detectives on the Tricky Dawson case.'

I knew what he was going to say. I had known before I left for Australia.

Mick said, 'They now think that the drink was tubed into him.'

'Oh, really. How do they now think that?'

'Look, these things take time,' Mick said and stuck his jaw out. 'There's a chip missing from one of his lower front teeth. Initially the post-mortem thought he'd hit his mouth on the table as he fell, but after more detailed examination they're now sure that the tooth was chipped when a medical instrument known as a laryngoscope, which was used to open his throat, slipped.'

How had all this happened? was my predominant thought. I felt a chill inside me.

Mick closed his eyes. 'They've also been looking into the circumstances of Lou's death, Joe,' he said softly.

And this was the exquisite finale of my torture.

Mick said, 'They're pretty certain that someone messed around with the brakes on her car.'

I felt detached and slightly crazy.

'How long has this been known?'

'A few days.' Mick leaned forward. 'You've been in no shape, my friend.'

'And – what's being done?'

Mick offered his podgy hands, palms up, in a gesture of helplessness. 'It's taking its course,' he said. 'There are no obvious suspects at this point. But the reason I'm out here is that the lads want to talk to you about Landy and Steer and all that. I've told them everything you told me.'

'How do I nail Guy Steer?' you're thinking. Problem is, if he did have Tricky killed, I'd bet any money that whoever did the job has no idea who they were working for.

Sam's words resounded in my head.

'Steer had them both killed,' I heard myself say. 'I'd bet the business on that.'

Mick frowned. 'Guy Steer lives in Los Angeles and other such places. He has never even been to Ireland. There's not the slightest shred of evidence to connect him to these deaths.'

'Tricky was going to expose him. After his death Lou came out here. She held me responsible.'

I could feel Hanny looking.

I said, 'She gave me the impression that she had the low-down on Steer that Tricky had come up with. Probably on disk.'

'I'm sure the lads will nail him,' Mick said.

'Sure,' I said.

Ten minutes later I walked with him out to the road and watched as he drove back into Dublin.

25

The following day two detectives from Special Branch came out to my house and spent five hours debriefing me. They were sincere, hard-working men who had dedicated their lives to putting away criminals; but although they made reassuring noises about keeping Lou's and Tricky's files open, it was clear to all of us that optimism in this case was not the appropriate perspective. They thanked me and left.

I didn't sleep much that night. Or the next. Hanny knew. She wrapped me in her arms and kept me alive. More days went by, then weeks. One morning I came downstairs and found myself face to face with Stella, the cleaning lady. For a moment I had no idea who she was. But she understood. She put her hand on my arm and said, 'I'm so sorry.' It was the worst time of my life.

July gradually ebbed and August came in with a blaze of good weather. I felt strange walking down a street, as if everyone could tell who I was and read my mind. Indifferent to my business, lacking appetite for anything, I allowed Hanny to take me for long walks along the seashore, where the forlorn cries of gulls and oyster-catchers seemed to echo my desolation. I lost fifteen pounds and began to go grey. It happens like that, I've read, life changes as if on a hinge. I tried to recapture all the moments of our childhood together, as if by doing so I could spare Lou from oblivion; but each time I tried the memories faded further and I was left perplexed and bereft. I couldn't even begin to address the issues that I'd caused between us these final months. It was as though I had finally and in the most conclusive way failed in my mother's instructions to bring Lou home safe.

In the second week of August, as every square inch of beach seemed to be taken over by families with parasols and deckchairs, my grief began to harden into something cold and heartless. I slipped into a glacier where all emotion was bled away, where peripheral details vanished, leaving just stark objectives and the means to achieve them. Time ceased to be limited by convention or reality. I went deeper, became entombed.

When I emerged it was the third week of September. Hanny had worked from my house those past weeks, doing assignments that kept her around Dublin. I knew she was watching me. And she must have known better than to hope it was all over.

'I'd like to talk,' I said one warm evening.

We were sitting out the back. I'd gone into Howth and come back with crabs' claws; I'd boiled them for exactly seven minutes, then opened a bottle of Chablis. I broke one fat claw with a nutcracker. The shattered shell fragments fell around my feet.

'I'd like to talk to you about what I'm going to do.'

I didn't need to explain to what I was referring. But I needed her on my side. I needed all the help I could get.

Hanny crossed her legs. 'I've been waiting. Hoping, too, that you wouldn't say this, but waiting.'

So I told her. The plan that had come into my mind in Australia had been cast in the cold furnace of these last weeks. When I had finished, all she said was, 'You really think it will work?'

'Yes.'

'It's dangerous.'

'I know.'

'You must do it,' she said.

I took her hand and brought it up to my mouth. 'That means everything to hear you say that.'

'You're crazy, but I know what you have to do.' She frowned. 'Are you going to tell Mick?'

'Of course,' I said, 'but after I speak to Sam Landy.'

'Mick won't like it.'

'That's irrelevant now,' I said.

We ate the crabs' claws and then we made love, looking out on the golden evening sea. I crept from the bedroom when she was asleep and walked down to the water. It was warm and full of hope. I swam under the rising moon for almost an hour; then I went back inside and rang Australia.

26

It was raining five days later when the early-morning Aer Lingus flight touched down at London City Airport and I made my way by cab to Sam Landy's house in Albemarle Street. Sam had put up fierce resistance when I telephoned him in Mount Landy; but in the end I had called in the promise he had made me. Now he had flown from Sydney the day before – but my proposal had simply meant he had had to bring forward his plans by a few days.

The house was the only one I could see without a brass plate or a cluster of bells. I rang once and the door swung open.

'Good morning, sir.'

'Jacquimo.'

Some things never change. He stood back like an undertaker opening the door to a mortuary and I entered. Sam was in a large room at the back, sitting at a desk by a French window that overlooked a garden. He came forward, his hand out.

'I'm going to try and dissuade you from this, Joe,' he said.

He could try all he wanted: this was going to happen. Sam picked up a phone. 'Silken, Joe has arrived.'

Jacquimo brought in a tray with coffee that looked a ringer for his tray in Mount Landy. As he was pouring, Silken came in.

'I'm sorry about your sister,' she said and kissed me on the cheek. She smelled of something better than roses.

'Thank you.'

'Joe, this isn't going to work,' Sam said with finality. 'I don't know where you got the idea from.'

'I got it from something Silken said in Mount Landy,' I
said.

'What did I say?' she asked.

'You said that Steer's need for cash drove everything the
time he and Sam teamed up. You said Steer would have
done anything for Sam during that period, that whatever
Sam wanted was his.'

She looked at Sam. 'It's true.'

'This is a man whose entire bloodstock operation is
sustained by its ability to introduce a fresh source of cash
at regular intervals. We know what happens to a new
victim – you're an example, Sam. Yet, there is a point – to
use Silken's phrase – in the courtship phase when the victim
gets full entrée into the inner circle. Becomes Steer's best
friend. Gets to know everyone in the operation. Of course,
the victim is gullible and sees everything through unsuspecting eyes. Steer is a charming new companion, a
wealthy man like the victim himself.'

'OK,' said Silken cautiously.

'But neither is Steer suspecting anything. This new
bloodstock partner is a mark – Steer is concentrating solely
on getting him in. This is the point at which Steer's guard
is dropped – if only because he suspects nothing. A lot of
things can be revealed in such a situation.'

She looked at Sam, but Sam shrugged, as if to say we'd
been through this before.

'And who exactly had you in mind?' Silken asked
quietly.

The picture of Lou as a little girl in a party dress flashed
before my eyes.

'Myself,' I said.

27

I was thinking of my time in Beirut and of the many ways I had learned to uncover information from unwilling informants. Sizing up the person, then learning the best way in. It was like prising open an oyster. Now and then you found a pearl inside.

'I've done my research,' I said. 'In five days' time, the Newmarket Houghton Sales will be held. As you know far better than me, these sales are where the cream of British and Irish bloodstock is sold every year. People like you, Sam, and Guy Steer and the Sultan of Tamil go head to head to buy the best at the Newmarket Sales. Steer has to be there to stay in the game. I'm going to show up, and with your contacts and knowledge I'm going to outbid Steer on the horses he wants to buy.'

'That's crazy!' Silken cried. 'You don't know anything about bloodstock!'

'Precisely,' I said. 'But you and Sam do.'

Sam opened the windows to the garden and stood there for nearly a minute.

'If we believe that Steer had Tricky and your sister killed,' he said slowly, 'then he won't hesitate to kill again.'

I said, 'Just think about that for a moment. For Steer to have had that done shows how desperate he must be. He couldn't afford to let this information come out because of the consequences. He's near the bone, he needs fresh money, fresh victims. Therefore what I'm proposing is exactly the right way to get inside his guard.'

Silken sat on a cushion near Sam. 'All he has to do is find the connection between you and Sam and you're exposed.'

'I agree,' I conceded, '*if* he does. But why does he have to find a connection? Sam's investment in Grace Equity is through a company in California called Boyd investments. You don't sit on any boards with me, we've met only once before this year. How would he find out?'

Sam grimaced. 'He's a perfectionist. He'll turn over every stone you ever imagined, he'll grill your people in Dublin.'

'He won't get very far,' I assured him.

Sam was still unhappy. 'He'll see a company like Boyd on your share register and he'll have someone over to California the next morning.'

I said, 'With respect, surely we can cover that. I mean, he doesn't know you own Boyd, does he?'

'No, he has no idea.'

'So, Boyd apart, where's the connection between us?'

'I'm just saying', Sam said, 'that you can't underestimate this man. And if Steer manages to find out we're in this together, then that immediately puts you at huge risk.'

I said, 'I'm not risk averse.'

Silken said, 'He'll connect you to Lou.'

'I've thought of that too,' I answered, 'and I realise he may connect me, but I consider it unlikely. She had a different name, she and I had virtually no contact for thirty years. Nor is there any connection between me and Tricky – unless he's going to trawl right through every phone call Tricky made in the last weeks of his life, which is unlikely.'

Sam sighed. He looked at Silken. She shrugged. His old face was now a study in preoccupation. 'Part of me says yes, I want this bastard behind bars if he killed Tricky and your sister. And part of me says why take such a risk? Life will go on. There's so much more to do and play for. And even though I was at fault myself I do not take readily to the idea of revenge.'

'Justice can stand on its own without revenge,' I said quietly.

'That I also appreciate,' Sam said. 'You know something – and I don't want to sound presumptuous, Joe – but I feel every bit as strongly about what Steer did to me when my wife was dying as about what he did to Tricky and Lou. I hope that's not outrageous, but he showed Elizabeth no respect. Now you may believe that Steer is responsible for two murders, carried out because he feared an exposé in the press and subsequent problems with his bankers, and that is a terrible, terrible thing. But it is unproven and maybe unprovable. What you are suggesting is high risk – not only because you may be uncovered, but because, at the end of it all, there may be nothing to be gained. In other words, he may not have had Tricky and Lou murdered, and so everything you do may be for nothing. I'm not worried about putting money into this side by side with you. But I am trying to put the risk into context.'

'How much might I have to spend to steal the best offerings in Newmarket from under his nose and get his attention?' I asked.

Sam said, 'A minimum of twenty million sterling.'

28

Sam retired early. He was still jet-lagged from his trip. He said he'd give me his final decision in the morning, although I'd told him I was going to do it anyway and that time was running out.

'Where are you staying?' Silken asked.

'I'll book someplace,' I said.

'Nonsense. I'll have Jacquimo make a bed up,' she said and put her hand up to forestall my protests. 'There are eleven bedrooms in this house and only a few of them are ever used.'

'Then the least you can do is allow me buy you dinner,' I said.

We walked up Piccadilly and into Soho, where we found an Italian place.

'The real world,' Silken said as we ordered fettuccine. 'Wine at fifteen bucks a bottle. Check tablecloths. I spend more than a month around Sam and his world and I find myself craving for the normal. For houses without servants, for a kitchen, for meals like this.' She smiled. 'Without Jacquimo.'

'What's it with old Jacquimo?' I asked.

'He's been with Sam for thirty years. Before that he used to wrestle for a living.'

'I'd believe it.'

'Sam uses him as a kind of butler-cum-bodyguard. Jacquimo's been professionally trained. He's incredibly strong. I've seen him lift a pony.'

'I'd say he'd eat one too,' I observed.

'He used to look after me when I went to Slow Creek as a child,' she said. 'He's a bit possessive.'

The restaurant was full of noise and on the high tar side of smoky; but the ambience was good. I poured the wine and chewed on a piece of crispbread.

'Who looks after Mount Landy while you two are away?' I asked.

'Sean,' she said. 'He likes nothing better than to be there on his own.'

'He likes you,' I said, remembering the secret look that had passed between them when we'd been out on the horses and Sean had appeared on the quad.

'There was something a long time ago, but that's over,' she said. 'By the way, you ride well. Someone taught you early on.'

'My old man,' I said. 'Taught me to ride, to box. To fish and shoot.'

'To shoot? Like, a six-gun?'

I laughed. 'A twelve-bore. You get a couple of dogs, coming up to Christmas when the frost hasn't been too hard, and you find a big open heather bog. That's where you find snipe. Small birds with this incredible wingspan. Shoot them and you can shoot anything. And great to eat.'

She looked at me curiously. 'You're like him – your father, I mean. I can tell.'

'In some ways.'

There was always pain in there for me, for I had wanted to be like no one else on God's earth; but then one day he had walked out from under me and I'd been on my own ever since.

The pasta arrived, hot and creamy and aromatic.

'What were you doing in the States before Sam asked you to keep an eye on his horses?' I asked.

Silken smiled. 'I wanted to become a film producer – like everyone else in LA. I worked in movies for almost seven years. Saw how life is a series of illusions.'

'Doesn't sound as if you liked it.'

'It's exciting, but it's not life, not the way I want it.'

'Is this?'

'Maybe. At least something tangible is being created. Flesh and blood. It's intensely primal. It seems important.'

We were both, I knew, thinking back to the scene in the covering shed six weeks before, the urgent sexuality that had spilled over and made us aware of each other. We ordered grappa and a single order of ice-cream.

She looked at me. 'You have a woman.'

The grappa burned its way south.

'You make it sound like a jungle.'

'It is.'

I sat back, feeling my need and suddenly, with it, hers.

Silken said, 'Tell me about her.'

I didn't feel comfortable discussing Hanny in the circumstances; but yet I needed to affirm my relationship with her, so I told Silken about us and the types of thing we did together, and how long we had been doing them.

When I had finished, Silken looked wistful. 'You don't have to go through with this scam. It's new territory for you. Forget about it and we can still be, you know, just friends.'

'I know.'

We walked out and along the street. The bars and clubs were going full blast as hot air barrelled out from them. We walked for half an hour, her arm linked lightly through mine. In Leicester Square we watched a couple of buskers for a few minutes.

'Let's take the Underground home,' she said.

We rode a down escalator deep into the earth. The platform was three deep, full of happy people returning home after a night on the town. I felt strangely reassured by their presence. The electronic signal board showed one minute to the next train. We began to make our way to the front so as to be sure of getting on.

I was thinking about what was going to happen when we got back to the house. She wasn't the sort of woman to take kindly to rejection, nor, from the look in her eyes, who liked spending a night in London alone. I felt the rush of warm air made by the approaching train. Silken was standing to my left. I saw her face in profile, the lips slightly parted. Christ, I thought, she's beautiful. I heard the clatter of the train. Then I was hurled forward.

No pain, not yet. As I fell, I heard my own scream. I grabbed air in frantic, useless fists. The train loomed over me. I was checked – by someone else's reflexive gesture. The train slammed my face, but now a glancing blow. I spun. Hit the platform, blessing it even as I did so. Then a thousand voices, some of them irate.

'. . . get yourself and everyone else killed, mate!'

'Is he drunk?'

'Someone call the police.'

A ring of faces. A young man in uniform with a luminous yellow jacket. I got to my feet. A slowly growing realization that I was bleeding.

'I'm all right.'

'You come with me.'

A firm hand on my arm. The passengers, shaking their heads, were now boarding. Then Silken was there, wide-eyed.

'What – *happened*?'

I saw the frightened face of the young official.

I said, 'I slipped.'

'Are you hurt? Jesus, you're bleeding.'

'I'm all right,' I said.

We walked together out of the station with the disembarked passengers.

29

I went to bed alone and exhausted – the kind of exhaustion that comes from knowing someone's tried to kill you. It could have been an accident, of course: the platform had been overcrowded and people had been pushing forward all the time. Yet the blow to my back had not felt accidental. But who? And why? Silken had insisted on bathing my head with warm, aromatic water before saying goodnight. I went to sleep and when I woke up I had a golf-ball-sized bruise on my forehead.

'What in hell happened to you?' Sam asked.

Breakfast was served in a bright room at the other side of the garden. Sam's eyes clung to my wound.

'I slipped,' I said, not sounding any more convincing with my explanation than I had the night before.

'He tried to fall under a train,' Silken said, sitting down.

'Maybe it's an omen,' Sam said. 'Maybe someone up there is trying to tell us something.'

If there is, I'm on message loud and clear, I thought. I asked, 'Have you made up your mind?'

Sam's mouth went grim. 'It is only if we do what we know to be unquestionably right at all times that we deserve to ever be lucky. And bringing this man to justice – if he is guilty – is unquestionably right.'

I blinked. He was behind me.

'Thank you, Sam,' I said. 'I appreciate this.'

'There is one condition,' Sam said. 'I'll get into this up to my elbows, give you all my contacts, share the cash risk, do whatever is needed. But I reserve the right to pull the plug on the whole operation if it gets too dangerous. To say – enough and no more. And I must be kept informed at all times, by whatever means, of what is happening.'

I said, 'Agreed.'

'Your showing up like this in the market is going to upset a lot of powerful people who are unconnected with Steer – I'm talking about people like the Sultan. None of us likes being outbid by an upstart, which is exactly what's going to happen – and the Sultan is highly unpredictable. Man's got his own army at home. He may well take your arrival on the scene as a personal insult. So if I think that it's getting too dangerous, I'm going to wind it up. I want you to agree to that.'

'Agreed,' I said. Remaining alive seemed like a reasonable compromise. I said, 'But I too have a condition.'

'OK.'

'The only people outside the three of us who are to know about this are Hanny and a cop in Dublin named Mick Davitt.'

Sam frowned. 'Explain the cop,' he said.

'If Steer is guilty, we need to set him up,' I said. 'The murders took place in Ireland. We need the Irish police on side.'

'Deal,' Sam said and we shook hands.

'I agree,' Silken said.

Sam stood up and looked at his watch. 'We don't have much time. I've called my office and told them I'm working on a project, that I'm going to be unavailable for the next forty-eight hours. Where do we start?'

'You've got to teach me how to become the world's newest and biggest buyer of horseflesh,' I said.

I was joining the idiots.

30

'What makes Steer tick?'

We were in Sam's study. Silken was cross-legged on the floor by her father's feet. I'd spent the whole day swotting at bloodstock registers, racing journals, horse-sales catalogues and photographs of the key people who made up the international thoroughbred industry. I'd watched videos of yearlings and of horses in training. Now Sam drummed his fingers on the arm of his chair. As we'd focused on the project, his enthusiasm had stepped up a gear and his complexion and general demeanour had become more vigorous.

'Money, and more money, and more money,' he replied. 'It's as if he is trying to compensate for some inner lack. Everything he does or owns must be the best. This extends to every aspect of his daily life: expensive is best and Steer is the best so he only buys the best. It's like a religion.'

I wondered what religion he had in mind.

Sam said, 'I mean, you and I are not exactly in the poorhouse, but we can occasionally sit down and have beans on toast. Not Guy Steer. We're talking Cartier watches, quarter-inch-thick, twenty-four-carat gold bracelets, bottles of wine at a thousand pounds a throw – every single day. And perpetual motion. The man is never still, he's on the move the whole time, as if to pause would be fatal. So, after Newmarket in a few weeks' time, he'll go to California because I know he'll have horses running at Santa Anita. Then it'll be either up to Canada, or back to Europe, or down to the Caribbean. Never still. There's no one place he calls home.'

'Must be a hard person to serve a writ on,' I remarked.

Jacquimo appeared like sunshine itself and replaced one silver coffee pot with another.

Sam said, 'I first met Steer's people at dinner in the Belvedere Restaurant of the Peninsula Hotel, Beverly Hills. He has an Englishman called Tony Friar, an accountant by trade, who oversees the nuts and bolts of the investments. Friar is a cold fish. He's known behind his back as Friar Fuck since he also functions as chief procurer.'

Sam glanced down at Silken.

'Sam, I grew up in Hollywood,' she sighed.

Sam said, 'If there's any glue other than money that binds the Steers of this world, that keeps them loyal and hunting in the same pack, then that glue is sex. Also at dinner that night was Davey Delgado, a chronic alcoholic who works as a bloodstock agent. You'll recognize him by the colour of his nose. He's a worthless individual, but he did Steer some favours in the old days, when Steer was still feeling his way into bloodstock, and loyalty is a sacred cow where Steer is concerned. Then there was Alan Steer, Steer's older brother, a man utterly programmed to do whatever is required. And Fizzy Wilson, Steer's famous American trainer. The meal was splendid, the wines all cost a minimum of $1,200 a bottle and Delgado was roaring drunk before the main course arrived.

'Steer loves this sort of scene. Davey Delgado was being outrageous. Suddenly Friar whispered in Steer's ear. Steer listened, looked at his watch, nodded. Minutes later, we were all in an elevator, heading for one of the suites on the top floor. "I have a surprise for you, Sam," Steer said. The suite was in semi-darkness. There were at least five young women sitting in various poses on a huge, circular bed. All stark naked. Delgado immediately waded onto the bed, unbuttoning his clothes. "Take your pick, Sam, or if you wish, take them all," Steer told me. "But you'd better hurry

– Davey looks like he's going to get there before you." I understood clearly that this was some form of initiation ceremony.'

'What did you do?' I grinned.

'I told him I had a heart condition and left,' Sam said.

31

Jacquimo appeared and whispered to Sam. It was six in the evening. Sam looked up at me.

'Seems you have a visitor.'

I had called Hanny and she had said that she was going to be in London. Now she walked into the room. She was wearing gold-coloured leggings under a very mini skirt. I saw Silken look her up and down. Hanny kissed me on the lips.

'This is Sam', I said, 'and this is Silken.'

'I tried to tell him that he's crazy,' Sam told Hanny as Jacquimo brought her a honeybush tea. 'But I guess you know that already.'

'I like crazy,' she said.

'You think this is going to work?' Sam asked her.

'Joe's plans always work,' she smiled. She turned to me. 'So, what horses are you going to buy?'

'A good point,' Sam said. 'Silken has narrowed them down to the ones likely to make the biggest money.'

Silken had been watching Hanny with cool interest. Now she picked up a thick sales catalogue from the floor.

'There are several colts in here that, subject to them being exciting, physical specimens, Steer will want to bring home,' she began and went to markers in the catalogue. 'The first is a bay colt by Rainbow Quest out of a Be My Guest mare.'

'Northern Dancer line,' Sam said. 'Who's sending him up?'

'Crabtree,' Silken said. 'The dam, Post House, ran second in her three-year-old prep race before retiring injured. If he looks the business, he'll go for anything between four and five million UK.' She flicked. 'Another bay colt, by Kingmambo out of Massorah. She was the champion three-year-old sprinter in Italy.'

'Steer likes Kingmambos,' Sam said.

Silken agreed. 'He'll think his only opposition for this one will be the Sultan. He'll hate to lose such a colt. And then there's a Royal Academy colt but I've never heard of the mare, although she goes back to Neartic. Those are the top three, in my book.'

Sam said, 'We need to check these horses out a million per cent. If we're going to sting this bastard, it's got to be with horses that he doesn't already own.'

'How do you mean, "doesn't already own"?' Hanny asked.

'This is a business where the identity of the ultimate owner of a young horse is often unknowable to all but the most meticulous students of the industry,' Sam explained. 'Mares and foals are registered in a labyrinth of cross-partnerships. Often Steer will bid on a yearling, making it seem as if he is genuinely trying to buy the horse. Then at a strategic moment, the price in the rafters, he'll stop bidding and the auctioneer's hammer will come down, leaving the other bidder the owner.'

'Do I get to have my own racing silks?' Hanny asked.

'I'd start thinking about the colours right now, if I was you,' Sam smiled.

Hanny left at eight. As much as Silken had been sizing her up, I knew that Hanny too had missed nothing – in fact I was sure that the purpose of her visit, which was to relay a message to me that Mick wanted to talk, could much more easily have been done by telephone; Hanny had wanted to see these people, and Silken particularly, for herself.

We worked on into the evening. It was like cramming

for an exam: I went to bed having been tutored all that day; when I awoke we all met for breakfast and the tutorial resumed. It had been agreed that, even though Sam and I would go in fifty-fifty on any horses I bought, I would personally fund the whole venture: it was too risky to have Sam chipping in cash to my account just at the moment when Steer's men would be looking hard at everything I did. I'd called Tim in Dublin and told him to put the funds in place.

'There's a driver-cum-bodyguard called Bill Ruth,' Sam said. 'He'd go through a brick wall for Steer. Ruth is in charge of overall security. I know for a fact that he checks out hotel suites with an electronic surveillance detector before Steer checks in. He also uses a radio transmission scanner. Watch him.'

Silken said she had some business calls to make. I followed Sam down a corridor and was surprised to find a large swimming pool had somehow been incorporated here, deep in the townhouse. A skylight window let in a shaft of sunlight. Sam's old flesh hung off his frame. He waded in and floated on his back.

'In addition to the people I've told you about, Steer's main adviser is a Dr Simon Markowitz, who was actually a very respected equine veterinarian in Kentucky before joining the Steer operation full-time.'

'No women?' I asked.

Sam looked away. 'He's married to an ex-model, Cheetah by name.'

'You've met her?'

'Sure. I'm not sure how well she and he gel as a couple. She knows what his social life is like – I mean, Delgado regularly turns up with a hooker in tow, so she'd have to be rather stupid not to get the drift. And Cheetah's not stupid.'

No one is stupid when this amount of lolly is floating around, I thought.

Sam said, 'Guy's UK horses are trained by a woman – Diana Bigge, whose father is Lord Bridgewater. The softest thing about Diana is her wooden leg, as they say.'

'You serious?'

'Lost the left leg from the knee down as a child in a riding accident. Takes no prisoners, runs her stable like a Gestapo commander, but she's won the Derby three times. And his principal agent is Heather Hunt, an Australian who's lived in England for twenty years.' Sam paused. 'Modesty does not permit me to tell you one of her nicknames, but suffice to say that otherwise she is known in the business as the Piranha.'

It was as if a parallel world to my own was being revealed.

Sam resumed, 'Of course there are layers of management people I never met, accountants, managers, clerks. This is a big operation – but although racing is Steer's passion, it is not the only source of his wealth. You must also look to commodities. Base metals. Copper, tin, lead and zinc. The fastest game in town. Guy is one of the big players.' Sam smiled faintly. 'Just don't get involved, if he ever suggests you do. Even I don't have the kind of cash to support a losing streak in commodities.'

He clambered out.

'Let's have lunch and wind this thing up.'

Lunch was served in the garden by Jacquimo. He wore white gloves, which made his huge hands look like bakers' trays.

'I've decided on your agent,' Sam said.

This was a problem the three of us had discussed at length. No one, no matter how wealthy, would ever consider buying expensive horses without a bloodstock agent. I was therefore going to have to employ an agent cold: trouble was, the majority – and particularly those who were any good – were already committed to such people as Steer or the Sultan. We also decided that Landy's own agent, an Englishman called George Scales, was too near the bone: he might somehow recognize the connection, and if he thought that Sam was buying through a front, that would cause further complications.

'His name is Dunty Rainway,' Sam said.

Silken rolled her eyes. 'He's the only agent certain not to be retained by Steer,' she said.

'Dunty's good on his day,' Sam said, and added for emphasis, 'on his day.'

'He drinks,' Silken said.

'An understatement,' Sam said. 'Never drunk, mind you, but never entirely sober either.'

Sam explained how Dunty Rainway, a sixty-year old Anglo-Irishman was one of dozens of Almost Made It people who still lived on the fringes of the horse business. He was honourable, had made some legendary buys in his day, was known by everyone, but he drank.

Silken said, 'Dunty will never agree to buy a horse that's fundamentally wrong. Where his judgement is suspect is in separating out the top point one of one per cent into the truly great and the simply very good.'

I asked, 'So what do I do if he wavers? I can't ring you up for your opinion.'

Sam waved his hand, as if batting away my doubts. 'Use your intuition, Joe,' he said. 'It's like buying a company. You'll know a good one when you see it.'

'From the moment on Monday that you appear, Steer will be on to you as opposition,' Silken said. 'Rely on it.'

'We need to have a means to communicate that doesn't give away the connection,' I said. 'Assume, if he's suspicious, that he'll have all my regular phone lines listened to. Same for cellular phones – scanners are ten a penny. I suggest I get my people to set up seven telephone numbers in Dublin, one for each day of the week. We communicate by calling the appropriate number for the day and leaving a message. We're the only ones who know the password to access the messages – which we do only from a payphone.'

'You done this before?' Silken asked.

'I've done everything before,' I said and picked at some homemade noodles.

32

I rang Mick from my room.

'So what are you up to?' he enquired.

I told him, although I got the impression as I did so that what I was saying wasn't entirely news to him. He and Hanny considered my ongoing welfare their personal responsibility.

'Oh boy!' he said when I had finished. 'Look, if we're right, then whatever Tricky was on to was serious enough for someone to hire international contract killers to fly in and take him out. Same for Lou. And now you're going down the same path. Worse, you're actually proposing to go into partnership with Guy Steer.'

'What else do you propose I do? Sit back and wait for a couple of years until your colleagues in Dublin bring a case against him? That's not going to happen.'

'How long d'you think you're going to last?' Mick said. 'I mean, one wobble and you're toast, mate.'

'I'm gambling he'll just see my money. He needs money. We've set it up that when he researches me, he'll see only a bottomless pool of wealth.'

'And then?'

'That's where you come in. What do I need in order for a cop like you to arrest him?'

Mick sighed heavily. 'You need him to incriminate himself.'

'You mean, record what he says?'

'Exactly that.'

'Then I need advice.'

Mick's uneasiness all but clogged up the phone line. 'It's essential you have good-quality gear, excellent voice and sound reproduction, otherwise no court will accept it. But I don't believe we're having this conversation.'

'Keep going.'

'So when the time comes and you think you're ready to go, call me and I'll see if I can set all that up. As to the entrapment itself . . .'

Mick paused and allowed the word *entrapment* to float out and crystallize somewhere over the Irish Sea.

'. . . you need first of all to get him to identify himself. So the conversation needs to make reference to his identity. The fewer other people present, the better, just you and him would be perfect. No room for confusion. Then, whatever he says that can reasonably be interpreted as connecting him to Tricky's death – enough to put hand-cuffs on the bastard and mount a case against him.'

'In Ireland.'

'Otherwise it gets messy – extradition warrants, his being the citizen of another country. Tricky and Lou died in Ireland. That's where we have all the clout.'

We discussed some minor problems that might arise. Then Mick asked, 'How do you know you can trust Landy?'

'It's a value call,' I said.

'When are these horse sales?'

'Day after tomorrow.'

'I suppose there's no point in suggesting that you forget this,' Mick said. 'I mean, if you were to change your mind, I could fly over and we could go on the greatest piss up of all time.'

'I'd like nothing better,' I said, and I meant it, 'but this has to be done first.'

I could imagine Mick doing his shrug. 'I know,' he said, 'but I thought it was worth a try.'

33

I put one of the videos into the VCR in my room, poured myself a Jameson and sat back. It was footage of The Hunter in his paddock. The stallion was grazing at the bottom end. When he saw the camera he lifted his head, broke into a canter to the middle of the field, threw his muzzle this way and that as if asking by what right someone else was there, then abruptly resumed his grazing. I wanted just to look at him, to try and get some idea embedded in my mind of a perfect horse's conformation. No more elusive science existed, I knew. It was not just the stallion's muscular physique, but a whole host of other, minor matters which went into the making of a good horse.

I thought of top athletes, how they dominate their environment, but also how they often appear slight. Like Tricky Dawson. The Hunter trotted in a wary arc. I could see that he was not by any means a big horse. Then there were his legs. Most horses fail, Sam had told me, and the main reason for their failure is their legs. A horse weighs on average one thousand pounds. He or she gallops at speed for a living. If the legs that carry that weight are not properly engineered by nature to begin with, sooner or later one of the legs will give and the horse will break down. The Hunter's forelegs were neither straight nor angular, rather tapering down gracefully into each wide and round hoof. His hind legs were still powerful limbs, muscular to the hock, then the sling-like curves of the fetlocks. The Hunter had never broken down. Sustained a few stone bruises along the way, but had otherwise carried through life the gift of perfect soundness ordained by nature. There, in the paddock in New South Wales, I could feel the excitement that this animal must have generated.

'Doing your homework?'

Silken had come into the room behind me and I hadn't heard her. She was wearing a towelling robe.

'I thought you might like a moonlight swim.' She was smiling at me like a teenager who has escaped from the school dormitory. 'How about it?'

'I have no togs.'

'Oh my goodness,' she said.

I went to the bathroom, put on a robe and we walked downstairs and down the corridor to the pool room.

'You really are going to go through with this, aren't you?' she said. 'I mean, you could call the whole thing off now and there'd be no loss of face. No one would think less of you.'

I thought of Lou and of myself. 'I'm not sure that's entirely true,' I said.

She asked, 'Are you nervous?'

I considered the question. 'No is the truthful answer, which in itself makes me slightly nervous. I should be.'

Moonlight fell on the surface of the pool, but there was no other light. She went to a switch on the wall and turned it. A humming began in the machine room and the surface of the water began to move.

'Last in buys the drinks,' she said.

The robe had slipped to the ground and her ivory body glistened like a knife as she dived full length into the lapping waves. I followed. Currents tugged and teased my body. I swam two lengths, but the wave machine was on full tilt, making it difficult to see where she was. Treading water in the centre of the pool, I suddenly saw her at my feet. She burst upwards in front of me, put her two hands behind my neck, bent forward and kissed me deeply. She was naked.

There was something desperate about her approach, which I would not understand until later. I held her close. She shoved her knee between my legs and again probed her tongue into my mouth. Her wildness and raw excitement seemed all at once the opposite of Hanny's cool, Teutonic poise. The current was satin smooth on my shoulders as she put her hands there to keep her balance. I leaned back against the lapping water, as if against a warm, undulating wall. Silken swam upwards, then let the water guide her down deliciously, little at a time, on to me. Slowly, thrusting, I went under and found her breasts with my mouth. The water was like a giant amplifier – I could hear my own blood pounding, and Silken's, and above us both, way out there somewhere, a deep, almost mechanical growl. At some point, joined, my legs enwrapped her and we floated, as one.

'Oh Jesus, Oh God,' she said, as we both surged.

Later, we lay for hours, it seemed, on cushions, watching the moonlight. Had she been trying to keep me, I wondered afterwards? Did she have a far sharper appreciation of the dangers facing me than I myself did? Or was she giving me every reason, when it was over, to come back to her? I would always remember her body. Its vitality. Its need. The way she had clung to me, as if she really feared losing me. She didn't show up the next morning as I was leaving. And then I understood: she didn't expect to see me again and the night before had been her farewell.

Part Three

Part Three

34

The butler eased out the cork from the bottle of Bollinger, tilted the glass flute to catch the soft, white froth, then bore a silver tray with the champagne and a plate of sushi over to the perspiring, tweed-clad, middle-aged man on the sofa. The man shook his head, once.

I remarked, 'You don't like sushi?'

'I don't much care for it, thanks, no,' said Dunty Rainway, his eyes flitting around Claridge's £3,500 a night penthouse. 'To be absolutely candid, I don't care for anything Japanese.'

He grasped the champagne glass and, nudging it briefly in my direction, took a generous pull. His release was palpable.

'Father was a Burma POW,' Dunty said, sitting back and lighting up a cigarette. He had a jaw like a potato spade, which remained rigid as he spoke. His voice, a gravelly, nicotine-coated drawl, seemed to originate somewhere near the top of his stomach. 'Bridge over the Kwai and all that. Remember seeing photos of him coming home like a skeleton. Never got over it, ruined his chest. Made a lasting impression.' Two bright red patches had appeared as if by magic on Dunty's cheeks. The butler refilled his glass. 'Hasn't helped me in my line of business, of course, but there you are.' He chuckled briefly. 'Rum little chaps, you know. I was in a trainer's yard in Chantilly a few years back –'. The agent paused, as if suddenly considering the company. 'You know, north of Paris, and three limousines full of these people arrived. All dressed in black suits, bowing and scraping and chattering on, dreadful racket. They had half a dozen horses in training there, it seems. Anyway, my man had to show them around, so I tagged along. I'm sure half of them hadn't the remotest idea what they were looking at or what was being said. Then we came to a box and a colt that had won his last four races was pulled out. "Now", said the trainer to the head Jap, "this one was a *very* good buy."'

Dunty emptied his glass and began to chuckle, a noise like a dog gargling. Cigarette ash tumbled down his tweed front.

'And do you know what happened? They all chanted, "very goodbye," and bowed, and ran over into their cars and fled the place!' The agent wiped his brow with an enormous silk handkerchief. 'Swear to God, that's true. "Very goodbye!"'

I recalled what I had heard from Sam about this man and decided that two more glasses of champagne and the meeting would be a waste of time.

'I'll look after this, thanks,' I said, taking the bottle from the butler, who melted out of sight like an obedient gun dog. 'I'm kind of tired, Dunty,' I said, filling his glass to halfway, then taking the bottle to the table beside me. 'I'd like to get the business out of the way now, if that's OK with you.'

'How did you hear about me?' enquired Dunty, his red-veined eyes following the bottle. He scorched the side of another cigarette and drew deeply.

He was a likeable man, I could see, but at the same time probably lost on the great battlefield of life. If he became drunk on two glasses of champagne, clearly he was now only topping up.

'I have people who find things out for me,' I said. 'I asked them to find me a top-class agent who was completely independent.' I made knowing gestures with my head. 'They came up with you.'

'Good for them.'

It was two in the afternoon. I'd checked into Claridge's at noon and managed an hour's kip. I'd awoken midway through a vivid dream of Silken astride me in the basket of an airborne balloon. Symbolism was ruining my life.

'Your list of horses,' Dunty rumbled, putting down his flute with some reluctance. 'D'you mind me asking how you came up with these particular ones?'

'A little bit of research, a few phone calls, a look at what's been winning the big races recently,' I said solemnly.

'Ah.' Dunty drained his already empty glass. Maybe it was the sniff he was after. 'Decided who'll train?'

'I was considering Tim Haines,' I answered, mentioning a competent Newmarket trainer who had been suggested by Sam.

'Good choice,' Dunty gurgled, putting down his empty glass with more than a touch of regret.

'Let me tell you how I come to be here, Dunty,' I said.

I gave him the agreed spiel about my lifelong interest in racing and then settled back as Dunty, keen to add his own gloss of expertise to the catalogue, gave me his view of the three colts I had picked. I nodded to show I was listening, but I wasn't; in truth I was feeling cut off – from Silken, and also, in a way I found it hard to explain, from Sam. I was putting out into a sea I knew very little about.

'Don't you agree?'

Dunty, squatting under a cloud of cigarette smoke, was looking at me expectantly.

I said, 'I'm sorry, I didn't quite catch the question.'

'I was merely observing that there is little point in going head to head with the very big boys when we can do terribly well indeed, thank you very much, down at the next level.'

'Dunty,' I said gently, 'don't take this the wrong way, but

I've been going head to head with all the class – and winning – for as long as I can remember.'

Dunty blinked. 'I take it you've heard of the Sultan of Tamil?'

'Of course.'

'The Sultan will be very active tomorrow and, with respect, his money comes out of a hole in the ground. He gets upset if he's outbid. Same goes for Guy Steer. You've picked probably the three colts I happen to know he's keen on. The Rainbow Quest out of the Be My Guest mare is a stunner, I've seen him.'

'Northern Dancer line,' I said.

'Precisely. The colt has been seen four times already by Steer scouts. A lovely horse. As is the Kingmambo. So I wouldn't be doing my job correctly, Mr Grace, if I didn't tell you that these horses won't come cheap.'

'It's Joe. What's the matter, Dunty?' I asked, standing up, feeling irrational power surging through my veins. 'You scared of a fight?'

Dunty's eyes popped. 'Certainly not!'

'Well then, what's the problem?'

Dunty jumped to his feet. 'You want to take them on, sir, I'm your man!'

I showed him out to the hall. I'd have had a grand to a shirt button that he was headed for the bar downstairs.

I decided to go for a walk. As I crossed Claridge's chequer-board, black and white marble hall, a porter, unbidden, handed me a generous umbrella. I had once lived three months in London, but that was more than a dozen years ago. I strolled down Brook Street, in the heart of London's Mayfair. I wondered about the incident in the Tube station two nights before. I'd considered calling Mick about it, then changed my mind. Maybe it had been an accident. But if it had not been, then who was on to me?

I wondered what my attraction to Silken said about my commitment to Hanny. I'd been married twice before and each time had tried to give it my best; neither marriage had worked. Silken's wild side was irresistible. She was in my blood.

For twenty minutes I rambled by squares and streets with second-hand bookshops until all at once I found myself on the other side of Piccadilly from Green Park. The rain drizzled. Crossing, I walked with the sloping ground through Green Park until I came down to the end which meets the top of The Mall. Across the wide, busy thoroughfare the usual, curious crowd stood outside Buckingham Palace.

I crossed, not knowing why I was being drawn to one of the world's most obvious tourist spots. Then, as I stood by the railings to the palace, ahead of me the guardsmen stamped their feet and everything dissolved in an absolute and terrifying way: railings, guards with busbies, people. A little girl was holding a man's hand. A woman was linking mine. The man, as a joke, was stamping his feet in unison with the guardsmen.

'Sssh!' the woman was saying, but she too was now laughing.

The scent of her perfume gripped me. We'd come over on the boat, Lou, me and my parents. I was no more than six years old, Lou three. My mother would ever after refer back to this trip as to a golden age.

Thud! Thud! The hobnail boots hit the pavement. I leaned against the railings, wondering if I still existed, or if I was now simply an invention, a phantom, condemned to look in on old scenes from behind one-way glass.

'You all right, gov'nor?'

An elderly man collecting cigarette ends with a stick and claw was looking at me.

'Am I . . . ?'

'Just thought you came over funny as I passed you, no disrespect.'

'I'm OK,' I said and thanked him. 'I'm just tired.'

'Takes a lot out of you if you're not used to it, guv'nor,' he said and made his way down along the railings.

I flagged down a cab and went back to my empty suite and to bed.

35

At seven on the first morning of Newmarket Sales I rang Mick.

'What the fuck's going on?' he asked.

I described in detail what was happening, the plan that had evolved and was now being put in motion. When I had finished, Mick's laughter rang down the line.

'Oh boy!' he said. 'What a fucking scam!'

'I'll keep you posted.'

'Just mind yourself,' was the last thing he said.

Then I called Hanny.

'Are you OK?' she asked, her voice tense.

'Why wouldn't I be?'

'I don't know. I don't like that woman.'

'Silken?' I said, and felt the usual tug of guilt. 'She's helping out. She's OK.'

'There's something about her,' Hanny said. 'I don't like her.'

'Look, forget her. When this is over, you and I are going to begin a new phase of our lives,' I heard myself say.

'How can I believe you?'

I had this sudden impulse. 'Might you agree to marry me?' I asked.

'I might,' Hanny said, 'but not on the telephone.'

I promised I'd be home in a few days, then went downstairs and got into the back of the black limousine.

Dunty Rainway was outside the main entrance to Tattersall's Park Paddocks, hopping from one foot to the other as if his shoes had ants in them. I'm sure he thought this was all too good to be true.

'We may be in a bit of luck,' he said from the side of his mouth. 'No sign yet of Mr Steer – and normally he would be very active by now if he was going to bid.'

'Good,' I said and my heart sank at the thought of us failing at the very first hurdle.

Upwards of sixty separate training establishments and over four dozen stud farms could be found within a few minutes' drive of Newmarket town centre, Sam had told me. Tattersall's, the family firm that had begun selling horses in London in the late eighteenth century, now carried on this business from extensive premises in the centre of the town.

The yearlings were housed in a series of different stable blocks, some of them a considerable walk from the sales arena. These blocks, which at any one time had to cater for nearly seven hundred horses, were interspersed with rings in which the horses could be lunged or exercised or walked or whatever horses did when they weren't hanging around waiting to be sold. There were snack bars and offices. The enclosures were busy. I looked around me and saw the stock figures I remembered from racing: old jossers dressed like gentleman farmers on a day out, tweeds and cords and caps with the type of double peak that otherwise were worn only by characters in books by P.G. Wodehouse.

'The Rainbow Quest's up in an hour so we'll have a look at him straight away,' Dunty said, forging ahead, catalogue wedged beneath his arm.

We walked down a row of boxes. A woman was coming towards us. She wore a green headscarf and the sort of padded green jacket that is only licensed to horse people. She walked with a limp.

'Morning Dunty.'

'Diana.'

Dunty let her get out of earshot. Then he said from the side of his mouth, 'Know who that is?'

I told him I had no idea.

'Steer's trainer, Diana Bigge. She's probably been down here looking at exactly what we're interested in.'

Several people got to their feet as we reached the box: Dunty was clearly expected. I was introduced. Warm handshakes, ruddy country smiles. These were the breeders of this horse and any additional punter such as myself, who might bid the price higher, was clearly welcome. The stable door opened and the groom led out a gleaming colt. The horse was well muscled and threw his head around with high-bred impatience, dancing sideways and scattering the onlookers. He was pissed off with this routine, I could tell. Instinctively I found myself evaluating his scope, the size and shape of his head, the way he looked at me, the space between his ears, the width of his chest, the length of him, the structure of his legs, his hooves, the way his quarters had developed and, then, on top of all these individual attributes, the indefinable sense which he transmitted to me, the sum of all his qualities and more. In this case, the sense was overpoweringly of more. This was a horse.

'What do you think?' Dunty murmured as we stood to one side, evaluating.

The Rainbow Quest colt was being put through his paces, trotting up and down the level ground beside the boxes. He moved well. There was nothing crabbed or tight about his action. He threw out each toe with confidence, the same way, one hoped, that he would attack the final furlong in a great race.

'Well?' Dunty asked again from the side of his mouth, out of earshot of the stable people. I could see the veins on his nose standing out like raspberry vines. His was, of course, a question founded on politeness and tact, since

Dunty would not expect his average client to have horse knowledge beyond that gleaned from *Black Beauty*.

'You're the professional. What's your opinion?'

Dunty almost groaned with relief, for he was now in sight of a real transaction. 'I'll tell you what my opinion is,' he muttered with the utmost seriousness, 'I think this is the type of horse who could go on and win the Derby.'

'Well then, let's go and buy him,' I said.

We thanked the colt's consignors, Dunty with more than a touch of familiarity. I wondered as we walked towards a snack bar whether Dunty was on commission from them: for Dunty was now valuable to them whether or not I bought the horse; the mere fact that he was going to bid meant the price would go up. The fact that such a financial arrangement ran directly contrary to the interests of the person whom Dunty was meant to be solely representing – me – had never been an impediment to this practice in the horse industry, Sam had explained.

'Have you considered an upper limit, Joe?' Dunty enquired, looking at his watch and simultaneously sinking his teeth into a pork pie. In fifteen minutes' time the colt would be offered for sale – Lot 216.

'Not really.'

'They're unlikely to let him go for under three and a half,' Dunty said and belched.

'I didn't think this was going to be cheap,' I said.

Dunty sucked down lungfuls of smoke as we moved out of the snack bar and towards the sales arena. A check-jacketed man red of hair and face came and shook Dunty's hand. I recognized him from the photographs in Mount Landy as Tom Haines, my trainer of choice. He looked as if he had just climbed down from a tractor, and he spoke with one of those English regional accents that reminded me of advertisements for cider.

'This is Mr Grace, who hopes you can train for him,' Dunty said as he introduced us.

'I look forward to it,' Haines said jovially. 'By the way, Dunty, a quick word . . .'

He drew the agent to one side. There was a brief discussion, then Haines hurried away.

'He's interested in the Rainbow Quest himself,' Dunty observed darkly. 'He asked me if we were interested in a partnership.' Dunty looked at me sideways. 'I told him I didn't think so.'

I managed to keep a straight face. A partnership with another owner would not only lower the price, it would also halve Dunty's hand-back, if one were in place, since now Haines too would be involved.

'Quite right,' I said and we entered the Newmarket sales pavilion.

36

With high tiers of seats and steep steps arranged around a small arena, it was very like a theatre. We made our way up a busy flight of stairs to an upper tier known as the Gods, where, apparently, Dunty always sat. Everyone had their traditional place at Newmarket Sales, Sam had explained, perhaps because that was where they had stood when they first made a purchase here that turned out to be lucky. So, the Sultan of Tamil always stood in the tiers known as the Bidders, opposite the Rostrum, and Guy Steer's position, if he was here, was to the right of the auctioneer. And Dunty Rainway always sat in the Gods.

Lot 216 was being led in. From our position, the animal appeared far below us, as if in miniature. The auctioneer, a man in a regulation tweed jacket with half-spectacles perched on the tip of his nose and, from our position, substantially bald, stood to the fore of a wide rostrum, from which sprouted a slender microphone. It could have been the scene for a political rally. Either side of the auctioneer stood two further, younger men, also in country jackets. Dunty gave me the thumbs up. When I looked at him quizzically, he whispered, 'No Steer!'

So much for planning, I thought. I now had to decide whether or not to pay at least £3.5 million for a colt in which Steer had not had enough interest even to show up and bid for.

'Lot 216, by Rainbow Quest out of Post House by Be My Guest by Northern Dancer . . .' The auctioneer's voice was that of an actor playing an English officer in a nineteenth century epic involving Zulus. 'His mother was a winner, he comes from a family that embodies stamina, he's every inch a winner. Look at him, ladies and gentle-men, who'll put me in at two million?'

The colt whom thirty minutes ago I had smelled and run my hand over, strode around the ring. There was a rustle of interest from the auditorium.

'One million then, who'll put him in? All ·right, seven hundred and fifty thousand, but I'll not take a penny less,' scolded the auctioneer. 'Half a million I'm bid, thank you, sir, half a million, and fifty, thank you, and six hundred thousand I'm bid for the Rainbow Quest. Who'll say seven?'

I saw Dunty's eyes twitch. He moved his catalogue a quarter of an inch and the man to the auctioneer's right seized the movement immediately and relayed it.

'Seven hundred thousand from the Gods, thank you, am I bid eight, eight hundred bid, and nine, and nine, nine hundred thousand guineas.'

Dunty moved his catalogue.

'One million guineas.'

Not bad going in under a minute, I thought. There was a time not so long ago, near enough to remember clearly, when I'd owned a car but I'd not always had the cash to put petrol in it. The bidding stepped along merrily. It was quite difficult to appreciate that this was real money. We crossed effortlessly from one million plus to two and then to over three million.

'Three point three million, I'm bid, and I'm selling at three point three million!'

The auctioneer's cries echoed. I tried to get a grip. If the auctioneer said he was selling, it was because he had reached the seller's reserve. Lot 216 was now on the market. Dunty's catalogue was ticking like a metronome. But the whole point of the exercise, outbidding Guy Steer, seemed to have failed since Steer was not even present.

Down in the Bidders a knot of dark-skinned men conferred urgently each time Dunty bid. One of them in particular was sending us up looks of naked hostility.

'Three six, three seven, three eight, three nine,' hollered the auctioneer with zeal, stepping a hundred grand a time with ease. It was hard to comprehend that each twitch of Dunty's hand, represented more money than the average man would ever see in a lifetime.

'Four million I'm bid – against you in the Gods. Can I say four one?' asked the auctioneer and the entire auditorium turned its head and looked up at us.

'What do you want to do?' Dunty whispered grimly, sweat transforming his face into a dripping phantasmagoria of purples and livid reds.

'Who's bidding against us?' I asked.

'The Sultan stepped off at three and a half,' Dunty hissed. 'Not pleased. Now, as far as I can see, we're against Diana Bigge. Fuck her.'

'Where is she standing?'

'To the right of the rostrum as you look at it.'

'I'm selling against you in the Gods for four million guineas,' said the auctioneer in the same sort of calm voice you might hear announce a train's platform.

I peered down. There, at the level of the ring, huddled to one side of a group of men and with a telephone to her ear, was the green-scarfed and jacketed woman who had earlier said hello to Dunty.

'Do hurry!' Dunty whispered.

'I'm selling once at four million,' said the auctioneer.

I nodded to Dunty. Dunty twitched.

'Four one!' cried the auctioneer with satisfaction.

Now I could see the reaction to our bidding. The woman was clearly on an open line – but to whom? If not to Steer, then this was a gigantic waste of money. Then, emerging from the shadows, I saw the face of a man who had been standing behind the woman trainer. From the photographs I had studied in Albemarle Street, I recognized Alan Steer, Guy's brother. Displeasure at the prospect of his brother's plans being thwarted, was plain in his face.

'Joe?'

'Keep going, Dunty,' I said, and thought of Silken's face and the way her neck dived into her throat and the width of her shoulders. I'd have to get counselling or something.

'At four million eight hundred thousand, I'm selling him, ladies and gentlemen –'. The auctioneer looked down at Diana Bigge. 'Are you going to lose him for that?'

I looked at Dunty. He was quivering.

'Sold!' The crack of the hammer was like a gunshot. 'Four million eight hundred thousand guineas. Mr Dunty Rainway.'

I was dazed. I had not appreciated that our bid was the highest. Some people around us came and clapped Dunty on the back.

'Well done,' I told him.

'With the very greatest respect, Joe,' the agent gasped. 'I need a drink.'

37

I ate alone in my suite, treated myself to a £175 bottle of wine on the basis that everything is relative, then took a call from an excited, and well-oiled, Dunty Rainbow.

'We're the talk of Newmarket,' he said. His voice had moved up an inch from his stomach into his windpipe. 'No one can speak of anything else: the man who gave Steer his come-uppance.'

'So that was Steer she was bidding for,' I said, feeling £4.8 million worth of vindication.

'Steer was delayed in South Africa,' Dunty babbled. 'He sent his brother, Alan, who was standing behind Diana Bigge.'

I thought of the pale face that had floated out of the gloom below the auctioneer's rostrum. Nice people.

'Guy was bidding by telephone on his plane from Cape Town,' Dunty gabbed.

'From Cape Town to where?' I asked.

'To London, of course. He'll be here himself tomorrow.'

We rattled on for a few further minutes about sending the colt to Tom Haines, and about insuring the animal, which Dunty had already done. He also told me that the Sultan of Tamil had had a major fit of pique at being upstaged by a newcomer.

'Of course, who he thinks he is, I have no idea,' Dunty sniffed.

I needed fresh air. The evening was almost balmy as I left Claridge's. London went about its evening business, buses screeching, *Evening Standards* discarded for another day. I wondered how pissed Dunty was by this stage. I reached Bond Street, then at a public phone box took out the plastic phone card, which sported a cheerful face in dreadlocks from Notting Hill, and dialled the Dublin number for that day.

'Nice horse,' was Sam's voicemail. 'I would have bought him myself. By the way, tomorrow don't look so pale, Joe. When Dunty bid four eight I thought you were going to get sick.'

I was grinning as I walked back to the hotel. The fact that Sam had been in Newmarket that afternoon somehow made it all much easier.

I was in a deep dream. Floating in water. Silken in my arms. We floated. I lay back in the warm river. Silken lay above. My legs entwined her. My hands on her breasts. The river joined us in the most urgent, primal sense. Something, a spar of wood, knocked against the shore. Insistently. But the shore was distant and I only wanted to be more part of Silken than anyone had ever been. And yet the spar knocked.

I was out of bed and across the room in three strides. Fully awake, yet still acutely in the dream. The knock on the outer door was soft but firm. Who was knocking? The butler had long since bid me goodnight. I put the chain on and eased the door a inch. Eyelashes floated level with mine.

'May I come in?'

I closed the door, used the spyhole to confirm she was alone, took off the chain.

'Hi.'

She was tall, five-ten, with natural blonde hair. When she stepped into the hall she turned so that I could help her remove her coat. She wore a simple dress, black, two slim straps over the shoulders. Her skin was like an ad for Dulux satin finish. Her face had an aura of luminous innocence mixed with the Kama Sutra. She was nineteen, at most.

'Thanks,'

'Who are . . . ?'

She put a finger to my lips. 'I am your nightcap, Joe.'

'Sent by . . . ?'

She smiled. 'An admirer.'

I should have, in the general plan of things, opened the door again and given this beautiful girl money for a taxi and told her to behave herself and go home. But I was curious to know exactly who my admirer might be under the circumstances, so I stood back and she walked by me, looking back over her shoulder, saying, 'I'd like to take a shower, if that's OK.'

Be my guest. It had to be Steer, I reckoned, and yet something about the crudeness of the approach disappointed me. When she came back in, I was in bed.

'May I get in?' Her face defied the notion that she could have been a hooker, even though no other explanation was possible.

I said, 'Only if you tell me who sent you.'

'The truth is I don't know who's paying.'

'So what happens if you leave now?'

'I lose five grand,' she said.

'Then sleep on the sofa,' I said.

She made a face. 'Don't you like me?'

'I like you a lot,' I said. 'It's me I don't trust.'

'I can do anything you want.'

'How old are you?'

'Seventeen.'

'Come on.'

'All right, I'm twenty. But you can do anything you want. Anything.'

'Can I take you up on that?'

'Sure,' she said, sitting on the bed. She dropped her voice and ran her finger down by my ear. 'Tell me what you'd most like to do. I don't care how naughty it is – if you want to do it, you can.'

'I'd like to go to sleep,' I said and closed my eyes.

I slept lightly and when I awoke it was dawn and the girl was sitting on a chair in a towelling robe, drinking coffee.

'I went ahead,' she said.

'Fine.'

She was, she told me, in her second year studying architecture in London; that she did a gig like mine only very occasionally; that it was all set up by a film agent – a pimp, in other words – who lived in Belgravia. She had no idea who was paying. She was truly beautiful, whatever she did. I enquired how she had got into Claridge's in the first place and she replied that she had a room on the second floor.

I wondered if she had really been sent by Steer or if there was someone else out there who could not make up his or her mind whether to kill or woo me. I showed her to the door ar seven and she kissed me chastely.

'If you ever want to call me, there's no charge,' she said.

I watched her saunter away down the corridor. Sex was the glue of the horse business, Sam had said. And this was the business I was now in.

38

I arrived in Newmarket at the same time as I had the morning before. As my car pulled up to the main entrance, I saw a big bruiser of a man dressed in a brown suit go to the driver's door of a maroon-coloured Rolls Royce. His appearance was not dissimilar to that of a brick shithouse. He looked once in my direction before getting into the car and driving off. Dunty was waiting again; by the number of tissue patches on his face, it looked as if he had shaved that morning with a broken tumbler. I stepped out of the car and a man exploded a camera flash in my face.

'You've become an overnight racing celebrity,' Dunty blurted happily. 'Have you seen the newspapers?'

I had not.

'You've made the front page of the *Racing Post*,' he chortled. 'Not bad for a chap's first day.'

There was a marked difference as we walked down through the boxes. Our arrival was being noticed. Dunty was taking the brunt of it, and in his stride; I could imagine how in the past clients such as myself had been prised from his hapless grasp, probably with a bottle of champagne. For now numerous attempts were made to engage us – to meet me, in other words – as Dunty battled his way through for both of us, his face like the scarlet prow of a magnificent if disorganized ship. At a narrow passageway into the row of boxes, a man stood, unyielding. He was enormously fleshy and wore the wide-brimmed, leather hat of a big-game hunter.

'My congratulations on yesterday. Long overdue, if I may say so. I am so happy to see you back in the big time.'

Dunty, glowering, mumbled, 'Thank you, George,' then

couldn't but add, 'my client, Mr Grace. Joe, this is George Scales.'

'Ah, a great pleasure,' said Sam Landy's agent and we shook. 'You're in the best hands, let me tell you,' Scales said, his small eyes performing an intensive inspection. 'Now, Dunty, you're going to see the Kingmambo, I take it. How much will you give, eh?'

'We haven't even decided if we will give,' Dunty said.

'I've just inspected him for old Sam,' said Scales. He pursed his lips. 'We're very keen. This one would fill the bill for a nice back-end campaign next year, then a crack at Newmarket in May. What do you say, Mr Grace? I assume you know who I represent.'

I was intrigued to think what Sam would make of this approach, which had to be unauthorized. Sam had obviously told the agent not to bid on the colt, but here was Scales, like all agents, trying to manoeuvre himself into a position where he could buy an expensive animal.

'Maybe another time,' I said politely and stepped around him.

'We will speak again,' said Scales, gone cold all of a sudden. Fat prick, I thought. He added, without enthusiasm, 'Good luck.'

Quite a few people were gathered around the box as we approached it. A dark-skinned, bearded man straightened up from running his hands down the legs of the colt, who was standing inside, a groom at his head. The man spoke to someone in the shadows of the box. Another face emerged, sallow, clean-shaven, but with the arrogant gaze of a hunting hawk. He held my gaze steadily as if I were a below-average species of rat. I didn't need to be told I was eye to eye with the Sultan of Tamil. As the Sultan withdrew, looking to neither left nor right, Dunty took me to one side.

'This is undoubtedly the prize offering of these entire sales,' he whispered. 'You know the breeding as well as do I. However, for my own part I would be remiss if I didn't say that I have never seen such a magnificent colt in forty years. The Sultan wants him, Landy wants him, Steer wants him. You want him. Well, here he is.'

Dunty's melodrama apart, the colt before us exuded an aura of serenity that it was hard to not be affected by. He was a big-boned, athletic specimen with Classic written all over him, but in addition his temperament and intelligence overrode the physical and told you that this horse, if treated with the respect he deserved, would be a champion. At least that was my opinion.

We stood aside as the colt was lead out and trotted away from us. Perfect action to my apprentice eyes.

'He's one to die for,' Dunty said wistfully.

I hated it when people talked like that. As we made our way to the snack bar, I wondered how many times Tricky, when he had been a trainer, had dreamed of getting a horse this good. Every other night was my guess. Like the great majority of small trainers he would have come to these sales and spent his time looking at horses on behalf of owners whose decision to go an extra ten thousand meant the difference or not between an empty box over the coming winter. The cash needed to buy the kind of horseflesh we had just seen put through its paces was phenomenal. Once he had lost Sam Landy as an owner, Tricky hadn't stood a chance.

'Well, look who's here.'

The woman who walked up to Dunty as we entered the snack bar had extremely long legs, matted, golden hair and the type of tan that comes out of a bottle.

'Heather,' Dunty jawed and tried to walk on.

'Aren't you going to introduce me, Dunty?' She turned

to me. 'I'm Heather Hunt, you must be Mr Grace. I'm just another horse agent, but Dunty's afraid of me, Mr Grace. You see, he's being a naughty boy and he's afraid he's going to be punished.'

She had a way of standing right up close and decanting her words, not to mention her chest, into your face.

I said, 'Dunty's looking after me fine, thanks.'

The woman strafed me with her tacky, grey eyes, then turned away so that her shoulder was between me and Dunty.

'Just remember one thing,' she growled, but not so low that I could not overhear, 'you poached yesterday and got away with it. But once is enough. Guy was not amused.'

'I was not aware', said Dunty, suddenly pale, but not without dignity, 'that my function was to amuse Guy.'

The woman's eyes flashed as she looked at me over her shoulder. 'Guy said to give you a message: back off, in case you have any further ideas. Otherwise, when your current pigeon has flown to another coop, you might find it very difficult to deal with your old friends.'

She looked once at me, winked, then walked out. Had these people never heard of the Ten Commandments? Dunty ordered coffees and, quietly, a whisky for himself, which he decanted into the styrofoam mug.

'Bitch,' he sighed. 'They give you one or two small jobs, then think they own you.'

'Tell me more,' I said. I had deliberately up to then not shown any interest in Steer.

'Guy is a genius,' Dunty said. 'He is the most aggressive, most talented operator to appear in this business in the last fifty years, but he is also a highly skilled manipulator.'

As well as being someone with little value for human life? I asked myself.

'People like me . . .'. Dunty allowed himself a brief

moment of modest reflection. 'I've had my ups and downs.
About three times a year I get jobs from the Steer camp –
Mickey Mouse assignments, to be honest. I'm sent to
Deauville to bid up some horse they want puffed, or I'll be
dispatched to the November Sales in Ireland with a mission
to make the running on some mare or other they want sold
without reference to them. It's scraps from the rich man's
table. But they use those scraps to keep me at heel. There
is an unspoken deal – we'll give you some of our bits and
pieces provided you don't become a nuisance where our
big deals are concerned.' Dunty shrugged, smiled. 'Yesterday I became a nuisance. Do it again and no more scraps is
what that bitch was saying. She's not called the Piranha for
nothing.'

'Fuck them,' I said, feeling suddenly warm towards the
old agent. 'Let's go buy our horse.'

As I had done the day before, I followed Dunty into the
sales arena, but today I was conscious of people's stares,
and of being surreptitiously pointed out. Then I saw Sam
Landy. He was walking directly for me, in conversation
with his agent. My immediate instinct was to greet him – I
barely managed not to call out, 'Sam!' The agent, Scales,
had spotted us and had nudged Landy to look. But, apart
from a brief, professional glance in my direction, a
response to what his agent had said, Sam walked by
without a glance.

'I'll be just a moment,' I said to Dunty and made my way
into a toilet.

The colt we were about to bid on was going to cost
minimum seven million. I unzipped my fly, peed, then
flushed the jacks and came out of the cubicle. If I hadn't
realized it before, the size of the chips these people played
for was becoming clear.

'Mr Grace?'

I turned.

'The Sultan trusts you enjoyed your nightcap, sir.'

I stared. The man at the basin had chocolate-coloured skin and a dense, black beard. He was smiling at me with lazy complicity.

I said. 'What did you say?'

He displayed an upper row of teeth grouted with gold. 'The Sultan understands how men can be lonely when they are away from home. He would like to be your friend.'

I thought of my five-grand hooker. 'What may I ask does the Sultan want in exchange?' I enquired, wondering whether a black eye would change his complexion.

'His Highness wants only for you to be happy, sir. And in this instance, he begs to enquire whether you would do him the honour of being his partner in the Kingmambo colt.'

'Tell the Sultan he's been out too long in the sun,' I said and dried my hands.

'The Sultan doesn't understand people who don't want to be his friends,' the man said, still smiling.

'Then try "Fuck off",' I said.

The man shook his head. 'I'm sure you don't mean that, sir. In our country there is an old saying: "Foolish the man who disturbs the lair of the tiger."'

'In my country we say, "which do you not understand?" The "fuck" or the "off"?' I said and made to walk out, but the man's arm shot out to the wall and formed a barrier in front of me.

'Don't be a silly boy,' he whispered. 'You have no idea what you're doing here.'

'I know this,' I said and brought my fist up hard into the unguarded joint of his elbow.

The man's dark face contorted and he doubled in pain.

'See you inside,' I said and made my way out to Dunty.

39

Dunty had not outlined his strategy for purchasing Lot 498, but now, up in the Gods as beneath us Lot 496 was being auctioned, he revealed it.

'It's not going to be cheap, whatever happens,' he confided from the side of his mouth.

Cheap was like leprosy in this business, it was never mentioned. 'I know,' I said.

Dunty nodded grimly. He had, I thought, gained in confidence since our first meeting, as if now, finally, at this time in his life he had joined what he called 'The big boys' and found himself equal to the task. Or maybe he was just pissed. He looked around him and took a deep breath.

'I think, essentially, if you're prepared to buy him at any price, then you should let the others fight it out, then come in when the horse is about to be knocked down to one of them. Believe me, when you're a buyer and that happens, when new blood suddenly appears against you just when you think you've won, it guts you.'

Dunty looked as if he'd been gutted more than once. I peered down. The arena was much more crowded than it had been the day before.

'You think that's better than demonstrating early on that we're determined to get him?'

'I think so. Bid from the start and you have to take everyone on. Wait till all but one is done, then at least the others have made a decision in principle to quit.'

I smiled at the older man's intense face.

'Dunty,' I asked, 'truthfully, have you ever been in this position before?'

Dunty blinked. He sucked in his stomach and made

himself proud. 'Very many times, Joe,' he said. He turned to the ring and I heard him add, almost imperceptibly, 'in my dreams.'

'*Lot 498. A bay colt by Kingmambo out of Massorah . . .*'

As the auctioneer began to describe the colt, I looked down. The place was packed – it was more difficult to pick people out than it had been yesterday. This horse, it was widely anticipated, would make the high price of the sale. Quite a few faces were upturned towards our position. I could see the Sultan in the Bidders, surrounded by his knot of dark, intense-looking advisers including the one I'd recently encountered, who was still holding his arm. My heart bled. As yesterday, Diana Bigge stood below and to the right. My eyes searched the crowd, shoulder to shoulder, but if Steer was there I was unable to spot him.

'. . . always a pleasure, but sometimes, as in this case, a privilege to offer you a truly magnificent son of champions,' intoned Bertie Wooster. 'Who'll put him in at three million? Two and a half? Two then? I'm bid two million guineas. Thank you.'

Dunty's hands gripped the seat in front of him as if he was in the carriage of a train. Below us, as the colt walked around in long, unhurried strides, the bidding went without much pause to five-point nine million guineas.

'The Sultan and Diana Bigge,' Dunty whispered and a large bead of oily sweat rolled down the side of his nose.

'Five nine, I'm bid,' said the auctioneer, leaning out over his rostrum and speaking directly down to Bigge, 'against you at five million nine, I'm selling him all the while, at five million nine hundred thousand guineas . . .'

I saw the tweed-jacketed spotter to the auctioneer's left tug the impresario's sleeve.

'Six million guineas!'

The auditorium buzzed.

'It's Guy Steer!' shivered Dunty. 'He's bidding through the Piranha!'

But still I could not see him. Beneath us and to the right, in the tiers known as the Bidders, the Piranha's blonde hair stood out like varnish. Now she was locked in eye-contact with the rostrum.

'Six one,' called the auctioneer calmly and I looked over to see if Dunty had bid, but instead he was leaning back, eyes closed, shaking his head.

'The Piranha's gone head to head against the Sultan,' he said and winced. 'I told you it would be expensive.'

I think it genuinely hurt Dunty to spend other people's money; I made a note, when this was all over, to tell Sam Landy he could do a lot worse than give Dunty Rainway a few decent chunks of business every year. Below, the bidding had slowed to increases of fifty thousand. In the circle around the Piranha, I searched to make out Steer. I could not.

'Are we all done at six million six hundred thousand? He's cheap at the price and you're going to lose him,' called the auctioneer, addressing the Sultan directly. 'His dam was the champion of France. I'm selling once at six six, twice –'

Dunty looked at me. I nodded. Dunty's catalogue flapped once. Down on the rostrum, the spotter caught it and grabbed the auctioneer's arm. All faces turned to the Gods.

'Six million seven – a new bidder!' cried the auctioneer with triumph. He turned to the people in front of him. 'Can I say, six eight? Six eight, I'm bid.' He looked up. Dunty flapped. 'Six nine.' Back to the Piranha. No hesitation. 'Seven million guineas I'm now bid for this son of Kingmambo.'

As I watched the horse beneath us make his circular way without concern, I was aware of a groundswell of noise, like that at a prize fight. An atmosphere thick with tension and high drama and someone else's money. I was as good as detached from the fact that every time Dunty twitched his catalogue, another hundred grand was leaving my bank account.

'Seven million guineas. Against you in the Gods. Will you leave him go for another bid? Come on, don't get beat, he looks a good one,' oozed Bertie Wooster.

Dunty leaned back, his face drawn and sweat soaked.

'This is madness,' he gasped.

I know, is what I felt like saying, but instead, I said, 'Keep going.'

'I'll take fifty thousand,' the auctioneer cajoled, his face for us alone. 'I have seven million and fifty, thank you. Seven one, seven two, seven three . . .'

The bids ticked on with smooth and well-greased unreality. Dunty's mobile phone began to ring. He snatched it from his pocket.

'Seven million four hundred thousand . . .'

'Joe?'

I looked at Dunty. His face was contorted by fear.

He said. 'It's for you.'

I took the phone. 'Hello.'

A voice said, 'This is Guy Steer.'

I felt my breath catch. I peered down and suddenly saw him standing in the bidders, two above the Piranha, looking up at me, a phone to his ear. Behind him and to one side stood the brick shithouse I'd noticed on my way in.

'Welcome to Newmarket, Mr Grace.'

The voice was soft, cultured.

'Hello,' was all I could think of saying.

'I'd like to buy you a drink afterwards.'

'Thank you.'

'I'm sure we will have much to talk about, but –' Steer chuckled '– time at the moment is literally money, so I want to make you a very brief proposition.'

I could see the outline of his face, more particularly his eyes, very large and dark, something the photographs had not got over, for some reason.

'Seven six, seven seven . . .'

'Call Dunty off and we'll stand in halves on this colt – but do it now!'

'I'm not sure I understand.'

'Seven million eight hundred thousand I'm bid . . .'

'Partners, fifty-fifty.'

'I want the animal,' I said, 'for myself.'

'He can run in your colours,' Steer said. 'Deal?'

'Certainly not,' I heard myself say.

'Seven nine . . .'

'Then this is going to cost you, sir.'

'So be it. Goodbye.'

'Eight million guineas!' came the cry from the rostrum and a loud murmur rose from the assembly. 'Eight one!'

Some people actually clapped

Below me, Steer, phone put away, had now turned and was standing, somewhat hunched, hands in the pockets of his coat, looking into the ring. I wondered if I had done the right thing – for there was no doubt that he was now aware of me and had even offered me a partnership before we'd met. Had I not achieved my objective? Or, indeed, were I now to call Dunty off, to let Steer prevail at eight point three million, currently the Piranha's bid, would I not alone have achieved my purpose, but done so saving money? Then I thought of one of our many discussions in Albermarle Street. Sam's voice: *You have to beat a man like this, at his own game, in front of his home crowd, to gain his respect. Believe me, nothing less will work.*

'Eight million four hundred thousand,' spoke the auctioneer in response to Dunty. Immediately the Piranha responded and the bid went to eight and a half million guineas.

I thought of Steer's phone call and all at once I knew what would work. It had been something in his voice, something beyond the smooth patter of instant friendship and final, raw threat. What I had also heard had been a degree of pleading. Unconscious, perhaps, but nonetheless real. Steer was hurting. I thought of Lou.

'Against you in the Gods, I'm selling to the Bidders at eight and a half million. Have you quite done in the Gods? You're going to lose him. I'm selling once . . . I'm selling twice . . .'

'Bid ten,' I said to Dunty.

The agent stared at me. He gasped. 'Are you mad?'

'Do it!'

'I'm selling three times . . .'

Moving his body so that only the rostrum could see his hands plainly, Dunty briefly spread the fingers of his left hand and flexed them, twice. The auctioneer wasn't slow.

'Ten million I'm bid!' came the ringing cry. 'Ten million I'm bid for the Kingmambo!' To Guy Steer, 'I'm selling him against you.'

I found it hard to hear, so full were my ears with the sounds of my inner disbelief and turmoil. But then I looked down and what I had somehow known would happen was happening. Steer and the Piranha plus half a dozen others were moving in a knot and leaving the arena. The crowd was parting for them.

'. . . I sell at ten million guineas.' The explosion of hammer on gavel. 'Mr Dunty Rainway!'

Applause broke out. Dunty turned to me, his eyes glazed.

'We bought him,' he said in a small voice. 'We beat Guy Steer.'

'You beat him,' I said.

'That's right,' Dunty said in a dazed voice, 'I did.'

40

I slept deeply that night and did not dream. Reluctantly I had agreed to meet Dunty for dinner at Le Gavroche and had then sat for two hours on my own, waiting for him to show up. He didn't. I was damned if I was going to call him – the man had made his pension out of me these last two days, the least he could do was to sober up enough to buy me the dinner he had suggested. I had gone home and for the second night eaten alone in my suite. From there I'd called Hanny, but she was out, so I left a message saying I missed her. Finally I called the Dublin number for that day and got the whine of an empty mailbox. No one, apparently, wanted the man who'd paid the top price that day in Newmarket sales. I went to bed. It seemed I'd been under only a few minutes when the bedside telephone rang.

'Mr Grace.'

I felt something happen to my scalp hairs as I recognized the voice.

'Yes.'

'I trust you had a restful night.' He made no attempt to introduce himself; he knew I knew. 'Do you like Manx kippers?'

I said, 'Occasionally.'

'Then let me order you some. I'm downstairs in the dining room. You've made all the papers, by the way. See you in what – twenty minutes?'

He hung up. I took my time shaving and noticed that what I called my Tube bruise was still there, as if it had taken a lease on that part of my forehead. I showered slowly, then dressed, trying to work out the moves. He had

come to me, which was exactly the way we had planned it
in Albemarle Street. I tightened the belt on a pair of slacks,
left the top two buttons of the Charvet shirt unbuttoned,
stuck my feet into a pair of Gucci loafers and went downstairs, trying to feel as if I knew what I was doing.

Guy Steer was seated behind what looked like an acre of
white linen. As I walked in, a waiter pulled out the table
and Steer stood up. About the same height as me, broader,
probably fitter, were my instant impressions. Square, flat,
competent hands. The round, searching eyes. A vital,
handsome man. Caught my hand in both of his as we
shook.

'It's Guy.'

'Joe.'

'A great pleasure. Please.'

We sat.

'How's the other guy?'

I looked at him closely. 'He took off like a train.'

Guy Steer laughed. 'I've always thought kippers are the
best-kept British secret,' he purred as a silver-domed dish
was put in front of me and the dome removed to reveal
what resembled a partially dissected anatomy lesson. 'By
the way, congratulations. Took balls to bid ten big ones.
Good luck with him.'

He studied me with an almost frightening intensity.
Then he raised his cup of coffee. Mine was empty and a
vigilant waiter rushed in and topped me up. We clinked
cups.

'Who'll you send him to?'

'Tom Haines,' I replied, feeling the kind of old panic I'd
last had when facing oral examinations.

'He's straight.' Steer made a face. 'As straight as any of
them.' He smiled at me as if to put us both on the same side
of whatever chicanery had just been inferred. 'So what

brings you to the party, Joe? Not that it's any of my business.'

'Always had an interest in racing. Thought I'd indulge myself while I had the opportunity.'

'The best reason to do anything,' Steer said, buttering toast. 'It's quite a small club here that you've just joined, you know. My guess is that no more than half a dozen people control the top end of the trade.'

' "Control"?'

'Maybe that's the wrong word. What I'm saying is not many people have the kind of money you spent yesterday. Fewer still are willing to gamble it on a horse. So I suppose what I am saying is it's a kind of club, in the best English gentleman's sense of that word, and so here I am this morning to extend the hand of friendship to our latest member.'

'And a kipper,' I said.

He sat back and laughed. It did not seem possible that such an engaging man could have had the slightest part in killing Lou or Tricky Dawson.

'Look,' he was saying, 'we're both grown-ups, we don't need mother's permission to enjoy ourselves any more – right?'

Now his smile was that of the naughty companion, a lad out on the town. His intense stare again locked on me for an instant. All this eyeballing was getting tiresome.

'We all do what we must,' Steer continued, slipping smoothly from loaded generalities into the specific purpose of this breakfast. 'You saw two nice horses, you bought them. I lost them.' Steer shrugged. 'Had I known about you, we could each have had a piece of them for a fraction of what you paid.' He put up a hand. 'But you knew that anyway and made a choice. Fine. Like I said, we don't either of us need permission anymore.'

I looked at my watch. 'I've got to get going, Guy. I need to be in Newmarket to see a horse.'

He winced. 'The Royal Academy?'

I nodded.

Steer smiled. 'Where on earth did you get Dunty, by the way?'

'Seems like a nice old guy,' I said and wondered what sort of shape Dunty was in this morning. 'Knows his horses.'

'Sure, sure.' Steer's lukewarm approbation was transparent. 'I use him from time to time – because I like him. I'd hate to have him making any big calls on my behalf, mind you. Man must have a liver the size of Manhattan. However.' The hatchet job of Dunty completed, Guy looked at me intently. 'You've bought two out of the three horses I most wanted at these sales. What'll you pay today for the third? Four big ones? Five? Six? He could go for six – if I want him as well. And I do. But if I don't want him, what'll he make? I'll tell you – a couple of million quid at the most. That's four million quid less than he'll cost you – or me – if we both bid. Why am I here? I'll tell you. To save us both money. OK, you don't want a stand-in. Fine. Here's what I propose. Let's toss a coin. Whoever wins goes out and buys the colt unopposed by the other. What could be fairer?'

I said, 'I don't like losing.'

He spread his hands. 'Even if you lose, you've won twice already this week. That's a great score by any reckoning.'

I had to decide whether or not I had hooked him by now. Was what I had already done enough? Was this the beginning of his play for me? Or did he need another sharp kick where it hurt most before he'd set out to ensnare me? Decision time.

'Why not?' I said.

Guy nodded vigorously. He took out a round silver coin.

'An old Irish pound coin,' he said. 'Useless for anything nowadays but making decisions like these. Waiter.'

An elderly waiter approached.

'Sir?'

'Toss this, would you?'

'Certainly, sir.'

Several heads had turned from other tables.

Steer said, 'Let it fall on the floor. OK, Joe? Your call.'

The waiter poised the coin on his thumb, flicked. Up spun the glittering coin.

'Heads,' I said.

It hit the carpet square and rolled on edge two yards before falling flat.

'Heads it is,' Guy Steer said. 'You win again, Joe. I'm impressed.'

We walked out together and across the hall to the main entrance. The outside-toilet-sized man I had noticed at Newmarket and whom I now identified as Bill Ruth, got out of the maroon Rolls and opened the back door. The colour of his brown suit resembled the stuff you scrape off your shoe.

Guy said, 'I genuinely wish you the very best of luck with all three horses.' A smile crossed his face, and now he was suddenly in another role, that of the incorrigible rogue. 'By the way, there was one part of that bet I forgot to mention.'

I gave him a cool look.

He said, 'Winner buys dinner tonight – all right Joe?'

I suppose I had technically just won four million quid. 'My pleasure,' I said.

He got into his car and I watched him drive away. Ten

minutes later I rang that day's mobile number from a payphone two blocks from Claridge's. The number clicked into its answering mode.

'We're in,' I said.

41

I walked down the Strand, relishing the evening breeze. I had had my driver drop me at Trafalgar Square. In Newmarket that afternoon I had purchased the Royal Academy colt for exactly two million pounds. Not Dunty Rainway. Me. Dunty had not shown up, nor did he respond to his mobile.

'It's phenomenal!' trainer Tom Haines had blathered. 'I know for a fact that the Piranha saw that colt three times. They *wanted* him – but when they saw you were interested they gave in without a fight! Phenomenal!'

Haines had done his level best to have me check out of Claridge's and come to stay with him in Newmarket until further notice. So easy to make friends when you're spewing out cash like water from a burst hydrant. But now I was walking in the direction of the Savoy, responding to a message from Guy Steer's fixer, Tony Friar: Guy was genuinely delighted that the colt had been knocked down to me and he was also looking forward to dinner, Friar had said. However, he went on, Guy had been detained with business and wondered would I do him the honour of joining him for a pre-dinner drink in his suite in the Savoy? Around seven? The invitation had been relayed in the smooth, conciliatory tones of a wheedling skunk. I walked down the spur road from the Strand.

I was thinking of Hanny and the fact that she had taken such a dislike to Silken. Had she felt threatened? Or, where I saw just a beautiful girl, had she seen something more? Hanny rarely took dislikes, but for some reason this had been different. I stepped out of the lift. The door to the Savoy's River View suite opened to my knock and I was

looking up into the expressionless face of Bill Ruth. He
stood back to admit me and I heard him call, 'Mr Guy.'

'I like the suit,' I told him and felt his breath like toffee
on my neck.

'Joe! How very nice to see you!' Steer gave me the two-
handed treatment and once again looked at me with such
intensity that I felt that he was trying to see into my fillings.
'Thanks, Bill. Joe, this is Bill Ruth, he looks after me.'

'Mr Joe.'

My hand was lost in the other man's. His eyes were so
deeply set that it was impossible to tell if they were open; on
the other hand, he was unlikely to be asleep. Steer put one
protective hand at the small of my back and gently pressed
me forward into a room where blazed a fake log fire,
around which stood a number of people drinking Cristal
champagne. There were two televisions on, both showing
racing. I recognized Steer's woman agent, the Piranha, and
his brother, Alan. A woman with straight blonde hair and
freckles across her nose stood to one side. Six feet tall.
Razor thin, drop-dead beautiful. And bare-foot.

'Cheetah – this is our new friend. We flipped this
morning for the Royal Academy. Joe won. Joe, my wife,
Cheetah.'

'My pleasure.'

Her voice was American – Texas, I guessed. She moved
like a cheetah, or cheetahs moved like her. She was so thin
I could see her bones. At the final moment, she had a
problem with eye contact. The opposite to her husband.
Maybe he had burned her out. Or maybe it was just me.

Steer did the rounds – introducing me to the Piranha,
who winked at me, and to his horse adviser, Simon
Markowitz, the Kentucky vet, who was a slight, stooped
man with a goatee beard. And to Alan Steer, who was pale
and uneasy looking, a body-builder, by the look of him. He

just nodded when we shook hands: he looked about as happy as a mortician who has just heard that the Black Death is over. Tony Friar, on the other hand, greeted me as if we'd just done a moon landing together.

'You've got some nerve taking us on like that,' he joked. 'We had no fuckin' idea what was happening!'

'And this is his first time!' Steer said, his eyes huge. 'His very first time!'

'Tell him what he's let himself in for, Doc,' Friar cackled.

The vet shuffled in and made despairing motions with his hands.

'You went out and maybe you bought these beautiful creatures because they looked so good you thought they just had to be perfection incarnate – right?' he said.

'They were beautiful, that's for sure,' I said, falling for it.

'Hah!' The Doc threw his head back and I saw that he had an Adam's apple the size of a cue ball. 'Let me tell you what you really bought. You bought these massive one-ton pieces of mobile flesh and blood, that's what you bought! When they start to motor, half the time inside them it's going to be like an abattoir – blood splashing around like a Jackson Pollock canvas gone mad. And no fuckin' way can their legs take this weight, this pounding, pounding, day in, day out. They crack, they break down. They just collapse. And even if they don't, how can a beast this size, bleeding inside like a pig, manage to get enough oxygen through this tiny windpipe into its fuckin' lungs for the final effort? It can't. Those lungs, if spread out, would be each one bigger than one of those spinnakers they use in the America's Cup. The average horse's windpipe, in many cases, is not much bigger in diameter than my prick . . .'

'Which by all accounts is pretty awesome,' Steer chuckled.

I watched Cheetah Steer. She was drinking a fruit punch of some kind.

'. . . this *relatively* insignificant piece of equipment,' persisted the Doc to more laughter, 'has got to funnel enough air to do the job. It can't be done!' He clapped my arm. 'So you've just spent seventeen million big ones tryin' to win the America's Cup with somethin' the size of my prick!'

I laughed. The Doc seemed like a friendly enough guy, not someone who worked for a bunch of killers. But then I was easily amused.

Steer said, 'Here's someone who's an expert on pricks.'

We turned. A man of scarlet complexion, with eyes that peered through folds of fat and a long mouth curled into an expression of perpetual aggression, had joined us.

'Joe Grace, meet Davey Delgado.'

He shook my hand gruffly, took a glass of bubbly, swallowed half of it. The top of his head came to my shirt collar.

'Been readin' about you,' he said. 'Where d'you get all the money?'

I held his scowl. 'Same place as you guys. I stole it.'

There was a beat of silence, a missed footfall of time during which all the world could have disappeared down a plughole. Then the air resounded with laughter.

Davey Delgado grinned hugely and turned to Steer. 'Hey, I like this guy!' he bellowed and raised his glass.

Platters of warm hors d'oeuvres were doing the rounds. Steer and Delgado were constantly back and forth to the television screens; Friar relayed bets to a bookmaker who was based, I gathered, in Gibraltar. I could easily imagine how someone, knowing nothing of the background, could think that he had just fallen in with the nicest crowd in town. Decent people like Lou and Tricky.

'I *like* Dunty.' The Piranha's healthy front suggested she could blow out her birthday candles from the other side of town. 'But where was he today, poor old thing?'

'Indisposed,' I said, asking myself the same question.

She said, 'I mean, some people are put off by the fact that he's such a lush – but who hasn't got a vice, eh, Joe?'

It would be like going to bed with a roll of barbed wire, I thought to myself, as poor old Dunty was shafted yet again.

'I've been watching him these last days,' I said, wondering at my ability to bullshit. 'He doesn't drink nearly as much as people imagine. In fact, a lot of it is a front, in my opinion. Allows him to operate at his own pace. Smart.'

'Are you being serious?'

'Sure. I mean, which agent's client came away from Newmarket this week with the three best horses? Not you, Heather.'

She blinked. Then her tongue came out, a slender, deep-grooved organ that reminded me of a beaver, for some reason, and ran in a slow lick across her upper lip.

'You're a tough bastard,' she murmured, as if we were in some intimate, sexual ritual and she had been suddenly subdued.

As Davey Delgado ambled over and began to chat about horses and about who I thought the best jockeys were, I became aware of Alan Steer's eyes. They never seemed to leave me. His brother was in discussion with the Doc and Friar, and the Piranha was at the mantelpiece with Cheetah Steer, but Alan remained to one side, looking at me.

'You know Sam Landy.'

Like a knife the statement had been slid by Delgado into the conversation.

'Just who he is. I've never met him,' I said.

Delgado looked at me closely. 'Sam's an example of what I mean. Old money, old ideas. Just fuckin' old. He can't come up with the winners any more. My heart bleeds for him, pompous old prick.'

'Joe.' Steer had my arm. 'I've taken a liberty.' It seemed to be a habit with him. 'There are too many of us, so this evening's on me.'

'Numbers aren't a problem,' I said.

'Of course I know that,' he said endearingly, 'But the bet should have been, loser's choice – OK? This is my choice. Indulge me. Please.'

Friar was on the phone, calling up the cars. I saw Bill Ruth leave the room.

'You like Japanese?' Friar asked me as we trooped out.

'Sure.'

'Then you have a treat in store,' he grinned, as if his only purpose in life was to give me treats – which for the moment, I reflected, might well be the case.

I stood aside to allow the ladies out. Alan was behind me.

'Easy, isn't it?' he said in a slow voice that only I could hear.

'Sorry?'

'You heard me.'

'I hope so,' I smiled.

'So do I,' he said, but in his case the smile was missing.

42

The dining room was private and over a restaurant off Greek Street. The full oriental McCoy, it was decked out with cushions and upright posts, dim lights, and a succession of courses that looked like miniature items of abstract art rather than food. Sake was served in crystal decanters that came imbedded like sculptures in deep blocks of ice. It was as good as any wine and, Tony Friar made sure I knew, twice as expensive.

'They all live on these mountains, see? Fuckin' hundreds of families. There's one source of water, trickles all the way down the mountain, they all have to use it. The best rice is like the best anything – takes a genius to cultivate it. This stuff you're drinking is distilled only from the best. It would want to be at two grand a bottle – eh?'

Directly across from me sat Cheetah, then the Doc and Alan. Steer was on my left, discussing his US trainer, Fizzy Wilson, with the Piranha and Davey Delgado. I asked Friar how long he had worked for Steer.

'A long time,' he said.

'And Alan,' I asked quietly, 'where does he fit in?'

Friar bowed his head to one side for maximum discretion. 'You don't want to worry about Alan. Not the world's greatest diplomat. But hell will freeze over before the boss will ever drop him from the team. It's a long story.'

Amber glasses of fishy liquid came with worm-like spirals of spaghetti afloat. Japanese girls in silk dresses with generous side-slits kept the sake coming. I was beginning to feel light-headed, but in the quiet moments, when neither Friar nor Steer were trying to engage my attention, I became aware of Cheetah observing me from beneath lowered eyelashes. She drank none of the sake, I observed, but kept to still water. It was warm in the room and she had taken off her top to reveal a simple, golden halter which showed off her golden but too thin shoulders and arms. She was like a gilded fairy – the Christmas tree variety. I found myself being drawn back to her with each further glass of sake.

'. . . I mean, when was the big moment?'

I had not realized Steer was talking to me. His eyes held mine powerfully. I was going to have to get shades.

I said, 'Big moment?'

'You know, when you knew you had escaped.' He appeared to relax, leaning back and helping himself to sake. 'For me, it was the first day I had a million in the bank. I only had it in my account for about thirty minutes – but I knew then that I *would* escape. Get out from the throng. Do my own thing. Own my own plane. Be my own man.'

'For me it was a concept,' I said slowly. 'Knowing that I had an idea that would work. I could see the future.'

'And what a feeling,' Steer said and actually, for a brief moment, put his arm around my shoulders, 'what a feeling that is, Joe.' He sat back, leaning against the pole as if to get a better look at me. I hoped my nostril hairs were clean. 'Tony here tells me you run an investment outfit out of Dublin. Do I know any of your players?'

'I don't know, but I don't think so,' I said. 'Your name has never come up.'

Steer looked at me thoughtfully. I wondered how far they had got in their analysis of Grace Equity or how far they were digging. Because, of course, the bastards were digging.

'My main investments, other than horses, are in commodities,' he was saying. 'D'you ever look at them?'

I remembered Sam's advice.

'I know nothing about them,' I said, relieved to be able to speak the truth. 'Gold and silver and that sort of thing, you mean?'

'Yes, but also copper, lead and zinc, and platinum, and when the time is right, what we call the softs, such as coffee, cocoa and sugar. They're all cyclical, you know. It's just a matter of patience and timing.'

'What's good now?'

'Oil,' said Steer without hesitation. 'We're making good money trading oil right now, aren't we, Tony?'

'A fortune,' mouthed Friar, making a big play in pronouncing the 'f'.

'Nothing is guaranteed in life,' Steer said, 'but with certain friends I've always shared the good times. Right, Tony?'

'Absolutely.'

Steer looked at me intently. 'Tell you what – we don't know each other all that well, but I have a feeling we're going to be friends – yes?'

I said, 'I've almost never regretted making a friend.'

He offered over his wide hand. I shook it. We'd be kissing next.

He said, 'Good friends are a rare privilege. Let me make a suggestion to inaugurate our friendship, Joe.'

I shrugged. 'It's not necessary.'

'I insist. Let me invest a hundred grand in oil for you over the next week. Give it a run and see what happens.'

I made a swift if uncomplicated calculation: if this was, as it had to be, part of the groundwork to win my trust, then the bet was a sure winner.

I said, 'I'll write you a cheque.'

'No way,' Steer said sternly. 'If we lose, I'll bill you. All right?'

'Fine,' I said, and added, 'just don't lose more than the hundred grand, please.'

Steer showed that he understood my sense of humour. 'Where are you next week?'

'Probably California,' I replied, remembering what Sam had said about Steer's itinerary.

'So are we! Cheetah – did you hear that? Joe is in California next week.'

She looked directly at me for the first time. 'Then you must come see our horses run at Santa Anita.'

Texas, I decided, definitely Texas.

Steer chatted a bit about the Middle East, about Nigerian oil, about his coup a few years back in cocoa. Then the ladies were on their feet and, together with Alan Steer, were saying their goodnights. Bill Ruth had appeared at the back of the room.

'I'll look forward to Santa Anita,' said Cheetah, and gave me her cheek. There was an undercurrent in the way she had dealt with me from the start, as if she wanted to communicate something privately.

I said, 'Me too.'

'You boys behave, now,' said the Piranha archly and this time both her boobs sank into my chest. 'You ever want me to run my hands down the legs of anything you fancy, just give me a ring, Joe.'

It was obvious that we weren't all going and suddenly I became apprehensive.

'That was excellent,' I said, feeling the sake. I turned to Steer. 'I'll make my own way home from here.'

He winked at me as his wife's long, tanned back and legs were presented to us. 'Hang on a minute, Joe,' he said.

Friar ushered out the departing group and the Doc, Davey, Steer and myself made a semi-circle around the end of the table. One Japanese girl arrived with a box of Montecristo cigars, another with a bottle of Armagnac on which the date, 1890, was visible. The door opened and Friar reappeared, taking his jacket off. He'd done this before.

'All loaded and dispatched,' he announced and settled down on a cushion.

Further girls, made up in the traditional, pat, Japanese way, appeared. When I chose a cigar, one of them took it from me, knelt at my feet and placed it in her own mouth. Reaching for a balloon glass of Armagnac, she took the cigar from her lips and, her face a study in concentration, greased it slowly within the glass. Then placing the moistened cigar between her fine, white teeth, gums bared to me, she chopped. The severed butt in her lap, she wriggled towards me, inserted the cigar in my mouth, then flared a nine-inch match and very slowly allowed me to suck the Montecristo alight.

'You OK, Joe?'

Steer gave me the thumbs up as he puffed, his drink untouched.

'Never better.'

Extra cushions had been brought in and now the girls, moving about on their knees, were using these cushions to prop us all comfortably in a semi-circle. The end of the table had been cleared and the lights adjusted so that the area was softly illuminated. Then, as the sound of cymbals and reed music grew from the background, the girls began slowly to undress.

'This is somethin' else!' Davey cackled.

Their clothes seemed to float off them, revealing, bit at a time, a variety of bodies. Some were tawny skinned, some milk white. The music grew more languid. Cushions were placed to make a huge bed. One by one they paired off, kissing chastely, but not for long enough to escape interruption from one of the others, and the pairing reformed. There were five of them, and the twos and threes of lithe young bodies kept changing and coupling and recoupling, until an undertow of aggression entered their sexual pageant, then desperation, as if the all-too-brief touch of changing flesh was making them more and more frustrated. Sweat ran down their bodies. It reminded me of a game we used all to play with cushions at children's birthday parties: each time a cushion was taken away so that when the music stopped there was room for one less person. The girls began to cry out – but still their search went on, writhing on the pillows, rising, groaning, grappling.

'Fuck,' I heard the Doc gasp.

The music was frantic. One of the girls broke, went to the edge of the cushions alone, and began to work her fingers.

'Ah shit,' said Davey Delgado. He got up and the girl went to him with a look of pleading. She took him by the hand and they disappeared behind a black curtain.

The remaining girls now raised the stakes, whimpering with desire that had to be feigned but was so convincing that it didn't matter. Friar rescued one of them, banished from the cushions. The Doc went next, taking a small girl who had squatted down shamelessly in front of him and taken his hand between her legs.

I looked at Steer, thought of Hanny.

I said, 'After you.'

'I insist, you're my guest,' he said, his voice low.

This was the ritual Sam had described, but had cried off from, pleading a bad heart. The girl whose mouth had already held my cigar, was now kneeling at my feet, her eyes imploring. *Sex is the glue*. She led me out the back, through a curtain. The first thing she did was to put out my cigar.

It was one in the morning when I got back to Claridge's. As I went to the desk, a man in the type of suit that policemen tend to wear when they're not in uniform stepped out.

'Mr Grace? Can I have a word?'

We went into a manager's office, where the manager on duty was sitting. On seeing us, he jumped to his feet and left at a good canter. My new companion hauled out his ID, then put a picture on the desk. I felt ill.

'Know him, sir?'

'I've met him.'

'Seen him this last twenty-four hours?'

'Not since the afternoon of the day before yesterday,' I replied. 'Why? Is he all right?'

The policeman looked at me narrowly. Dunty's big nose seemed to shine from the black-and white photograph.

'I'm afraid he was found in waste ground near Canning Town this evening,' he said. 'He'd been very badly beaten. He may not live.'

43

Dunty Rainway's brutal beating made the front page of every paper next day. '£10 MILLION MAN MUGGED' one of the tabloids screamed. Guy Steer was one of the first to call me, just as I was checking out of Claridge's.

'I hope they find who did it and lock them away for ever,' he said.

These people were something else. Dunty had been found at the bottom of an embankment. His head had been rendered almost unrecognizable by an iron bar. They said that even if he survived, he would never walk or function again. I felt a massive burden of regret, as if everyone I came near was doomed. And yet, in the same way that a veil had been drawn over Tricky's death at first, the general opinion here would again be one of inevitability: what had happened was always going to happen, sooner or later. Dunty Rainway, a notorious drinker, had gone on a bender to celebrate the most successful horse transaction he had ever been involved in. He'd wound up that night in a backstreet nightclub, where his accent and bearing had marked him out. He'd been seduced, beaten and robbed. The story would not run for a second day.

I flew into Dublin and took a cab home to Howth. The original plan had been for me to go to LA having spent the weekend in Dublin: Steer had horses running in Santa Anita and I was now due to be his guest of honour. But Dunty's maiming had thrown a cloud over the proceedings. Just because I now owned three racehorses and had had dinner with Guy Steer didn't mean I had to keep going. I'd checked the voicemail, but Sam had left no message. Hanny wasn't coming back until Sunday. I called Mick.

We met next day in a pub near Sutton. Mick shuddered when I told him about Dunty.

'What are you going to do?' he asked when I had finished.

'If it wasn't for Lou, I'd step off now,' I said. 'But because of Lou I'm going to see it through.'

'You're crazy.'

'I know.' We chatted on for a few minutes about how Steer might drop his guard. Then I said, 'I may need to be wired.'

Mick sighed. 'Let me know where and when and I'll set it up.'

'Any progress from Special Branch?'

The curly head went from side to side. 'File is still with the DPP. But I'm keeping a couple of the lads informed of your shenanigans.' He looked at me over his pint. 'Cops hate amateurs.'

'I wasn't always an amateur,' I said.

When I got home there was a message from Sam. He was breaking the rules ringing me like this. I called him back.

'We need to talk,' he said and gave me another number.

I drove to Howth and called the number from a payphone. Sam picked up on the first ring.

'This is a disaster,' he said.

I agreed with him.

'Dunty Rainway never harmed a fly.' He paused. 'What are you going to do?'

'Someone wants me to pull out,' I said. 'The messages are very clear.'

'That wasn't an accident last week in the Tube station either, was it?' Sam asked.

'It could have been.'

'Christ,' Sam said. 'Look, I want to call the whole thing

off, but Silken flew out yesterday to cover the Boyd problem.'

'Fuck,' I exclaimed. 'That was fast.'

'I told you it would be,' Sam said.

We had recognized that before he went any further with me Steer would check out all my business connections, to see if there was any possibility I was setting him up. One of these connections was Boyd Investments in San Diego. Sam's ownership was held through a Panamanian trust fund and his name appeared nowhere in Boyd's records. That didn't mean that if one of Steer's men walked into Boyd and asked the right questions that he wouldn't learn of Sam's involvement. Quite the opposite. The job of covering what we came to call 'the Boyd problem' had been given to Silken.

Sam said, 'I told you he wouldn't hang around. He's checking out every angle that he can find. Friar is due in San Diego on Monday morning.'

'Then we have to keep going,' I said. 'We have no choice. It's as simple as that.'

'Tricky, your sister, Lou, now Dunty, or as good as,' said Sam. 'Who'll be next?'

'There is a phenomenon known as grotesque coincidence,' I said.

'I don't think so,' Sam said. 'Tell me what happened when you met him.'

I described everything – almost everything – that had taken place with Steer. 'They appear to like me – or almost all of them do. Guy's brother is an oddball and seems to have taken an intense dislike to me. There's some deep bond between them, so he can behave much as he likes.'

'He's mentally unbalanced,' Sam said.

I thought back to the Leicester Square Underground.

A madman might just have done that, I reasoned. Someone who saw me as a threat.

Sam said, 'My latest information on Guy is that he is hurting big on a number of fronts. He'll see you as a lifeline from heaven.'

'How big is big?' I asked.

'He needs to find between fifty and one hundred and fifty million US between now and Christmas to bail out short-term debt on his worldwide breeding operation.'

'That's big,' I said.

'Too big,' Sam said.

I walked the pier, then drove home. Hanny's car was in the drive.

44

I have Silken as my source for what happened subsequently in San Diego. I can see her face now, a study in concentration, as she related every detail. The chief operating officer of Boyd was a recently appointed career management operative named Thornton Bishop. Bishop was to know nothing of what was taking place – all he was asked to do was to oblige, for reasons unexplained, in one single tactic.

Silken had flown to LA and met a veteran B-movie actor of cameo parts called Donald Rellis. Silken had cast him twice in movies on which she had worked as co-producer. She had handed him a thick script. She hadn't been a producer for nothing.

All his career Rellis had played the role of the silver-haired patriarch, an endlessly reassuring older figure representing candour, integrity and security. Silken checked his availability – Rellis had just finished shooting a movie in studio and was planning a month off. Silken told him the deal. He had to be on permanent standby to fly to San Diego. Silken would meet him there. The fee for one hour's work: $50,000 in cash. One stipulation: he could not be recognized. He had to shave off his bushy, trade-mark moustache.

Silken was back in London, where she received a call from the secretary to Boyd's CEO. A man called Anthony Friar had just booked a meeting for the following Monday morning at ten am with Mr Bishop in Coronado, the city within San Diego Bay where Boyd's offices were located. Friar had described himself as a financial analyst. His was one of the names given to Bishop and his secretary to trigger the plan of action.

Boyd Investments was, of course, a private company which had no need to concede to the wishes of unknown financial analysts; but Sam had agreed that anything other than fully satisfying Steer's requirements could mean he would decide not to take the bait. And thus Boyd, Sam had decided, would portray itself as one of those lovable open corporate sweethearts that made time for assholes like Tony Friar.

'Thank you,' Silken told the secretary and put down the phone. Then she rang Donald Rellis's number in LA. No reply. *Shit!*

Silken booked herself on the next morning's New York flight with a connection which would get her into San Diego by six that evening.

The problem now was Rellis. His number didn't answer, although Silken tried it every ten minutes. He had no voicemail and his mobile was permanently switched off. He was unmarried. So much for being on permanent standby, Silken thought. At quarter to midnight – four in the afternoon in Los Angeles – Rellis's agent returned Silken's call.

'I found him,' the man said.

'Thank God – where is he?'

'He's in hospital,' the agent replied.

45

We lay in bed, watching the moonlight on the water. We'd made love twice in as many hours; now, limbs tangled, bodies still glistening, we just lay and watched.

'She's very beautiful,' Hanny had said earlier.

'Yes.'

'Did you screw her?'

'Of course not.'

It was as if the image of Silken was in the forefront of both our minds; the effect on me was arousal and a powerful desire for Hanny. Nor was Hanny immune. She was at her most physically aggressive, fighting for every ounce of pleasure, her fit body challenging me at every pass. She came in a shuddering burst which I prolonged until she lay back, exhausted.

'Let's swim,' she said.

'It's October.'

'So?'

We grabbed towels and walked barefoot through the garden. The tide was soft and warm and the moonlight rode the little waves like silver eels. I had told her how I'd met Steer and his people, how I was going to California to meet them again. I told her about Dunty. I left out the bit about the Leicester Square Underground on the basis that it might have been an accident. We sat in the shallows, where the water was warmest.

'It's become very dangerous, hasn't it?' Hanny said.

'Yes, and I want you to be careful,' I said. 'Just in case.'

'I'm not involved.'

'You are, I'm afraid. You know what's going on, so they may target you.'

She floated onto my lap. 'What do you want me to do?'

'Move out of here, when I leave. It'll only be for a week. Go back to your own flat. Be aware that this thing is coming to a head and that some people may want to try and stop it doing so.'

'Who?' she asked.

A kaleidoscope of faces rushed through my head. 'I really don't know yet,' I said.

Somewhere up along the dark beachhead, a dog began to bark.

'Is this always going to be our life?' Hanny asked. 'We said before that it wouldn't be.'

'This kind of thing will never happen again,' I promised her and then kissed her.

We lay there among the silver eels, watching the ash-like moon. A car suddenly sputtered to life behind the dunes – lovers going home. If anything happens to this lovely girl, I'll kill myself, I remember thinking.

46

Silken had no back-up plan, as she later told me. It had seemed so simple. If Steer's people got in touch, Donald would be installed at Boyd to cover the crucial meeting with Friar. Next morning as Silken crossed the Atlantic, she realized that she would have to have Boyd call Friar and reschedule the next morning's appointment – but to when? And who would replace Donald Rellis? Steer's suspicions would be raised at a crucial moment. In New York Silken took a plane for Los Angeles instead of San Diego and gritted her teeth.

It was three in the afternoon when her cab pulled up outside the clinic on Wilshire Boulevard in Beverly Hills. She had telephoned the hospital from New York and, when she had asked to be put through to Donald, had been told that he was in the gardens. If he was well enough to be in the gardens, Silken reasoned . . .

Beneath shade-giving palm trees and by cool fountains sat patients, some in dressing gowns. Donald's room was on the third floor.

'Silken! Darling!'

The veteran actor was sitting in an armchair, reading that week's copy of *Variety*.

'Are you OK?'

Donald explained that he was scheduled next morning at seven a.m. for surgery – a corrective procedure for a twitching eyelid.

'I can't be seen to twitch, Silken,' he frowned. 'I can't look them in the eye and at the same time twitch.'

Silken explained the nature of the crisis.

'But I can't just walk out of here!' Donald cried. 'They'll bill me for the operation!'

'Donald, I'll pay.'

Donald folded his arms. 'I don't think this is very dignified. I'm not well. This is a hospital, not a studio. Your project will have to wait.'

'Donald,' said Silken narrowly, 'we have a deal. You are meant to be available. If you don't get out of that chair now and walk out of here with me, I guarantee that you're going to need surgery for more than your fucking twitch.'

She drove directly from the hospital, down the 5-South. Donald never spoke. Anticipating that Friar too might have come down the night before, Silken checked them into a beach-front house in La Jolla owned by Sam, then drove south across town and over the bridge into Coronado, where the CEO's secretary had come in to meet them.

The office for the next day was allocated, the procedures to follow Friar's arrival agreed. Silken and Donald went back to La Jolla, where Donald, somewhat thawed, accepted the offer of a whisky. Silken cooked steaks. Donald read through the file again and retired early in order to be rested for his performance. And to shave off his famous, flourishing moustache.

Work started at seven-thirty in Boyd. Silken was dressed in a short skirt and white blouse, Donald in a double-breasted, light charcoal suit, white shirt, French cuffs, rose red tie. He exuded the confidence of the chief financial officer of a successful, modern company. Silken had been right about the moustache: the man who now sat behind the desk, his heels on its corner, bore no resemblance to the face in a hundred B-movies.

Friar arrived in Coronado just before ten, sat in
reception. Silken took a deep breath and walked down the
corridor of the executive suite to greet him.

'Mr Friar? I'm Jennifer, pleased to meet you. There's
been a slight change in the schedule . . .' Jennifer threw her
eyes to heaven and noticed Mr Friar's eyes on her legs. She
explained how Mr Bishop had had to fly to New York for
an unexpected meeting 'with a new customer', but that Mr
Bowles, the chief financial officer, would be more than
happy to take his place.

'You live around here?' asked Friar, as Jennifer led him
into the office suites.

The asshole was actually cruising her, she said
later. Jennifer replied that yes, she was now a San Diego
girl.

'Maybe you can show me the sights,' said Friar Fuck.

'Maybe I can,' Jennifer beamed.

The performance began well. Donald, as Donald
Bowles, was born to play the role of the confident, urbane
financial autocrat. He had a stack of financial reports and
other details on his desk, including the latest accounts of
Grace Equity. The large office – home to Boyd's personnel
director, who was on a two-week vacation – was divided in
two, with glass doors through to the secretary's office.
Jennifer sat at her desk and occasionally responded to
requests from Donald for files or reports to illustrate some
point or other he was making to Friar about an aspect of
Boyd's operation. Friar rolled along with his usual bullshit,
specifying unidentified investors, shooting the financial
breeze. If it had not been so serious, it would have been
amusing, Silken thought: two men discussing a subject
about which one, Friar, had no direct interest, and the
other, Donald, no knowledge.

Friar asked, 'I can't help noticing you have the accounts

of an Irish outfit called Grace. I've heard of these guys. Are you happy?'

This was Donald's cue to launch into an awesome monologue about me and my company, about high yields, price-earnings ratios and five straight years of growth. Boyd was a serious investor, Donald said gravely. Opportunities like Grace were few and far between.

'And Boyd itself,' Friar said casually, when Donald's spiel about Grace had at last concluded. 'I see the main share-holding is in Cayman. But who really owns Boyd?'

Silken held her breath. It simply had to work. Any hesitation from Donald, anything less than an Oscar-winning performance, and Silken would have to telephone me and call the whole thing off.

She needn't have worried.

'Well . . .' Donald's eyebrows went up and he puffed out his cheeks, as if to say, you're asking me a big question there, buddy. 'Look, maybe I've said too much already, so I'd appreciate it if you'd treat this as just background, just between you and me?'

'No problem,' said Friar solemnly. 'Nothing goes beyond me.'

'Can I reply by just saying two letters?' Donald smiled.

'Sure.' Friar was puzzled.

'G S,' Donald said and winked.

Friar took a second or two to get it. 'George *Soros*?' he said and actually gulped.

'I didn't say anything,' Donald beamed.

And so, on exactly forty minutes, it was over. In Friar's eyes, not only was I independently wealthy, but I had one of the planet's wealthiest men behind me. Silken saw Friar's face. She reckoned he couldn't wait to get back and tell Guy the treasure trove on which they'd stumbled.

She saw the men standing up. She came out to show

Friar back down the corridor, planning as she did so how
to slip out from under his next, inevitable come-on.
Donald shook Friar's hand, Friar smiled at Silken. Then the
main door was opened and a very tall man whom no one
in the room had ever seen before stood there, staring at
Donald behind his desk.

'Who the fuck are you?' he cried.

47

Although I had not told Tim the substance of what I was doing, I was keeping in touch with Grace Equity, going into the office in the early part of the following week, trying to concentrate on the flow of financial information and on the deals we had in the making. The previous Friday a request had come in from one of the big international accountancy outfits for detailed information about Grace Equity – allegedly on behalf of an interested investor. Very detailed sort of questions. They wanted to know who the Grace shareholders were. Then I got a call from Caulfield Cade, a Texan oil man and one of my original investors, saying that he had become aware of elaborate enquiries being made about him. Steer was doing all the basic groundwork and getting any doubts out of the way before he focused on me. On Thursday I drove Hanny and her things into Jervis Street.

'What about Salman?' she asked before we left Howth.

I looked at the cage and the psychotic budgerigar glowered back.

'Do you want to bring him?'

'I'm not always going to be there.'

'Stella will look after him,' I said.

Stella had become indispensable; I liked her, a cheerful, happy woman who always had a good word to say about something.

'Goodbye, Sally,' Hanny said and blew a kiss; but Salman just pouted.

We went out that night and ate monkfish kebabs and drank two bottles of Chablis. Back in Jervis Street we made slow, caring love, none of the aggression of the last time. I got up at six next morning and spent two hours with Tim in the office. Then I got a cab out to the airport and walked on to the flight to LA.

48

Everyone was paralysed, including Friar, who, in retrospect, may have thought the question was directed at him and, given his dubious credentials in the first place, may have been crucially wrong-footed. Silken later described what happened next, however, as one of the best pieces of acting improvisation she had ever witnessed. Friar was staring at the door, but Donald never missed a beat.

'You like it?' he asked, coming around the desk, and rubbing his hand over his face. 'You are the third person this morning!' As he passed Friar, he winked and said, 'Last Friday I had a tash. My own wife screamed when she saw me.' He had the gaping newcomer by the arm and was pressing him out into the corridor. Boyd's director of personnel had been on vacation in Acapulco, but when his eight-year-old son had broken his arm in a jet-ski accident he had cut the trip short and flown home a week early. Donald was saying, 'Have a look at me out here in the light.'

And now the secretary to the real CEO of Boyd was coming at a fast trot up the corridor, having been alerted, too late, to what was happening.

'I'm sorry to interrupt, gentlemen.'

The director of personnel looked like a man unsure of whether or not he was yet awake. Donald was attempting to let the light from a window hit his face, all the time drawing the man away from Friar.

The secretary said, 'You have an urgent call in my office.'

The director of personnel went back down the corridor, blinking. Donald turned back to his office. 'Vanity gets us all into trouble, eh?' he chuckled to Friar, then, with a sideways glance at Silken, winked knowingly.

'You bet,' Friar said and they shook hands.

Out in reception, Silken saw Friar off, took his card and promised to look him up in Los Angeles. Later, back in La Jolla, over several bottles of Californian Chardonnay, she and Donald went over what had happened in detail.

'You think he bought it?' Donald asked.

'He bought it,' Silken said. 'And you should be short-listed for an Academy Award.'

'Ah,' said Donald, his eyes far away, 'if only.'

It was his best-ever role and there had not been a camera in sight, Silken said.

She was right. Friar went back to Los Angeles and reported to Guy Steer that I was not just the genuine article but that I had access to virtually unlimited funds. And, following Friar's report, Guy Steer put in motion the endgame.

49

Los Angeles was a white, blinding mass. Take the map of a beautiful setting – mountains and ocean, exotic vegetation and unfailing sunlight – then upend a pot of tagliatelle on the map and you had the modern highway jungle of Los Angeles. LA had long been a mystery to me – amid its contorted, congested, highway-bisected, sprawling, smog-bound tangle of contradictions I had over the years done some of Grace Equity's best deals. Now here I was, back again, trying to cobble together a deal of a very different kind.

We took the slip-road exit off the 101 and joined the Ventura Freeway going east. It was Saturday. I'd got in the afternoon before, checked into the Peninsula and spent the rest of the day lying out on the deck beside my suite.

Traffic was moving well. The drive from Beverly Hills to Santa Anita would take about an hour, which meant we would be in Santa Anita by noon. I settled back into the deep leather seat of the Lincoln Town Car and thought of the man I was going to meet.

He was ruthless, that I could sense, not just in the way that all successful businessmen are ruthless but in a far deeper, more predatory way. This was a man who'd had to fight all his life just for survival; he was still fighting. No matter what he achieved he'd never be content, for the fighter dies the moment he lays down his weapons and turns his back. Guy Steer could never turn his back. Something within him – from his early childhood, I guessed – was forever trying to claw him back to the place he had once escaped from. This was his life, the edge; he used any weapons he could to win. Morals or laws didn't enter into it. This was the opponent I was taking on.

And yet, side by side with these characteristics, there was something I could not help but admire in Guy Steer. This was absurd: that I should admire a man I believed had had my own sister murdered. It was the power of his personality, a weapon in itself. I blinked and shook my head. Like some dark, lethal jungle creature, one of his killing tricks was hypnosis: he overpowered his victims with his magnetism before moving in for the kill. It was weird, but true. I thought of Lou and Tricky. And Dunty.

'Fuck you!' I said and the driver turned around, wide-eyed. I said, 'Sorry, I'm talking to myself.'

50

Santa Anita race track is found in a setting of considerable natural beauty. Pacific seagulls were riding funnels of warm air that rose in the foothills of the San Gabriel mountains. The racecourse is a manicured garden in the lap of those mountains, a cool retreat for the wealthy Californian owners of prime bloodstock. I took the elevator to the Turf Club area and then on up to the top level of the stands, to the Director's Box. The first person I saw was big Bill Ruth, Guy's minder, standing guard outside the door to the box. Uninvited guests would need a JCB to get in here without his agreement. I smiled at him in his trademark brown trousseau.

'You're looking very elegant today, Bill.'

He looked at me curiously, opened the door and called, 'Mr Guy!'

'Joe!'

Steer was hurrying from the head of the table. It was impossible not to believe that our friendship had been made in heaven.

'You OK?' His eyes searched my face with the probing concentration of an acne specialist.

'I'm good.'

Cheetah Steer, in a dress that allowed sight of most of her legs, came over and went through the ritual of allowing me to kiss her. Steer took me by the arm in dear-friend mode and brought me to a chair beside his, on the balcony. There were sweatshirts at each place setting decorated with a horse's handsome face and the name 'Contango', Steer's runner in the big one. Davey Delgado, the Doc and Friar all stood up and we grinned and shook hands. The unspoken goo in the air had 'London' and 'Jap chick' running through it like soy sauce. I saw Alan Steer come in and stare alternately at me and Guy. A glass of champagne was put in front of me.

'Welcome to Santa Anita!' Steer said.

It was the best table in the place. Directly facing the wire, high in the stands, the Director's Box was set back in a cool, wood-panelled room. Behind us were tables with a lavish buffet of salads and lobster and cold cuts. Another table was loaded with champagne in ice buckets. Normally I'd have been cooing in here. Now I looked down the table, past Cheetah Steer's always attentive eyes. Between Davey and the Doc sat three young women, bright eyed, blonde-maned, all wearing Contango sweatshirts.

'Joe, I have a little surprise for you.' Steer was speaking in his you-and-me-against-the-world tone. He handed me a slim leather briefcase, the type without handles and with one long zip that runs around the edge. Everyone else at the table was now leaning forward with expressions of happy anticipation.

'Go ahead – open it.'

'Here, Joe, let me hold it and you unzip,' Cheetah said and her long eyelashes batted down. She added, 'Or something.'

She held the briefcase and I ran the zip quickly open – too quickly because bundles of bound hundred-dollar bills fell out across the table and on the floor. The girls at the other end all jumped to their feet and yelped with excitement. I looked at Guy.

'What the hell . . . ?'

'In London you gave me the go-ahead – a hundred grand in oil, remember?' Steer plonked a big wink in Friar's direction. 'Or do you not remember what happened in London, Joe?'

'London?' Davey Delgado looked around him in a good imitation of a clown. 'Was I in London? Doc?'

'You made a hundred and fifty g's.' Steer smiled to me. 'Like I told you in London. Good friends are a rare privilege.'

A waiter had come over and, in the spirit of things, was helping to pick up the bundles of money.

'I had forgotten about it entirely,' I said, and I meant it. 'At least you must now let me buy lunch.'

Steer winked at me, his pal. 'The Santa Anita people pay for this,' he said. 'Have fun.'

As the early, minor races were run off, two waiters poured Château Cheval Blanc. It was indeed a beautiful day.

'Fizzy tells me he worked Contango yesterday morning over half a mile. The colt is bursting out of himself,' Steer confided.

Fizzy was Fitzgerald Wilson, Steer's principal trainer in the United States. With training operations in Kentucky, New York and here in Santa Anita, over the last six years his horses had won an unprecedented clutch of important races on both coasts. Television drank in Fizzy Wilson's sun-weathered face and cool, sexy good looks. Now on cue, he appeared, one-way shades glued to his big face, and the three girls between Davey and the Doc gasped.

'Champagne?'

Fizzy shook his silver head.

'This is my very good friend, Joe Grace,' Steer said.

The trainer sat in the chair that had been suddenly vacated by Cheetah. Davey and the Doc pulled their chairs nearer to us. Friar walked around behind Steer and sat down.

Fizzy looked at me with telegenic insincerity. 'Heard you bought some nice horses in England.'

'I think so.'

Steer said, 'I was just telling Joe that you're sweet on Contango.'

'He's a nice horse and he stands up well to hard work,' the trainer said and popped a sugar cube from the bowl on the table into his mouth. 'I've told Gerry – jump out, then drop back off the pace. Let him forget there's a race. Then going into the back turn, switch him on.'

'Gerry Knight is your choice,' said Steer evenly.

'In my opinion he's still the best jockey in California.'

'And the oldest,' Steer said. 'It's a big field. If he doesn't lie up, he runs the risk of not getting around the front runners.'

'Or getting caught with horses dying on the bend,' Davey said.

'You run him with the pace for the first quarter, you'll burn him out and have no horse on the bend,' said the trainer. 'I trust Gerry.'

'The horse has got the ability,' said the Doc. 'You just have to cod him along.'

'He's running in a hood today,' Fizzy Wilson said.

They talked along for a few more minutes. Steer's impatience was palpable.

'I have every confidence in you,' he said at last, standing up. 'See you in the saddling box.'

'Nice to meet you, Joe,' the trainer said to me and we drank from each other's eyes. I was getting good at this.

The girls, star-struck, followed Fizzy's departure.

'He's a legend,' I said.

'He's an asshole,' Steer said tightly. 'A fucking brain-dead moron.'

Davey shook his head. 'He hasn't managed to train a Group One for us in three years.'

The Doc said, 'Too hard on his horses. He's managed to

break down two million dollars' worth of Guy's blood-stock. I mean, *kaput*.'

'Two million,' said Steer dryly.

'I hope he doesn't work his boyfriends as hard,' observed Friar.

'They've got sore assholes if he does,' Davey retorted and the Doc let out a little snort.

'He's dead if he doesn't deliver today,' Steer said quietly, his face suddenly drawn. He drew his finger across his Adam's apple.

'Amen,' said Friar.

Steer's eyes were on me, but there was no way he was taking in what he was seeing. For a moment, he was a man on the back foot, trapped. Then his pupils became focused again and his ever-compliant face reset itself into a broad smile.

'We mustn't dump our problems on our guest of honour, gentlemen,' he said. 'Joe, let's go gorge on lobster.'

51

Tiny television monitors were mounted on the balcony end of the table. The runners for the next race came out: Friar handed the girls folds of fifty-dollar bills to go and bet with. The Doc had disappeared down to the saddling enclosure to look at horses. Davey Delgado drank Chivas Regal and made telephone calls to Vegas bookies on his mobile.

I tried to get more handle on the make-up of this man I wanted to entrap. If I had just met him here I'd have been sure that Guy Steer was a rough diamond with a sense of fun, a street kid who thrived on success but whose sense of fairness – he had handed me a hundred and fifty grand in cash, after all – was his saving quality. I was now getting to know him as well as I knew Sam Landy.

People came and went from the table: agents, trainers, other owners. Famous jockeys. Turf writers. Cheetah Steer walked away from the table and out across the box's carpeted lobby. She really was a most attractive woman, yet once again, as I had felt in London, her sense of unease predominated, her need to communicate her subterranean disquiet.

Steer and I were alone. He studied me quietly, his gaze as ever searching and intense.

'What do you want from horses, Joe? I mean, you're making your first steps into the market. What are your dreams?'

I thought, then said, 'All my life I've tried to be the best. I'd hope horses would be no different.'

'Let me tell you something as a friend. This . . .' Steer's airborne hands embraced Santa Anita, '. . . is a gigantic honey pot. Ninety-nine point nine per cent of all these people are flies, out for the day, the owners of one or two horses, or guys who think they have a betting system. They've all been seduced. They'll all end up the same way. Stuck in the honey, unable to fly again. And do you know what, my friend? They accept it! That to me is incredible. They hand over their money and shrug. Shucks, they seem to say, so be it. You see, Joe, they almost *expect* to lose.'

I had declined the cigar box and Guy was now puffing alight the standard Montecristo.

He went on, 'I don't accept that, never did. I realized straight off that the only way I could operate in this jungle was as a professional. I built up this team. A pool of expertise. A system. A proven way of operating. I think the results speak for themselves. We're on a roll.'

If Sam's information on his financial problems was correct, this man had some balls.

'Now, take you. Can I be straight? Ultra-bright guy, knows what he wants, thinks he knows how he's going to get it. But can I say something? You know a lot, but you still don't know anything. Everyone in this game is out to screw you. Everyone. Even if they're brain-dead like Fizzy Wilson, they'll screw you by reflex. There are so many ways to cheat. So very, very many ways.'

I could dive into the limpid pools of his eyes without the slightest fear. And yet I also felt a surge of satisfaction: he'd done all the checks and suspected nothing.

'So what if I were to make you a proposition? I'll be frank – I like you. So do the boys, so does my wife. I think we get along well together. I think we make a good team. So what if I were to say to you something I've never said to another person before? Let's become partners. Let me put everything I know at your disposal, upfront. Let me fast track you to the top of international racing. I guarantee you, you won't regret it.'

I sat there, watching seagulls riding the air currents against the hazy, blue background of the mountains. Down below, in the sunshine, people in shorts and shirtsleeves cheered on their choice as another race went down the back stretch. Up here, over lobster and champagne, were made epic proposals. For the question his overture begged me to ask was 'How much?' But, instinctively, I knew it was too early to ask it.

Then, to Steer's annoyance, Davey Delgado came in, his hand over his mobile. 'Hold on.' He turned to Steer. 'The best I can squirrel is fifteen-to-eight,' he said.

Steer made a disappointed face. He looked at me. 'You want to bet Contango, Joe? Davey's on to Vegas.'

I said, 'After you.'

'Have me on eighty grand,' Steer told Davey and Davey relayed the bet. Steer turned to me. 'Joe?'

There was no time with these men that I could be less than a hard-assed bastard.

I said, 'I'll pass.'

52

We had all trooped down to the saddling arena and then into the paddock, where we had observed the jockey in Steer's vermilion and black hoops being given a leg-up on Contango. On the way back up to the box, I'd excused myself and walked down an oak-panelled corridor to the men's restroom. I had just taken a leak when a toilet in a cubicle flushed and the door opened. I stared. The same Eastern man with the thick beard and the lazy eyes whom I had encountered in Newmarket was standing there.

'Mr Grace.'

I grinned. 'We keep meeting in the little boys' room,' I said.

His eyes went momentarily round. Then he rinsed his hands and said, 'Would you like to make some money today?'

I looked at him.

'The Sultan's horse is going to win the next race. He's called Kablah. He's a good price. Have what you want on him.'

I asked, 'What about Contango?'

'Ah.' The man was amused. 'Your friend Mr Guy Steer's horse. I'm sorry to ruin the party I know you're all having, but Kablah will win.'

'Did the Sultan *tell* you to come and tell me that?' I asked.

The man inclined his head. 'He sends his sincere wishes and advises that you take his advice,' he said. 'He still would like to be your friend.'

'Say I said hello,' I said and went out. But instead of

going to Steer's box, I went down into the Turf Club hall and had fifty grand of Steer's cash on Kablah, which was showing odds of eight-to-one.

Now I stood alongside Steer at the front of the box. Friar and Cheetah were watching on the TV monitor. Out on the track twin screens showed the horses in giant reproduction as they were loaded into starting stalls. I could see white sweat flecks on Contango's neck.

'He hates the big occasion,' Steer said grimly and peered through binoculars. 'To be honest, in my opinion he's a horse with a lot of looks and modest talent. Whether or not he wins today, it's his last race. If he wins, then we'll make a stallion out of him, promote him for his looks and as the winner of this race. If he loses –'

Davey looked over. He said: 'If he loses we'll shoot the fucker. And the trainer, if I had my way.'

The metal gates clanged open and the ten horses jumped out.

I could see Steer's hoops surge into the lead straight off. On the screen the jockey fought with Contango, sawing the bit. Fighting his ride. Froth flew from the horse's mouth.

'Shit!' cried Steer. 'I know I shouldn't have let him put that geriatric on board!'

The race-reader's voice rose and fell in tones of rich melodrama. Kablah, in gold colours, hugged the rails in mid-pack. Halfway down the back straight, I could see that the battle to contain Contango had been partially won, for now the colt was nose down and in along the rail behind the first three horses. But at what cost, I wondered? I thought of Tricky, whom I had never seen ride except on an old video. Part of his genius, everyone said, had been his ability to turn the switch on a horse to off, to as good as put the animal to sleep. No fighting or yanking at the animal's head, just an indefinable capacity to communicate a sense of inner calm. And equally to ignite the sleeping beast from its false slumber, to translate its potential into a single, race-winning surge.

Steer's cheekbones were popping. The horses had entered the long turn. The leader had suddenly kicked into a twenty-yard lead, but Contango, still on the rail, was now fifth. Kablah sat on Contango's heels.

'He has no room,' Steer said.

'We're fucked,' Davey said.

I glanced back into the box. Friar and the three girls were all on the edges of their seats, absorbed in the monitor. But Cheetah Steer was sitting to one side, hands on her lap, her eyes closed.

'Now!' Steer hissed. 'Go now!'

In the last third of the turn, the horse immediately ahead of Contango veered left to right off the rails, carrying the horse on his outside into the middle of the track, but leaving broad daylight for Steer's colt to go through. The crowd roared. On the screen, I could see the jockey ask. And for one or two strides, the colt responded. But then they were straightening up for home and the leader, a pacemaker, dead all of a sudden on his feet, came backwards as if on pulley wires and filled the gap that Contango had been unable to take advantage of. And although a whole wall of horses had made their way up on the outside and were fanned out across the course, it was the horse in the Sultan's gold colours who now held the rail and was punched into the lead.

'Kab-*lahhhhh*!' cried the race-reader and the crowd screamed.

Kablah's jockey had timed his run to perfection; for the horses on the outside had used up too much gas in coming round the long way. Kablah swept across the line, the winner by a length. Contango was down the field, only two horses behind him.

I couldn't show my pleasure, of course. I'd never won even four hundred before on a race, let alone four hundred grand. And it was obvious to me what had happened to Contango. The horse's energy had been spent in the first quarter-mile of the race as he and his jockey had wrestled each other. There had been nothing left.

An explosion came from my right. I turned. Steer had dashed his binoculars down on the parapet of the box, where they had disintegrated. Everyone froze. Glass and metal lay at our feet. From the side of my eye I saw Bill Ruth come into the box. Then Steer turned to me and the force of his stare was so strong that it made his eyes look as if they were burning.

'It's not the fact that the horse is worth no more than a ton of cat food,' he said. 'It's not the fact that the race was worth nine hundred thousand. It's not even the eighty grand.' He took a deep breath. 'It's the sheer fucking scale of the stupidity.' He looked at Delgado. 'Joe will excuse us,' he said, 'but we now have some overdue business to attend to.'

They strode from the box. Steer turned back. He looked at his wife. She was sitting, unmoving, as she had during the race.

'Cheetah, will you please look after our guest.'

53

The horses were going out for the fifth as we stood at the owner's entrance and a valet drove up Cheetah's two-seater, an open-topped Mercedes SL600. She sat in, removed her shoes, threw them into the cramped back seat, then smiled over at me briefly and we drove out of Santa Anita.

'Where to?'

'I'm staying at the Peninsula,' I said. 'I have a driver here, you know.'

She looked over at me. Her hair flew out behind. The sinews in her long, bronzed legs rippled down to the toes of her bare feet.

'This means I can get away from horses,' she said and booted for the gate.

I sat back as we weaved through light traffic, Cheetah's hand fondling the shift. I had a feeling of subdued elation – apart from the primal kick of having made so much money. Steer had made his play and it was now up to me to respond. Cheetah was driving too fast, but enjoying it. The car's power allowed her to exploit any daylight in the lanes ahead and she did so relentlessly, lips parted, eyes bright. She was intensely physical, her fit, skinny body luxuriating, it seemed, in dominating the car's power. It was like being near a bomb-disposal unit. I surreptitiously checked my seat belt.

I needed to plan the next phase – my response to Steer's suggestion. The entrapment phase, as Mick had put it. We were doing a hundred and thirty and somewhere far behind I heard the sing-song of a siren. The tip of Cheetah's tongue was between her teeth. The 210 Freeway had become the 134. We drove so near the back of a truck I thought we'd touch it. Cheetah's eyes were flicking to her wing mirrors. Dropping back ten yards, she opened up and in three seconds was back up at a hundred.

'*Watch out!*'

A car was meandering from right to left, looking for an exit. We actually sheared off its wing mirror. The siren was closer now. Cheetah flung the Mercedes across all five lanes of the freeway. Brakes behind us squealed. There was a blare of horns. Screeching in a tight curve, we came down onto the Glendale Freeway and, slowing, joined the new flow of traffic. She looked over at me, breathless.

'Sorry,' she smiled. 'I feel so cooped up at the races.'

Red-jacketed porters surrounded the car at the Peninsula. There was a smell of squandered tyre rubber.

'That was . . . quick,' I said. 'Thank you.'

'I enjoyed driving you.'

'You must be thirsty.'

We walked in together, her shoes in her hand. I was carrying my new briefcase. Even without her shoes, Cheetah was head height to me. The suite was dim and cool, the gauze drapes drawn against the outside glare. She went into the bathroom and a minute later emerged with water dripping from her hair.

'I'll get them to make up a fruit punch,' I said.

'Don't. Do you have vodka?' Her voice was husky.

'I'm sorry, I thought . . .'

'I don't,' she said.

There was a bar with an array of bottles. I poured a vodka into a tall glass.

'Ice?' I asked.

'Just as it comes.'

She was sitting on the sofa, her head back. She looked suddenly exhausted.

'Pity about the horse,' I said, handing her the drink.

'It's one horse,' she said.

'I don't think you like racing.'

'Is it that obvious?' She got up, went to the bar and came back with a teaspoon. 'I used to race quarter horses when I was a kid.'

'In Texas?'

'Sure.' She laughed. 'Quarter horses mean Texas – right?' She opened her purse, took out a glass phial of white powder. Then she filled the spoon with neat vodka, tipped powder in and brought the spoon up to her nose. Pressing her right nostril closed with her thumb, she inhaled sharply, a brief, well-practised snort. She lay back again. 'Used to be quite good, until I grew too much. Boy, could they go! Wow.'

She stretched, then repeated the vodka and powder routine.

'Guy likes you. He's slow usually to make friends, but I can tell when he likes someone.'

'I like him,' I heard myself say.

She lay back and crossed her legs. 'Who are you really, Joe? Why are you really here?'

54

I could suddenly hear tiny sounds, like the soft purr of the room's air-conditioning. She was waiting for my answer.

I said, 'I don't understand.'

'Like, who's the real you? Or the real me? In my case, I've long forgotten.'

My breath being released must have sounded like that of a punctured truck tyre.

'I know what you mean,' I said.

'Do you? For example, what do you think of me?'

'I don't know you, Cheetah.'

'I was raised in a trailer park outside Baton Rouge. Do you know what my earliest memory was? Hunger. If I close my eyes right now I can drag up the dread of it.'

She shuddered.

'Guy and I have that in common, at least. We both understand hunger, how we both as children used to go to bed thinking of where the next meal would come from, and then dreamed that night of getting fed, and awoke in the morning with only one thing on our minds.'

'Yet you both escaped.'

'Hunger makes you learn real good. I learned never to give without getting more back in return. I did some modelling jobs, then moved west when I was twenty-one, to Los Angeles. A lighting technician said he'd get me a job in movies. I lived with him for a bit. Then one night I met Guy. Next morning we flew up to Reno and got married. I've been around ever since.'

'It must be difficult if you don't like horse racing,' I said.

'Sure. But then, I ask myself – what else is there? I mean,

what do I want that I don't have?' She looked at me curiously. 'Did you ever feel trapped?'

'Once or twice.'

She combed her hair back with the fingers of both hands. 'Everything has a price. I'm sure you pay a price for – all this.'

'What price do you pay, Cheetah?'

She took another snort of vodka. I could see the pupils of her eyes dilate.

'Those people you see like Tony Friar and Davey and the Doc, Guy controls their lives. They're all millionaires, but they also owe a shit lot of money to banks for horse partnerships in which they've invested. Guy controls all that.'

'A good team,' I said.

She laughed. 'Would you, honestly, if you had the choice, spend serious time with Tony Friar? He'd sell his children for soap – not that he has children. And Davey? Jesus, OK, he's picked out a few yearlings in his day, a winning brood mare or two, but he doesn't function as a human being.'

'Yet they're all loyal.'

'They're in the gutter without Guy. Me too.' She drew her bare legs up and put her hands around her knees. 'He keeps me on a leash. Scrutinizes every credit-card trans-action I make, gives me a monthly allowance and if I blow it, then that's it.'

'He's a businessman.'

'I'm a woman.'

'You could walk away.'

She laughed, this time without mirth. 'What could I do? I'm qualified for nothing except to look well. How long will that last? Another six years? Ten at the most. If I hang in here, at least . . .'

'Do you love him?'

'Love him? – Probably, in a funny way. He looks after me. I'm scared of what's out there. Guy knows what's out there and he looks after that. He's not like other men, you see. He knows what it is to kill in order to survive.'

55

I was breathing too hard. 'I didn't know.'

Cheetah shook her head and closed her eyes. 'Guy and Alan grew up together out in the Ontario lake country, three hundred miles north of Toronto. Alan is three years older than Guy.'

It was the 1960s, Cheetah said. Their father was a brute who worked a few land claims; their mother fled for good one night leaving two small boys. Alan was fifteen, Guy twelve, small for his age.

'They often went three days without cooked food if the old man was on the whiskey. The boys hunted raccoons and wild turkeys. They fished trout. When their father was drunk he beat them. Once he beat Guy so bad that had Alan not interfered, he might have killed the child. The nightmare went on for nearly a year. On one such night, when their father had collapsed on the floor beside the fire, Alan went out to the woodshed, took up the axe, came back in and chopped his fucking head off.'

I watched this beautiful, stoned woman as she recounted the story. The kids fled east. They were taken in by Christian missionaries near the town of Levack, nickel-mining country. And for the next six years, until Guy was eighteen, Alan looked out for him. He became a surrogate father to Guy and Guy adored him.

'And then without warning, right out of the blue, Alan began to get pains in his head. He'd wake up in the nights screaming that he saw faces. He began to think someone was coming to get him. It was a classical case of delayed trauma around their father, but the local doctor decided that Alan Steer needed to be put into an institution.'

Alan was put into a maximum security hospital, initially for tests that were due to last six weeks. He stayed there for eleven years, during which time he killed another patient, allegedly in self-defence. In the meantime, Guy learned the mining business, took over his father's old land claims and started out on the road that would make him his fortune.

'As soon as he could afford to, Guy came back, had Alan discharged and brought to Toronto for assessment by psychologists. Ever since then, he's been in and out of the best private clinics.' Cheetah sighed. 'Guy takes him out for a month or more at a time. Like now. Flies him around the world. Alan has nowhere else to go and Guy loves to have him near. But Alan is trapped in this role of Guy's protector. On his own, he's sweet and kind, but once Guy appears he's like a guard dog – he just wants to attack anyone who's a remote threat to the person he still regards as his responsibility.'

She was calm now and checked her watch. Then she looked at me for a moment with such frank, sexual curiosity, that I felt my mouth dry out. She reached over and put her index finger on my lips.

'Can I ask you to do me a real favour?'

'Just ask.'

'I'm a little short of cash this month,' she said in a low voice.

I could see how maintaining a habit like hers would eat into a monthly allowance.

'I saw you got some from Guy today. I was wondering, just for a week or two, if I could . . .'

'No problem, just tell me how much.'

'Would twenty grand be OK?'

I opened the briefcase. The amount of cash was embarrassing. I handed her over wads. 'Here's fifty,' I said. 'Pay me back whenever you want. No hurry.'

She took the money and ran her tongue over her lips. 'I could pay you the first instalment right now,' she whispered.

'No need,' I said. 'I'm flush.'

We walked to the door.

'You OK to drive?' I asked as she dropped her shoes and stepped into them.

'What do you think?' she asked, but before I could reply, kissed me, full on the mouth, and briefly let her tongue slip into mine. 'Am I OK?'

'You're OK,' I said.

56

I didn't have to wait too long for Steer's next move. It came on the Monday morning. A telephone call to my hotel in Beverly Hills from Tony Friar.

'Joe?'

Friar's unctuous voice was like bad news – instantly recognizable.

'Hi.'

'Guy asked me to call. He wonders if you could join him for a barbecue tonight? He says you and he need to talk.'

I told him, sure. And then Friar told me that where Steer had in mind was his beach house on the tiny Mexican island of San Felipe.

'He has a plane set up for you out of Burbank,' Friar said, mentioning that Steer was already on the island.

I didn't want to think too long about flying to a remote island and staying there with the man who, I was sure, had had my sister killed. In Dublin Mick had given me a number to ring in LA when I was ready; now I did so. It answered on the second ring. Ninety minutes later I was sitting in a darkened office in Century Plaza with a stout man in tie and shirtsleeves who introduced himself as Paul.

'Michael asked us to fit you out,' he said, referring to Mick. He paused for a reflective moment and looked out the window, or at least, at his down-angled venetian blinds. He wore old-fashioned, metallic armbands at his elbows. 'It's our pleasure. We've always held Michael in very high regard. We've had some good moments together.'

I wondered how many so-called Irish patriots, Americans who had fooled themselves into thinking that smuggling guns would result in 'Irish freedom', had been nailed by Mick and this honcho.

'Let's start with the location,' Paul said, returning to business. 'I need to know everything: where it is, who'll be there, what you'll be wearing.'

'All I know is that I'm going to an island in the Sea of Cortez ,' I replied.

Paul made a long face. He shook his head as he listened.

'Too risky,' he said at last. 'In fact, it's crazy. One, you're going to be on his territory; two, on an island in the Sea of Cortez. Worst possible scenario. Three, you'll be wearing minimal clothes, shorts, T-shirts, maybe less. Where do you hide the equipment? You can't. Even if you think you can and then they discover you're wired, how do you get out of there? You can't. Forget it.'

We talked for a few more minutes, but the FBI agent, if that's what he was, was implacable. What he said made sense. But I had already accepted the invitation, so now I was going to have to go through with it.

'Get him on the mainland someplace, no problem – we'll look after you,' the agent said.

And so on Monday morning I got driven out to the airport in Hollywood-Burbank, where I boarded the Seneca V that Steer had arranged and flew south.

Around the time I was getting on the plane in Burbank, Hanny decided she would go to Howth and check on Salman. The truth was she didn't much like Jervis Street any more; she missed the sea, as she had written in her diary, and she missed me. So perhaps it was an unconscious need to be near the house that drew her out of Dublin that fine October evening. She drove out along the coast road through Clontarf, seeing the last of the light on Dublin Bay. She drove through Sutton Cross. The house had become the central axis to our lives and Hanny let herself in with her own key. The dying sun was shining from beyond the Dublin mountains.

The first thing Hanny noticed was the perfume. A subtle yet distinct airborne block of it, a spicy scent not unlike sandalwood. Stella, the cleaning lady, did not, as far as Hanny knew, wear perfume – not when she worked, at any rate. Hanny was puzzled as she walked into the kitchen and then saw Stella. She was looking up at Hanny from terrified but dead eyes from where she lay, neck broken, on the tiled kitchen floor.

I looked out of the window of the plane as the colours of the ocean deepened into ever-changing layers of blue. The twin-engined plane was done out with comfortable leather seats and was air-conditioned. One of the two pilots chattered in plane-speak with air-traffic control on the island of San Felipe. We swooped low over dense vegetation and tin roofs. The wheels squealed briefly as we put down and puttered over to a single-storey building. A bedraggled flower arrangement spelled out: WELCOME TO SAN FELIPE ISLAND.

57

Hanny screamed. And Salman, seeing her, began frantically to beat his wings with the loss of many feathers, to
shriek and to bang the bars of his cage with his beak. Still
screaming, the breath hot in her throat and caught there,
Hanny made herself step over the dead woman and walk
to the telephone. The budgerigar was going berserk.

Hanny saw the figure out of the side of her eye. The face
was covered with a pair of green, sheer tights, the effect of
which was to make it seem as if a lithe but terrifying frog
was coming for her. But Salman's warning had given
Hanny an inch and she ducked back as the side of one hand
came down where her neck had been. Her shoulder took
the blow and she fell.

She could see the innate athleticism of her attacker,
crouched and moving with the confidence of someone sure
of their power. Hanny picked up the heavy bronze of a
trout I had bought once in France; the frog flinched as
Hanny aimed; in the time created by this reflexive moment
Hanny pitched the statue at the double-glazed picture
window.

She was aware of nothing but the presence of death. It
seemed to have spread up from the dead woman on the
ground and to be hanging on the air. The frog came in for
her now, low and hissing. Hanny felt herself caught and
they went down on a carpet of glass shards. Her hair was
seized and her head crashed back. She wriggled beneath,
but the frog was much the stronger. Hanny's hand was
bleeding where glass had punctured it. And although it cut
her further to do so, she grasped up a splinter and plunged
it into the frog's side.

240 Peter Benjamin

The green head went back and hissed in pain. Hanny was hit hard and felt her jaw go out of kilter. But blood was leaving the frog in a fizzy arc and it rolled to one side, cursing and trying to stem it. Hanny scrambled out the hall, but she could not open the door quickly enough and turned instead for the stairs.

58

I walked through Customs and found Cheetah Steer sitting in a Mini-Moke.

'You have a good trip?'

'The best.'

She accelerated away with the same regard for speed that she had shown in Los Angeles.

I asked, 'How's Guy?'

'He's all fired up for your visit. He can't wait to know if you scuba.'

'I scuba.'

She flung the little jeep around a slow-moving truck. I could see thin ropes of muscles rippling in her arms. 'He's set up a dive this evening. I gather it's the best time.'

'It's when the fish start to feed,' I said. 'You don't?'

'Texas girls can't swim,' she said. She was in shorts and, as usual, she drove barefoot. She shone with athleticism. Not bad for a coke-head, I thought. 'Joe? All that stuff I said the other night? About Guy and how I was afraid of him?'

'I've forgotten most of it.'

'Look, I was stoned. I hate it when a horse loses, I mean, when it's meant to win. I said stupid things.'

'We all do.'

She looked over at me. 'I'd really appreciate it if you didn't mention it.'

'It never occurred to me.'

She reached over and took my hand and brought it to her face. 'And thank you for the loan,' she said. 'I needed the cash.'

I bet you did, I thought. 'My pleasure.'

We passed through a dusty village of yellow earth and ramshackle houses, drove out a neck of land to where, in a clump of trees, a house was set overlooking the ocean.

'Nice place.'

Cheetah shrugged. 'It gets too hot and the air-conditioning doesn't really function,' she said.

Two house boys in white linen coats ran out.

'Welcome to Rancho Felipe, sir!' one of them called.

The illusion that this was another world might have been complete, but for the fact that Bill Ruth was standing in the shade in his regulation brown suit, observing my arrival.

'Mr Joe.'

'Hi, Bill. You going to a wedding?'

His lips parted and I saw a row of uneven teeth bared in what for him went as a smile.

I really was becoming one of the family.

The house must have cost a fortune – each block of amber sandstone had been set snug with careful attention to detail. Cross-beams the size of trees. Deep windows with teak frames. Timber floors.

'You know how much I paid for this?' asked Guy Steer.

We were sitting out on a terrace beneath enormous umbrellas, drinking iced tea. I'd been shown my room, which was as good as eye-level to the surf, thought about Hanny, showered and napped. Now the sun was slowly going down somewhere over Venezuela.

'A lot.'

'*Nada*,' Steer said. 'Not a dime or a dollar.'

I smiled at his engaging roguery.

'A few years back I sold a horse to a Californian commodities trader, a friend of mine – at the time.' He grinned. 'Price was two million dollars, it was entitled to be because this horse had won the Remsen in Aqueduct and then gone on to win the Hollywood Futurity by five lengths. Thing was, the buyer only had a million in cash – he was all fucked up in copper margins in London, but thought he only had to wait a week or so to get his money. And he was in love with the horse.'

Steer lit a cigar. Cheetah was in a bikini in the still hot sun, beside the pool fifteen feet away. I could count her ribs.

'So, being a friend, I said no problems.' Steer's eyes twinkled. 'I said, just give me some comfort. So he said, ah, Jesus, it's just for a week, three at the most, come on; but I said, a million bucks is a million bucks, friend or no friend. So he said, OK, I'll put up the horse.'

Steer drew on the cigar and chuckled.

'Now this was something else – I was being offered the horse I'd just sold as collateral, but the truth was I'd sold him because the Doc swore the bastard had a heart murmur, and now here I was being asked to take him as security. So I said, no dice, I just sold the fucking animal, I want my cash, or I want something that isn't going to gallop away into the night. Now here's the thing . . .' Steer emphasised what he was about to say with his cigar, '. . . people never expect the worst. My friend was long of a shitload of copper and fully expected to be rolling in a week or three. But I knew his position. I know commodities. I could only see copper going south, so I said, give me something else.'

Steer beamed. He looked around him.

'The only thing the man had unencumbered was this place. He threw it *and* the horse in as collateral – payable within six months if he defaulted. And, of course, copper went south and the banks moved in on him. And eight months later I got the horse back and this place as well.'

My host shook his head and laughed quietly. 'Funny thing is, the Doc was talking through his ass. There was nothing wrong with the fucking horse. He ran third in the Swaps the following year and damn near won the Travers. Just goes to show. You should never rely on a professional opinion.'

59

Hanny looked around the first-floor office, of my house. It was a bombsite. Every drawer and file had been dragged open and the contents scattered. Hanny heard the frog again, like wind through trees, as it came at her breath whiffling, both hands covered in its own blood. Screaming, Hanny began to throw whatever she could. Books, files, a stapler and a paperweight. She missed with all of them. The frog had a knife now, blade popped and ready, and was selecting the way to best finish it. Hanny screamed. The frog came around the desk, kicking away the chair. Hanny picked up a laptop and flung it. This time she was lucky and the laptop caught the frog on the temple. Yet the attacker was not deflected. The frog held the knife straight-armed and had trapped Hanny into a corner. Her attacker's alien appearance became clear in every hideous detail: the flattened nose, the oval eye cups, the straining neck sinews. The killing intent. Hanny was mesmerized. She was about to die and she could not move for fear.

And then she and the frog both heard the same thing.

Steps cut into the rock curved down from the pool terrace to a small jetty, where a thirty-foot launch was tied alongside. In shorts and a white T-shirt, Steer led the way. He was well built and fit, although his skin had not been exposed much to sun recently. Tight brown hairs covered his legs and forearms.

I looked back up and saw Alan Steer's pale face, looking down from the terrace. He had appeared an hour before and had greeted me in his usual, engaging manner.

'This is Sandy, this is Mr Grace,' Steer said as a

muscular, white-headed Mexican in shorts stepped on to
the jetty from the boat. 'Sandy knows the reefs here like
his back garden, I've been diving with him for ten years.'

'Mr Steer likes the *bi-ig* fish,' Sandy smiled and made his
eyes round.

'You got big ones for us this evening, Sandy?' asked
Steer as we got on board.

'I do my best, Mr Steer,' Sandy said and the boy at the
engine opened the throttle.

Bill Ruth was already sitting up near the bow; although
still in a suit, he was now, bizarrely, barefoot. The scuba
gear, three sets, sat up neatly on a bench in the stern. Single
bottles with regulators attached, and weight belts, fins,
face masks and snorkels. We put half a mile between us
and the shore in a few minutes. The lights of Rancho Felipe
glowed. To our right and left some other boats our own
size were heading out in the same direction. Tough life.

'You want wet gear?' Steer asked me. 'The water
temperature is about seventy.'

'I don't think so,' I said to myself and smiled as I recalled
the icy temperatures in the seas off Howth.

'Big man came down here twenty or so years back,'
Sandy recounted. 'Wanted the top of a wetsuit no matter
what the sea was like. Evening dive, just like this.' Sandy
picked up a wetsuit and fingered the plastic zip tag. 'Those
days these were metal, all shiny. We go down. Back of the
reef, big barracuda leaves his shoal, thinks this little
zipper's a fish. Wham!' Sandy's hand mimicked a spear.
'Went right through him, left a hole this big.'

'Take no notice of Sandy,' Steer laughed. 'He always
tries to scare the shit out of my friends. It's as safe down
there as it is in your bedroom at home, isn't that a fact,
Sandy?'

'Whatever you say, Mr Steer,' grinned the boatman.

We went out far enough for the shoreline to be almost lost to view, then Sandy let down the anchor. The nearest other boat was three hundred yards away.

'How they know where these reefs are beats me,' Steer said, as I strapped on the bottle and checked the regulator. Sandy helped me find fins that my feet went snugly into and I buckled on a weight belt.

'Take this,' Sandy said, handing me a knife.

I secured the knife sheath to my right calf, then took and spat into the inside of a face mask and dipped it over the side and rinsed it. I fitted in the snorkel beside my ear. Sandy strapped a depth gauge to my wrist.

'Sixty feet to the top of the reef,' Sandy said, putting on his own harness. 'Anchor should be another twenty feet or so lower down. You dived this time of day before, sir?'

I shook my head.

'Easy get lost. You'll see this light.' He picked up a large-sized torch in rubber casing. 'We go over, meet at the bottom of the line. We stay together – OK?' He gave me the diver's OK sign, thumb and middle finger joined in a circle.

'OK.' I looked over at Bill Ruth. 'You don't dive, Bill?'

'I don't swim, Mr Joe.'

'Any trouble, be still,' Sandy said. 'Don't get excited. These fish aren't mean, they're just hungry.'

Steer and I sat on the side of boat, facing in. As we brought down our face masks, Sandy reached behind and switched on our air. Steer went over, sending up a big splash. One hand to my mask, I keeled backwards and saw the blue sky for an instant before I hit the water.

It was suddenly dusk, but above me, where the water was white and crystal, I saw the shape of Sandy coming down, surrounded by a mass of bubbles. I'd not dived for years, but neither had I forgotten the fundamentals: that when you've got a couple of hundred million tons of water

between you and fresh air the only two speeds are slow and
slower; that extreme depth on a dive like this was only for
idiots; and that when you come back up you only do so
after your bubbles.

I sank and saw the outline of the reef to my left. Spears
of daylight held bands of multi-colored fish as if within
translucent cones of glass. Steer was holding on to the
anchor line on what was a high shelf of the ocean bed.
Sandy joined us then, switching on the torch, motioned us
to follow him.

Despite all our planning in London we had failed to
anticipate the pace of events, how the play would unfold
once I was inside Steer's guard, the timescale of the
endgame. Or maybe Steer knew what I was attempting and
was playing me on his own line, at his own pace. Unlikely,
but possible.

The only sound was the echoing exhalation of my own
breaths. Fish swarmed in coloured waves on either side of
us as we glided over shimmering silver ferns and coral that
shone in the dimness. Sandy's shaft of light picked out rock
formations, the steep sides of the reef, the black mouths of
caves. Beneath us and about twenty feet ahead, a massive
stingray erupted from the apparently smooth seabed in a
cloud of sand and flapped away, tail swishing.

I watched the tips of Steer's fins as we glided in and out
of crevices, across quivering sea urchins and coral that,
despite the near darkness, still shone. We were making a
leisurely circuit of this part of the reef. At the extremity of
distance, I could see the occasional glow of another light –
divers from one or more of the other boats that had come
out from shore around the same time. Sandy held up his
hand, pointed. Ahead of us, swimming in a slow, circular
pattern, was a shoal of barracuda. The fish did not seem to
mind the light. We edged closer. The barracudas' lower

jaws protruded like the tips of serrated knives. At least thirty fish. Occasionally, when a small fish was imprudent enough to venture into their orbit, several of the barracuda snapped out of formation and tore it apart before resuming their ritual.

I remembered a similar play that had taken place years before when I'd been in the Middle East. We'd set up, or so we thought, the interception of some high explosive to the Druze militia; at the very moment of the pick-up, our observation post – a room over a carpet shop – had been almost torn apart by gunfire. They'd been watching us the whole time when we thought we'd been watching them. They'd turned our plan around and used it on us. The result: two dead Marines. And they got away with the explosive.

Something caught my arm. I whirled. Steer nodded and held up his circled thumb and forefinger.

'OK?'

'OK.'

The reef shelved deeply. Sandy took us down into a crevice and in the beam of his light I saw a small shark come out of the darkness, turn for a moment threateningly, its mouth white and mean, then, like a sullen dog, lope away. We were gliding over ever-more cavernous territory, deep, inky gullies. Sandy finned straight down into one and Steer went after him. I suddenly wondered what I was doing here on a Pacific coral reef with a man who I was sure had murdered my sister. The weight of the water was making my head light. I felt the pressure on my face mask getting tight; I hung back at the upper level, still ninety feet below the surface. Any deeper and there would be no natural light. I watched the torch beam below me, suddenly small, as it probed needle-like into the fissures of the reef base. From the corner of my eye I caught the movement above me. A fish was my first thought. Then, as I saw the edge of the diving fin, my air supply ceased.

60

A police siren grew out of the darkening window. The frog froze. Hanny could see the eyes widening. Then she flinched as the frog feinted towards her. The knife whistled in. Hanny began to scream. The siren was right outside. She watched the green head cock and listen anew. Then a decision was made.

If Hanny hadn't broken the window, it was later agreed, no way would the police siren have been audible inside the house's double-glazing. For the frog disappeared. That simple. Hanny couldn't move. The fact that the police siren had been passing by and was unconnected with the killer's presence was, like Salman, another factor which had contributed to the fact that she lived.

Mick got her call around ten o'clock. When he got out to Howth forty minutes later, he found Stella's body in the kitchen and Hanny locked in the bathroom upstairs, her hands in ribbons and trembling so badly she couldn't speak. Mick put his arms around her and took her and Salman home with him to his own house in Portmarnock.

I was finished. Tumbling in a world of crazy bubbles. Seeing the other diver above me already almost lost against the reef. My air pipe had been cut. I dragged the useless regulator from my mouth, I knew I couldn't make it to the surface alive. Tucked my chin to my chest and with a pain already flowering in my chest, kicked down to Sandy's light.

Death, my overriding thought, was followed closely by the irony of my situation: my only hope now rested with the man whose freedom I was trying to terminate. The

impossibility of what had happened existed side by side
with the fact that it had. Who had done it was a
bewildering and, in a sense, maddeningly frustrating
question, because I realized I would never find out. I
kicked, but it was as if great forces were pulling me in the
opposite direction. Now Sandy and Steer's leisurely pace
seemed far too fast, for with every further stroke the water
was hard and unyielding. Steer was still twenty yards
below me. I resisted the urge to use my arms, useless under
water for speed, and air sapping, but kept them rigid to my
sides, and flailed with the fins. With a detachment I found
surprising, I knew what would probably happen: sooner
rather than later, I would have to let out the paltry supply
of air still husbanded in my lungs and succumb to the
massive but fatal urge to inhale. At which point my limbs
would abruptly stop functioning. At a hundred feet, my
current position, I would drown silently and very quickly.
The others would, in just a minute, come across my body
floating aimlessly and in apparent peace across the reef.

My pipe had been cut less than sixty seconds ago, but
now, as I struck desperately for Steer's receding figure, as
my chest seemed crushed by a massive anvil of pain, I was
overwhelmed by regret, by a sweeping dismay for the
extent of my own failure. I had let Lou down. Tricky too.
And Hanny. Anger played its part as well, for I knew this
was not deserved – more, there was something inherently
ignoble about sneaking up on a man in this environment,
as someone just had on me.

The word endgame kept pounding my ears. I'd been
beaten in the endgame. Now it was all but over. I could not
hold it any more. Red mist formed within my face mask.
Not just my chest now, but my head too wanted to burst
open. The thought was a comfort. To let it all out. Become
part of the cool ocean. No more pain. My mouth was

open. Another beat and I wouldn't see. I stopped because I had to. Began to fold. Let out my tiny air reserve in a single, beautiful bubble. Smiled, I think. Then, ahead of me, Guy Steer turned.

61

I was aware of him catching me. My remaining reflex had been not to inhale. Now I felt the blessed rubber of his regulator as he rammed it into my mouth. I breathed.

The sensation of the compressed air alone nearly killed me. But even as I stared, pop-eyed at Steer, the red mist began to clear and my hands could move again. He was nodding frantically, telling me to breathe in and out. I did. He took back the regulator, breathed deeply from it himself a few times, fitted it back to my mouth. In a glare of light, Sandy arrived, and he took over. Steer's eyes were full of concern; I was no good to him dead, I understood, but this seemed genuine. Sandy guided me very gently upwards, five feet at a time. With each breath he leaned back his head and exhaled, showing me to do the same – for the greatest impulse in such a situation would have been to gulp air and rush for the surface. But do that and you arrive on top dead, I knew. Your lungs explode. So we came up ever so gently, the three of us, our bubbles big and small floating up like millions of silver balloons, up through the brightening water and bevies of tiny, rainbow-coloured fish, until after what seemed like hours but was in fact no more than ten minutes, we broke the surface of the Sea or Cortez and I lay back, luxuriating in the air.

'Christ, Joe . . . you OK?'

Steer was treading water beside me, his face ragged.

'I'm OK,' I said. 'Thanks to you.'

'What the fuck happened?' he gasped.

'I dunno.'

Sandy was in the water behind me. He held up the severed hose.

'Must have got snagged on a blade of coral,' he said, troubled that it had happened on his watch.

'Yes, I guess that's what happened,' I said.

'Jesus Christ.' Steer shook his head. 'Last time I'll dive here.'

Our boat lay a hundred yards away. We fitted our snorkels and made our way towards it. I noticed, as we swam, that there were no other boats in the area. And when we reached the dive craft Bill Ruth, still in his suit, helped us up on board.

The two houseboys cleared away the last of the dishes. The port was delicious, at least fifty years old, a deep, almost black-ink colour. Cheetah had withdrawn. Alan had been standing on the terrace when we got back in on the launch, in the same position he had been in when we set out for the dive over an hour ago. He had not changed his clothes. His hair was dry. Now Steer and I sat with cigars together on an elevated veranda, listening to the ocean. Alan sat away to one side, a bit like a sentry.

'How are you feeling?' Steer asked me.

'I feel good.'

He looked at me with deep, almost brotherly concern. 'That was too close,' he said. 'I would never have forgiven myself.'

'It wouldn't have been your fault,' I said and realized I meant it.

I had run the possibility that he had stage-managed the whole accident in order to be able to save my life; but that was too high risk, even for a high-stakes gambler like Steer. I had come much too near the ultimate dive for events to have been of his choosing. Which left precious few options.

I said to him, 'It was an accident.'

'Still,' he said and poured for himself from the decanter.

I was drained, of energy and clear purpose. Part of me
actually wanted to like this man, I realized, not for the
corny reason that he had saved my life – I wanted to
like his personality, his roughness, his audacity. I
marvelled at the power he exerted and at my own
inability to hold him in continual contempt. It went
without saying, as his story about how he had come to
own this house showed, that when it came to business, he
was ruthless, but that made him no different from the
majority of successful men. My exhaustion, I recognized,
came partly from trying to keep in the forefront of
my mind that this man was my prey. The fact that
someone was emerging at regular intervals and trying to
kill me didn't help my energy levels either. The fact that I
did not know who that person was left me acutely
debilitated.

'Joe, I asked you down here because I wanted to make
you a business proposal. However, after today's events,
you may not be in the mind to hear it.'

Steer's feet were propped on a stool. He wore a dark
blue silk shirt, the cuffs rolled up to just beneath the
elbows, white chinos, no socks, highly polished leather
shoes. Beneath us, the sea that had tried to claim me earlier
boomed on, but now distantly, it seemed.

I said, 'I assume we're talking horses.'

'Let me first of all describe the operation. Let me tell you
how I get these winners.'

He sat up and began to speak. I was struck above
all by his obvious passion. This went beyond merely laying
a line of chat on an unsuspecting victim, this was his life.

He was saying, 'The whole concept is based on the very
foundation of thoroughbred racing: mares must breed to
thoroughbred stallions. They cannot be otherwise insem-
inated. That is the cornerstone of the industry, the bible.

'So . . .' he spread his hands like a priest at Mass, '. . . I learned the bible.'

He outlined the workings of his operation on four continents. In Rhode Island he employed a statistician to record the details on computer of every two-year-old horse race run in America. What he was looking for was the exceptional horse.

'Ninety-nine point nine per cent of them are shit. They're beautiful-looking plodders. But now and again one pops up. He has this quality of consistency – he can run all his quarters in good even times.'

The Doc was then dispatched.

'We know the horse can run, but we want to know what he looks like inside. Does he have the heart that can win the Derby? Or is he going to bleed to death out there in front of fifty thousand people?' Steer shrugged. 'Of the point one of one per cent we examine, nineteen out of twenty fail at this point.'

'But then you bet the bank on the one that comes through,' I said.

'I want just one stallion a year,' Steer said quietly. 'From yearling purchases and horses in training, out of a total each year of maybe a couple of hundred horses – and you always end up with more than you bargain for – I want just one. Because, Joe, that one horse will pay tenfold for all the others. Yet, at the point of purchase, at the beginning of the campaign, everything that can possibly go wrong, will do so. You saw it yourself last week in LA – a dumb trainer puts up a jockey that's too old on a difficult horse. You know where Contango is now? You saw how beautiful he was, the excitement he generated in the crowd? Poor bastard, he's on a shelf someplace in a tin of dog food.'

Steer sat back and shook his head.

'That's more than I have ever told anyone before, believe me.'

I said, 'I appreciate it.'

'Sure, it's a risky business – which is why I need a partner of equal business strength. Someone who can be passionate about horses. Someone like you, Joe. I make the following proposal.'

Steer sat forward again, his eyes intently on mine.

'Join me in becoming the world's most successful owner of thoroughbred breeding stock. I'm pretty much on the way there already – but together we can scale the heights. Join me. I'm talking about a pool of horses that in five years' time will be worth a billion dollars. Maybe more. Mares from all over the world coming to mate with them. Everything we do together will be utterly mutual and transparent. In five years you'll be the most famous owner of racehorses in the world.'

I sat there and, for a moment, whether it was a trick of the balmy Mexican night, or of the nearby sea, or perhaps a delayed hit of euphoria at simply still being alive, I believed him. I was sold on his proposal to such an extent that I felt the thrill of it course through me, a sense of physical wellbeing, even as I realized that it could never happen. How many other people had heard this spiel? How many men, for whom horses represented glamour but no more, had pulled out their chequebooks at this moment and filled in the numbers asked for by Steer? Quite a few. Sam Landy was one. For this, I had to make myself believe, was the story Tricky had been on to. And had died for.

'How much?' I asked.

'Nothing,' Steer said, 'not now. Just a commitment. From now we do everything together. Equal partners. To do that over the next twenty-four months, we need jointly to commit five hundred million dollars.'

62

Jesus Christ, I thought.

I said, 'You want a two hundred and fifty million dollar commitment from me?'

'There's no point in fooling around with small numbers here,' Steer said. 'I think we trust one another? That's what it will take to achieve our objective.'

I was glad now that I wasn't wired. Not only had we not anticipated the pace of these events, neither had we anticipated that Steer would try to take me for quite so much. Night clung like inky marshmallow.

'I want to think about it,' I said.

'Of course – but in principle?'

'In principle, I'm interested,' I said.

Steer picked up the port decanter, filled my glass, then walked to the wall of the terrace and perched there.

'Think about it, Joe. It's a lot of money.' He was far too professional a hustler to press home any more. 'Whenever you're ready, I'm ready.'

I looked out over the dark ocean.

'I think I'll turn in,' I told him. 'It's been a long day – nearly too long.'

He smiled sadly to show that he hadn't forgotten the diving accident.

'Where are you next week?' he enquired as we stood up.

'Back in Ireland,' I said.

Steer said, 'I'm in Paris in ten days. Do you play golf?'

'Badly.'

He laughed. 'Not as badly as me. I'm a member of the best club in Paris – it's in Saint-Cloud. You want to join me? And then maybe we can decide where we're going on this thing. I'll send the plane.'

'Perfect,' I said and we shook hands. He was leaving at five the next morning, he had told me. He had a meeting on Wall Street at eleven. I said, 'See you in Paris.'

'My friend,' he said, my hand still in his, and then, he came inside my grip and hugged me, shoulder to shoulder.

'I would have died if anything had happened to you out there this evening, Joe,' he said.

I doubt it, I thought. I said, 'I know. Thank you, Guy.'

He held me out from him. 'Not many folks go through a thing like that together, eh? It's like we're partners before we ever begin.'

I lay in bed with just a sheet for bedclothes, listening to the sea below me. The house was on three different levels, cut into the cliff and connected by winding steps. My bedroom was on the bottom level, nearest the water; Steer's, two floors above, commanded the best views. It was sticky warm and the air-conditioning was erratic. As I had made my way to bed, I had passed a makeshift gym in which the light was on. Cheetah was in there, alone. She was working on a weights bench, her long, wiry arms pumping the iron. I drifted in and out of sleep. At some point I heard raised voices: Steer's, perhaps, and that of a woman. She was shouting. Abruptly the voices ceased. I slept again. I don't know what time it was when I heard the engine of a car. I dreamed of Tricky and Lou. Tricky punched a victory fist in the air as he passed a winning post someplace and the crowd cheered.

There was a part of me that suggested that whatever Steer had done, as far as I was concerned at least, he had earned a reprieve. Saved my life. I should now call it quits and walk away. It was an attractive idea.

I couldn't sleep. I put on a robe and walked out on the private terrace. I had missed calling in to Sam for over two days now. The house seemed empty. Steer's and Cheetah's departure for the airport had been what had awoken me. I picked up the telephone and dialled the international number. I heard Sam's voice.

'Wherever you are, whatever you're doing, drop it and contact Mick. This is priority.'

63

I sat on the flight to New York, JFK, wondering if I knew my own name. I still could not understand nor believe it.

'*What* did you say?'

I had called Mick from the airport.

'She's all right, but it was close,' he said.

'Jesus Christ!'

'This has got too deep,' he said. 'I called your man, Landy. He wants a meeting with you. He's in New York.'

I couldn't breathe.

'It could have been a coincidence,' I hear myself say, at the same time remembering the coincidence on the coral reef the day before, and in London two weeks ago. 'A messy burglary.'

'Listen!' Mick's tone suggested he was pissed off with me. 'There are now an unacceptable number of people dead, Tricky being the first and an innocent mother of five, Stella, the latest on the list. This is a personal vendetta, Joe. I can't help you any more. Just thank God that I'm not here telling you to come home for Hanny's funeral.'

I wanted to curl up somewhere and sleep.

Mick said, 'Go see Landy. He told me that events have overtaken your scam, whatever that means.'

'And what's your position?' I asked hollowly. 'Are we going to let this all just – I don't know – *go*?'

'Go see Landy,' Mick said and hung up.

In cold rain, I boarded a JFK shuttle bus. I took one complete loop of the airport and when I was happy I had not been followed, got off at the Sheraton. The room was on the sixth floor. I rapped on the door and it was opened immediately. By Silken. She stepped back as I came in. The bedroom was small and cramped. Sam was sitting on the bed. He looked exhausted.

'Joe, come in and sit down.'

Silken handed me a whisky and I told them about what had happened on the dive.

'Christ,' Sam said. 'Who do you think it was?'

I felt helpless to answer. 'There are a number of candidates,' I said. 'The obvious one is Alan Steer. Next, Bill Ruth. I've even wondered could it be someone who works for the Sultan.'

'What good are you dead to Guy Steer?' Silken asked.

Or to anyone, I might have added.

Sam was pondering. 'Alan is psychotic enough to want you dead. But why would Ruth try, unless Steer told him? And as for the Sultan . . .'

'Steer could have set it up so he could be the one who saved me,' I said.

'Who else is there?' Silken asked.

I thought of the attempts on my life and what I'd heard about Hanny's experience.

'Whoever he is, he's a professional,' said Sam, as if on the same wavelength.

Something about his words clicked in my mind. Why the presumption of gender? In my mind's eye, I had a sudden vision: of firm, attractive muscles rippling beneath the skin of slim, suntanned arms. Jesus, I thought, I'm going mad.

'Listen,' I said, 'let's not get diverted. I've done what I set out to do. Steer is now set up.'

'He may well be,' Sam said, 'but as of now I'm pulling the plug on this project. That's final.' He held up his hand to forestall my objections. 'Please hear me out. I had a call last week from an old friend.'

Sam described the call, from someone he referred to simply as Bob.

Sam said, 'Bob is chairman of the audit committee of a
major New York bank. One of their more troublesome
accounts is Guy Steer.

'About six months ago there was an internal shake-up
in the bank. New bank officials took over the Steer
account. One morning, one of these new people walked
into the account manager for his division and said, "I think
we have a problem."'

The bank's alarm bells began to go off. Steer was
hopelessly over-borrowed on what were, essentially, non-
realizable assets. Horses. In the high hundreds. He was
also losing heavily in his commodities operations. Bob was
called in and asked to head up a sub-committee with just
Steer on its agenda. They reached the conclusion that
anything they could salvage from the mess would be a
bonus.

'Three weeks ago they called him in,' Sam said.

'Between when we met in London and Santa Anita,' I
said.

Sam nodded. He set the scene. Nine in the morning on
the fifty-fifth floor of a building on Fifth Avenue a few
blocks south from Central Park. Bob in the chair. Two
nuts-and-bolts bank people, grey-suited mandarins with
chisel-cut faces. A senior executive, who was also a lawyer
with skills in bankruptcy procedure, a man with all the
charm of a career executioner. On Steer's side: just himself
and Tony Friar. Steer was ebullient, charming. Bob's
experience, he told Sam, was that niceties in such circumstances only delayed the pain.

'Mr Steer,' he said, 'we want our money back.'

Guy Steer blinked, but only once. He smiled. Then he
laughed. Friar too chuckled.

'You asked me here to tell me that?' Steer said without
rancour.

'Mr Steer,' Bob said, 'you may find it amusing that you owe this bank two hundred and ninety odd million, which with interest accruing at nearly sixty-four thousand dollars a day – and compound at that since you haven't serviced the debt in a month now – means that you'll be over three hundred million in to us within a few weeks – you may think this is a joke. We, on the other hand, do not.'

Steer leaned towards the men. 'What's the worst you think you can do to me?' he asked.

The bankruptcy guru patted the file at his elbow. 'We're ready to go. Seizure orders awaiting direct court execution, a simple procedure here in New York, to put eighteen named corporations, all owned by you into liquidation.' He rapped out a long list which included houses and horses, then he looked up. 'If you have a gold wristwatch, I'll want it, Mr Steer. And believe me, sir, what I want I get.'

'Let me tell you gentlemen how I spent my eleventh birthday,' Steer said. 'We lived in a wooden cabin three hundred miles from anywhere. Our father was either away hunting or at home, where he drank moonshine. This day he'd been away a week. My brother and I didn't know if he was dead or not. I kept a white rat as a pet in a cage under the bed. And so on my eleventh birthday, with our stomachs stuck to our backbones, we took out this pet rat, who was now as big as a little rabbit. He trusted me, so I held him over a bucket whilst Alan, my brother, cut his throat. Then we skinned him and boiled him to get the grease out. Then we spit-roasted him and ate him with our bare hands. We even ate his fucking tail, we were so hungry.'

The men were staring.

Steer said, 'Do you gentlemen really believe you can do any worse?'

No one responded.

'I have a proposal,' Steer then said. 'It entails you under-taking to get off my back for three months. No payments whatsoever, either of capital or interest. And a new working facility of twenty million dollars, separate to the main loans.'

'Why the hell should we give you a red cent?' asked Bob.

'Because within three months I will have introduced new equity to the tune of two hundred and fifty million,' Steer said. 'I'll take out two-thirds of your debt. It will happen. But pull the plug now, and you get nothing.'

'And they agreed,' Sam said. 'And although they asked him to tell them who it was, Steer refused.' Sam shook his head. 'He had just found you.'

64

Silken got up and again went to the window. She drew aside the curtains briefly, then let them drop back.

Sam said, 'The point is, Joe, that this man is going bust. The bank are going to lose, although they don't know it. He's going to lose everything. Steer now depends completely on your investment to save his organization. For him it has become, literally, life and death. As far as you're concerned, it's far too dangerous. We just stand back now and let the bastard swing.'

I looked to Silken, but she turned her head away. At that point, of course, I should have cut and run. But I said, 'So what's going to happen now? We walk away and let him flounder? Never find out what we set out to find out? And in three or five years' time, Steer will pop up someplace again, like these people always do, and we still won't know if he's the man who had Lou and Tricky killed.'

Silken looked at me grim-faced. I felt deep plates of longing shift within me. But they were all for Hanny. And for what I had landed her in.

'I'm sorry, Joe,' Sam said. 'We're out. It's over. I want to go home. I want to sit on the terrace and have Jacquimo serve me an Armagnac. You understand me, Joe? It's over.'

Something jumped in my chest. I suddenly saw a pair of massive hands, their veins standing out like tubes.

'Sam, where is Jacquimo right now?' I asked.

Sam held my gaze. 'He's back in Slow Creek. Why?'

I felt suddenly angry, always a sign that I was about to make a fool of myself. Because I didn't believe him.

I said, 'You may be out. But I'm going to see this through.'

And Sam said, 'Goodbye, Joe.'

Later, I took a cab into New York and booked into the
St Regis. I crashed on the big bed and kicked my shoes off.
My tiredness was huge. It always was at times like this.

For now it was just me and whoever else was out there
in the darkness, waiting to send me to oblivion.

Part Four

65

'Here is the position,' Mick Davitt said and made bookends of his two hands. 'Last week we got a call from the Dutch police. A Belgian national called Anton Crof was murdered the week before in Amsterdam. Crof had served in the medical corps of the Belgian armed forces, from which he was dismissed on suspicion of selling army drugs. He drifted into small-time crime and served two prison sentences for drugs-related offences in Holland. Crof's was an inter-gang killing, two big Amsterdam drug barons going head to head. Crof had apparently been making a nuisance of himself and so some nice people took him aside and injected liquid Polyfilla into his carotid artery.'

'Jesus,' I said.

'Charming, I agree,' Mick said and lit a cheroot.

We were sitting in the sun room of his house in Portmarnock. It was Saturday evening. I'd got in the morning before from New York and had telephoned Mick. Now Hanny curled her legs beneath her and snuggled closer to me. Mick got up and began to pace the room.

'The Dutch lads went through the usual motions and interviewed, among others, Crof's Polynesian lover, a man known, I believe, as Sweet Pie. Sweet Pie was devastated and gave the Dutch police access to all the information he could in the belief that he was getting even with his partner's killers. The cops were given all Crof's documents, which included bank statements. A picture emerged. Anton Crof had apparently been running a very nice little business, thank you very much, using his medical expertise to knock people off for a fee. He was a contract killer, in other words.'

I thought of Lou's face on my doorstep in the rain. I thought of what she had thought of me that day.

'He'd recorded his jobs in a very rudimentary code, which the police broke in an hour. Three unsolved Netherlands murders or suspected murders were instantly solved. Sweet Pie claimed he knew nothing, that good old Anton was gentleness and kindness itself. But then the cops came across an entry which was clearly an out-of-town job. It had apparently been carried out by Crof in Dublin earlier this year. The local cops handed it over to Interpol, Interpol put it into their computer. Hey Presto. The dates fit. This male version of Florence Nightingale was in and out of Dublin the day Tricky Dawson was murdered.'

'And the payment?' I asked.

Mick winced slightly. 'More difficult. It came through a middle man, a respectable drop. They've already gone knocking on his door – he's an antiques dealer, no convictions, he buys and sells all over the world, he's got foreign currencies going in and out of his bank accounts like maggots.'

'But he paid Crof.'

'Fifty grand, US. He says it was for an antique piece. Which is bullshit, of course, but he's holding firm. So they've got to get court orders in order to trawl through his financial stuff and see who paid him. Which will take time.'

'Steer will have run the money through so many intermediate points that he'll remain invisible,' I said.

'That remains to be seen,' Mick said, 'but at least we're closer to the truth than we were.'

He yanked the cork from a bottle of Chablis and poured three glasses. He came back from the kitchen with a plate of smoked salmon sandwiches.

'Don't you ever say you weren't looked after here,' he said.

Hanny chewed on a sandwich. 'Who's trying to stop Joe?' she asked. 'Who tried to kill me?'

Mick made big eyes and rocked his head. 'I'll leave that question to my learned friend,' he said.

'Suspect number one has to be Alan Steer,' I said, 'although he couldn't have carried out the attack in Howth since he was in Mexico at that time trying to drown me. Which means that the attack on you may be unrelated.'

Mick shook his head. 'Steer wants your cash badly. The brother knows that – why would he want you out of the way where you're no good to Guy? Someone wants you off the scene all right, but it's not Steer. They crippled the bloodstock agent to warn you. The murder of Stella and the attempt on Hanny were the same.' Mick frowned. 'What about Landy?'

'I've thought about him,' I said, 'and, yes, it's a possibility. He might have set the whole thing up from the beginning and now be playing along with me, convincing me and Silken that he's trying to help.'

I felt Hanny bristle. She said, 'I don't trust that woman.'

I decided to say nothing.

'Let this thing take its course,' Mick said. 'Ring Steer and tell him you've changed your mind, that there's no point in your going to meet him in Paris since you've decided against the investment. If he's guilty we'll get him in the end.'

I drew Hanny back to me. 'Or you may not,' I said. 'On the other hand, I've already spent a fortune getting in close to Steer. I'm in. I have to play this out.'

'There's somebody out there trying to kill you,' Mick said.

'I know.'

'You're an obstinate bastard.'

'I know that too. Sorry.'

Hanny put her hand to my head. 'Promise me you'll come home safe.'

'It's a promise,' I said and bent down and kissed the tip of her nose.

66

Rainwater flew in long slicks on either side of the taxi as we barrelled in along the A1 towards Paris from Charles de Gaulle Airport. I was obstinate, I knew. Maybe obstinate was another way of saying that I lacked either the instinct or intelligence for compromise; nor was this the first time I'd found myself in such a position. Which is to say: alone and up against it in a country that wasn't my own. I'd learned all about lack of compromise as a kid when I'd ended up leaving Dublin, aged fifteen, to finish my schooling with relatives in New York. There'd been a principle involved: the school bully had been picking on my brother John, a haemophiliac. I still considered what I'd done to the bully's face was justified. And now here I was again taking on another bully. It was the same, really, just that the stakes were much higher.

It would be neat to think that operations such as this always went according to carefully laid plans, that everyone remained in agreement as to the next call and that the baddies were always caught. My time in the Intel section of the Marines had taught me otherwise: very often all that remained unchanged in a mission was the original objective. This was what I was now locked on to, like a missile. And everyone knows what happens to missiles – whether they hit their target or not.

The taxi left the Pérephérique and took the route through the Bois de Boulogne. I'd considered calling Sam Landy, just to pinpoint his position. He owed me £10 million, half his stake for the three horses, and he hadn't said that pulling out meant he wouldn't pay. It was a lot of money and my bank account was looking distinctly unhealthy. And yet I couldn't really accept that all the advice and help Sam had given had been a sham, that he would have set up someone like Dunty Rainway and then have him beaten near to death. And yet Sam was a candidate, if only because there were so few others. Could it be the Sultan? Did he react like this to everyone who declined to be his 'friend'? I sighed. It would be nice for a change to meet someone in the horse business whose repertoire didn't include murder.

I looked out as we passed the stands for Longchamps and climbed uphill for Garches. The sun came out. I concentrated on the end game.

The eighteen-hole golf course at Saint-Cloud was accessed through a security barrier. Giant oak trees still retained most of their leaves. The taxi circumnavigated a flowerbed and came to a halt by the clubhouse door.

I was early. It had been six months since I had held a golf club. Now I made my way to the pro's shop. Twenty minutes and two and half grand later, kitted out like a tour professional and with Emile, the club's *professeur du golf* as my caddie, I made my way to the front of the clubhouse. Steer was standing just outside the glass doors. He saw me and raised his hand in greeting, but without enthusiasm. He removed dark glasses and I saw his haggard face.

'Joe.'

'Guy. Everything all right?'

He made a grim mouth. 'I had some bad news this morning.'

I said I was sorry. I wondered was I too late and if the bank had already moved in and pulled the plug.

'It's my brother, Alan.'

I thought of the pale face on the terrace in Rancho Felipe and I thought of the coral reef.

'He took an overdose in LA two nights ago,' Steer said and ran his hand through his hair. 'Alan has his problems – from when we were kids. He looked after me once. He's part of me.'

I made sympathetic noises, but inwardly I had to admit that I wasn't exactly despondent at this news.

'We can call off the game,' I suggested.

'I wouldn't hear of it,' Steer said. 'I spoke with him just ten minutes ago. He's OK, he's being looked after.' He managed a smile. 'Besides, I'm budgeting to make some money this afternoon.'

Bill Ruth appeared.

'Mr Joe.'

He had a set of brand-new Callaways hitched over his shoulder. A pair of spiked shoes. And his brown suit, of course.

'You ever heard of Nike, Bill?'

His lip curled. I introduced Emile, the golf pro, to Guy and we made our way to the first.

'How much do you want to lose?' Steer asked.

'Nothing,' I said truthfully and he laughed.

He said, 'Talk straight?'

'Sure?'

'This fucking game bores me unless it's for more than anyone should be able to afford to lose.'

'You name the stake.'

'Half a big one,' he said.

My heart included an unscheduled beat in its routine. 'Half a million?'

'Why not? You spent thirty times that screwing me at Newmarket,' Steer laughed.

'OK.'

The caddies set out ahead of us.

I said, 'Dollars or pounds?'

Steer shrugged. 'Why not play for both?'

We shook hands. I thought of how shit I was at golf and thought of my bank account.

We made our way to the first tee of the *parcours vert*, the green course. I stood up, took out a three-wood and hit the ball about two hundred yards straight. Steer took out a driver. Swung it a couple of times. He swung well. He connected with perfect timing. The ball flew into the distance. Further than mine.

'Good ball, Mr Guy,' Bill Ruth said and we set out.

67

The course curved away through a riot of autumn colours. Under the trees, amid oak and chestnut leaves, lay countless chestnuts, some of them still encased in their green shells. The day turned sultry as we finished the front nine. Steer was naturally athletic and had worked hard at his game. He had a manufactured swing, an awkward but effective punch-type shot. His game was remarkably consistent. He hit a long ball and putted well. His weakness was the short game: he lacked the telling shot from fifty to seventy yards. I was always behind him off the tees and with my mid-irons, but I hit the greens more often with my approach shots. In putting, I was about his equal. We had swapped the lead at the fourth, sixth and ninth. Now the match was square.

I kept thinking of Hanny and how, when this was over, I was going to marry her. We were going to settle down and have kids and do school runs and whatever else kids involve. A riding path ran all the way along the left-hand side of the golf course and occasionally I glimpsed horses and riders, and smelled stable smells over the tall trees. It was hard, it seemed, to get away from horses. I was just off the back of the eleventh green, Steer was in a sand trap. He swivelled into the sand with his heels, concentrated ferociously, then exploded the ball up and out in a cloud of sand. But not quite enough. The ball caught and stuck on the grass lip.

'Fuck!'

He threw down his sand wedge, asked Bill Ruth for the putter. It was my shot. I lined up, struck, and let the head go forward, smooth and loose. The ball came to rest eight inches from the hole.

'Given,' Steer said.

His own putt, to halve, was snagged by the short rough and never made the business part of the green.

We walked to twelve: I was one up.

Steer said, 'What a fucking game. It's like a woman. You think you're ahead of things, that you have her figured – like three up with four to play – and then the whole fucking thing falls apart.'

I said, 'Tell me about it.'

Hanny would be good at this game, I reckoned. She had the height and the limbs. The poise. Emile, the club pro, had managed to allow me to, if not forget, then to put to one side the fact that I was playing for a million. He had sized me up quickly and thereafter handed me the correct club each time. I was as relaxed as I could be. Steer, on the other hand, was becoming ever more tense. He wasn't chatty any more. Each time he hit a shot that was less than perfection, he was angry with himself. Losing the head game. I could sense the demands he made on himself, the imperative of winning. Which was what he craved. Yet the same desire to win was slowly losing this contest for him, causing him to become physically tense, contracting his swing, twisting his face into a knot every time he went to hit the ball. I was fucking heartbroken.

I had overplayed my tee shot on the uphill twelfth, a par four, and my ball had run in beneath the trees to my right. Steer's ball was twenty yards further on, sitting up on the fairway. I stood behind my ball and saw the stymie: I couldn't go for the green because of a tree immediately ahead of me. Three inches further left or right and I would have been fine. But, as it stood, I would have to chip out sideways and lose a shot in the process.

Emile was pondering my situation.

'Monsieur would know what to do,' he said with a Gallic shrug in Steer's direction.

I looked at him questioningly. Emile made a little kicking motion with his foot.

'He did?'

Emile nodded. '*Mais oui*. On the eighth and on the tenth. You should be three up.'

'Fuck him, no,' I said and took a wedge and hacked the ball twenty yards sideways into the rough.

'Well out, Joe,' Steer called, happy all at once.

He knew he had won the hole and that the match was square again.

The bridle path continued along the high perimeter for the next three holes. Occasionally I could see people on foot. At the steep downhill, par-three thirteenth, I missed a gimmie putt to go one up; Steer sank a thirty-footer to save. We halved the next two. Steer drove the green on the par-four sixteenth and very nearly holed an eagle putt; his birdie put him one up. It began to rain lightly. At seventeen, an uphill par five heading for home, I sliced my drive into a stand of trees and Steer was equally at fault in the opposite direction. With only one further hole to play, if I lost this hole and went two down, I lost the match. I watched Steer stride purposefully ahead of Bill Ruth and disappear out of sight. I thought of Emile's earlier remarks.

'Go and help him find his ball,' I said and Emile winked at me.

'*Bien sûr*,' he said.

I climbed into the tree cover. There was a house back here; dogs were barking. Within the trees it was all but dusk and eerily quiet. My ball was sitting on red pine needles, my next shot would be costly – but, perhaps, so would Steer's. He and Bill Ruth and Emile were out of sight. I needed to piss. Using my wedge like a walking stick,

I climbed up further, into deeper shadow where the trees
were planted much closer together and indulged myself in
what I had often heard my father describe as 'the last
pleasure left to man'.

   It almost was my last.

68

My head was jerked back so violently that it felt as if my neck had snapped. I had been jumped on by a wild animal, was my first thought. No such luck. The lack of air was terrifying. A length of cord was around my neck in an ever-tightening garrotte. My chest swelled as if a balloon were being inflated within it. Strength flowed from me. Vision blurred, my heels began to kick. I wanted to shit. Couldn't scream. Tried without success to turn, but knew I was pinned by superior strength. Reached desperately behind and felt the fingers of my right hand claw at a face. My attacker levered a knee into the small of my back and clinched the cord further. Yet, even as the strangulation moved to conclusion, I understood that there had been some flaw in its primary execution, that when my hands had sprung to my throat, the handle of the wedge had come with them and been trapped at my neck, inside the noose. My hands, flapping like fins, felt for the shaft of the iron. I could feel the strength and size of the attacker and hear animal-like grunts. We had come to a tree and thus had stopped going backwards. I knew one effort only was possible. I powered up with the club and felt the throttle give a fraction. I fell forward, head first, then tumbled downhill. I must have struck a tree, head first. I remember nothing more.

69

I came to looking at my golf ball three inches from my face.
I can have been out no more than a minute. My right hand
was blood-stained; I wiped it on the ground, then ever so
gingerly brought my fingers to my agonized neck. But for
the wedge handle, the cord would have crushed my larynx.
Even as it was, I could feel a growing weal. But there was
no blood there. The blood I had wiped off had been that of
my attacker, from the face or neck, where I had scraped it.
I was going crazy. I felt like a child dogged in the dark by
a monster. Except that in my case there was no one I could
cry out to.

Voices came to me from the other side of the hill. I
buttoned up the collar of my golf shirt. Emile was walking
back towards me, the corners of his mouth pulled down in
private disparagement. I got unsteadily to my feet. I had a
searing pain in my neck and left shoulder, and a white-hot
headache. In the distance behind Emile I saw Steer emerge.
Bill Ruth was not to be seen.

''E say 'e find 'is ball . . .' Emile said, his hands asking
very basic questions.

I took a bottle of water from my bag and slugged it. I
could barely stand.

'Where's his caddie?' I managed to ask.

Emile indicated the far side of the fairway.

I nodded to my ball. 'You play it,' I said.

Emile smiled that he was glad that I had at last learned
the rules. We were hidden from view by the trees. Emile
took out a six iron, closed the face, put his hands in front
and punched the ball through an opening no bigger than a
letterbox. The ball finished just on the edge of the green.

I craved Hanny. To be held by her.

'That was some shot,' Steer remarked, as I walked on to the putting surface.

'It was do or die,' I said.

Then, from behind a sand bunker, Bill Ruth hove into view. I looked at him and he held my gaze. Around his neck he had arranged a towel against the rain.

'Your shot, Joe,' Steer said.

His own had not been too bad, whatever its provenance. He was on the back of the green in an alleged three. As I bent over the ball, I thought my neck would crack. The ball slid by the hole. Steer put his to a foot.

'Your hole,' he said.

'Thanks.'

He looked at me. 'You all right?'

'I'm surviving.'

'I think the pressure is getting to you, Joe,' he said.

'You can say that again.'

I had never been more bewildered, yet I knew for certain that the same hands that had tried to garrotte me, had also cut my air hose and had tried to propel me under the London train. But who? I didn't know. Mick was right. I should go home and allow events to taker their course. But in the meantime there was the little matter of a million quid and the eighteenth hole to be dealt with.

Steer had already driven. I could scarcely swing the club – my drive went less than a hundred and fifty yards. Emile was looking strangely at me, trying to figure out the deterioration in my condition. I took my second shot with a three wood: the ball curved right and disappeared into a deep sand bunker in front of the green. Steer and Bill Ruth were still looking for his drive when we walked up. The fairway sloped to the left. I could see the outline of Paris in the distance. Steer's drive had been too good, in fact, for it

had obviously hopped into the semi-rough downhill. I
prayed to be out of there, to swallow some painkillers, to
drop my guard for a blissful hour. I wanted to lie down and
sleep. I wanted to curl like a kitten and, when I awoke, I
wanted to reach out to a beautiful woman and feel her
warm skin and allow her to hold me to her and to tell me
it was all over.

Emile was searching to my left, Steer and Bill twenty
yards further along towards the green. The Frenchman and
I saw Guy's ball at the same moment: it had come to rest in
a patch of ground that had been made wet by a nearby
leaking sprinkler head. Emile looked at me. We understood
each other. I nodded. Still making as if to search, Emile
walked with his full weight on the ball. It disappeared.

'Shit!' Steer said, walking back. 'Probably the best shot
I hit all day.'

'It's tragic,' I said.

We searched for a further three minutes. Then Steer
grabbed his driver from the bag and walked all the way
back to the tee to play the shot again. I felt Bill Ruth
inspecting me. I wondered had it been him back on the
seventeenth. And if so, why? I felt like lying down on the
grass and giving up.

Steer's tee shot was textbook; he was on the green with
his next, but with the two penalty shots I held the
advantage. The eighteenth green was tilted subtly into the
hillside – even had I been able to judge all the borrows and
angles, I could see how easy it would be to three putt –
that's if I got out of the sand. Steer was lying six feet from
the hole. I climbed down into the bunker, as if into a mine.
My ball was plugged. I looked up and all I could see was a
wall of sand. I stooped, picked up the ball and a handful of
sand and threw both high in the air over the lip of the
bunker.

There was a momentary silence. Then I heard Emile shout. I clambered out. He was running over towards me. I looked at Steer.

'Where did I finish?' I asked. I could not see my ball.

'In the fucking hole,' he said, his face drawn and empty. 'Congratulations.'

70

I got into my suite in the Hotel Crillon, locked the door and just made it to the bathroom toilet. My legs went. I knelt, head over the void for five minutes. It took me all my strength to make it back into the bedroom, where I swallowed four paracetamol then lay down, cold and trembling.

I was out of shape for this sort of thing. Both my body and mind were traumatized. I drew up the quilt over myself and shut my eyes.

Steer had written me out a cheque for a million pounds outside the clubhouse. Emile had driven me into Paris and got himself a two grand tip. Steer and I were due to meet that evening for dinner. I didn't think I would make it. When I opened my eyes again two and a half hours had passed and it was dark. I tried to get up from the bed, but my head wouldn't move. So I rang room service and had a housekeeper come and fill the bath for me. No point in staying in these places and doing it all yourself. The middle-aged housekeeper looked at me cautiously and asked could she do anything else. It was tempting to suggest she could take me home with her and mind me. I thanked her, made my way to the bathroom and did my best to scald my body back into some kind of functioning relationship with my brain. Then, pink but more mobile, I went back to the bedroom and on impulse dialled Mount Landy in New South Wales. The phone rang out. Bastard! I thought. Of course you can't answer it if you're not there!

'Mount Landy.'

'Could I – ah – speak to Jacquimo, please?' I said.

There was a brief hesitation. 'This is Jacquimo.'

I crashed the phone back down. So much for that theory. I began to dress. The plan had been for me to make contact with a number in Paris that Mick had reluctantly given me, and for me to be fitted out with a recording device. To get wired. But there was no way I could even reach down to put my socks on, so I'd decided to pass on that phase of the plan. My head spun. For the second time in as many weeks, I felt decisively outmanoeuvred.

My taxi pulled up beside the door of the pavilion-type building at exactly nine o'clock. A mile away in the dark woods of the Bois de Boulogne, long-legged prostitutes in fur coats huddled around bright bonfires along the roadside. I concentrated on emptying my mind of pain and confusion – of everything but the task ahead. Even of Hanny. I had something this man desperately wanted. He was going to have to spill out his heart to me to get it.

He was sitting at a round corner table. He stood up as soon as he saw me and moved in for the standard hug.

'God, that was close!'

He was referring to the golf. I would have liked to have told him just how close. He had already ordered pâté de fois gras as an appetizer, and a bottle of Château d'Yquem.

'D'you see those hookers on the way here?' he asked as the waiter served me the oily, fragrant wine. 'Brazilians. Most of them are men. Awaiting surgery.'

'So I've heard.'

'Were you ever tempted?' Steer smeared pâté on toast. 'I'm told they blow you better than any woman.' He crammed his mouth.

'My tastes are more conventional,' I said.

'I noticed – in London,' he chuckled. Then he looked at me more closely. 'You don't look very well, Joe. You OK?'

'I'm fine,' I said, 'I may have picked up a bug.'

'There's a lot of them around,' Steer said.

We talked about his horses and his trainers. We both ordered wild boar.

'Suggest a wine,' he said to the sommelier.

'Ah, m'sieu, after Chateau d'Yquem, the only possible strategy is to attack,' the sommelier said and came back reverentially with a bottle of Cheval Blanc.

As we ate wild boar and mushrooms, Steer described some of his greatest moments in racing, the thrill of winning the Prix de l'Arc de Triomphe in this very town, and I thought of Tricky Dawson and the appalling manner of his death at the hands of a contract killer hired by this man. How could Steer do that and carry on as if nothing had happened, I wondered.

'I've had a long think about everything we discussed in Rancho Felipe,' I said, as the plates were cleared away.

'Oh yes?' Steer said casually, as if up to now he had forgotten all about it.

'I have a few problems,' I said and wondered was my head going to burst wide open.

His face gave no hint that his entire future depended on my decision. He said, 'OK.'

'I'm on a steep learning curve here,' I said. 'I've had this horse dream for so long I can't even remember how it started. So as soon as I had the money and time, which was this year, I came to Newmarket. I understood during those sales how little I really know about horses. Now you've made a big proposal. My problem is: how do I know I can trust you?'

Steer frowned deeply. 'What do you mean? I thought we were friends.'

'Remember the story you told me in Rancho Felipe? About the horse and the million bucks? You told your friend back then, "this goes beyond friendship". You were right – a million is a million. And two hundred and fifty million is a gigantic piece of friendship.' I fiddled with the stem of my glass. 'You see, Guy, there's no way I can figure out, once I pay in the cash, how I can keep tabs on what you do with it.'

'So you don't trust me,' he scowled. 'Even though I saved your life.'

I let him know from my expression that this all pained me big time, which wasn't too difficult for me in the circumstances.

I said, 'Trust is a two-way street. Let me give you an example of how we used to work it as kids. We had a gang called the Black Knights. About five boys. Our sole ambition was to skip school, but we realized that our greatest danger was if one of us was caught and ratted on the others. We needed to establish trust. So each member of the gang had to declare to the other four a personal misdemeanour. Something that had never been found out. So one said he'd stolen chocolate from a shop, the other that he'd burned hay in a barn.'

'What was yours?' Steer asked.

'I'd got one of their sisters to pull down her knickers,' I said.

He laughed at length, his head back. 'I like it!'

'The point is it worked,' I said. 'No one of us could ever screw the other. We had too much to lose.'

In Albermarle Street, light years ago, Landy and I had planned the script right down to the last word.

Steer was thinking. 'That's a big call,' he said quietly.

I said, 'Think about it. It's quite simple. I just need to be sure that my money is underpinned, that's all.' I signalled for the bill. 'I really enjoyed today.'

And now, as I signed the card receipt, I heard the silence. For this was the point at which Steer, overwhelmed by need, would, we had calculated, play my game. Come on, you bastard, I thought. You need me!

He sat there, just looking at me. And yet, I could see a process of calculation taking place within those deep eyes.

'I have to go,' I said. I was through.

'I've got a car,' he said.

'So have I.'

We stood up. Relief and disappointment flooded me together. It was over. We walked from the restaurant.

'I'd like to keep in touch,' I said as we were helped into our coats.

'Absolutely.' He seemed to be in another world.

We shook hands. Our drivers held the doors to our respective cars.

'Give Cheetah my love,' I said.

'Of course.' Something dramatic was going on in his head. He seemed almost dizzy. 'Goodnight, Joe.'

'Some things are just not meant to happen,' I said. 'Goodnight, Guy.'

71

I walked towards my waiting car.

'Joe.'

I stopped, turned.

'Let's walk for a bit,' Steer said.

I fell in beside him as he walked out through the gardens and into the Bois du Boulogne. Fifty yards behind us, our cars trailed.

'Let me tell you about a friend of mine who owns horses,' Steer said, his shoulders hunched forward. 'A little while back he had some trouble. With the media. He could never understand these people, their motivation, their basic envy. They see someone successful and all they want to do is tear him down.'

Come on, I thought, come on, you bastard.

'My friend was targeted by a washed-up nobody, a vagrant who had somehow got a job as a hack in a racing paper. Suddenly this asshole wanted to blaze a trail of glory across the headlines – at my friend's expense, of course. Small-minded, pig-headed ambition. No other walk of life would have tolerated the kind of shit he was peddling. He called it research.'

'What – what was he researching?'

We were in deep darkness. Only the dimmed headlights of the first car behind us illuminated the road ahead.

'Some of the people my friend had had horse dealings with were fraudulently attempting to get out of their commitments. For some reason this hack took their side. I mean, without even asking my friend for his side of the story. It was as if his opponents were being given this free platform to say what they liked about him – and boy were they going to crow.' We stopped and Steer turned to me. 'You know horses, Joe. You know what can go wrong. How risky the investment is. All the marginal items on which success depends.' He laughed. 'These – *bastards*, who had freely accepted the successes my friend had had, now, as soon as he hit a rough patch, began to whine. And this little shit took their side.'

'That's ridiculous. Who was the hack?'

'Oh, it's not important who he was. He was no one, but now, for a brief moment in his life he had the means to act out his envy.'

He wasn't no one, I thought as I saw Lou's pretty face. He was someone's world.

'My friend found himself in a highly precarious situation. Here was someone who wanted to bring him right down. Into the gutter. Who hated my friend so much he wanted to paint a picture so dark that everyone else would hate him too.'

We had come round a bend and all at once there was a bonfire with figures in fur coats around it. Pop music blared from a transistor.

'*Bonsoir messieurs. Voulez vous faire l'amour?*' a beguiling face enquired from a fur hood. The figure let the coat fall open and long, bare legs were revealed beneath a tiny, leather skirt.

'Nothing is as it seems, Joe – is it?' Steer said.

'So – what did your friend do?' I asked as we resumed our walk, wishing I had all this on tape.

'He tried to talk reason. The opening of the British flat season was in sight. There was a danger that this nonsense, if published, was going to end up with the Jockey Club holding an inquiry into whether or not he was a fit person to have horses in training. I mean, can you believe that? He'd spent millions on horses in England over the previous few years, and now they were going to call his fitness into question all because of the ranting of some drunk!'

I stopped. 'He was a drunk?'

'Yeah,' Steer said. 'Yeah, he was a drunk.'

'Did your friend try to talk to him?' I said, hearing my own voice now as it seemed to rebound among the nearby trees – a hollow, unconvincing sound.

'Tried to,' Steer was hunched deeper, head forward. 'Offered to make a payment towards his expenses – not a bribe, just a gesture while they sorted things out. And when the word came back that the hack wasn't interested, my friend said he'd pay the same amount into the charity of his choice. What could be fairer? This thing was unproven, the people whose side the hack had taken were making allegations with no foundation, no sense. My friend got calls from two other turf writers within the space of twenty-four hours. Was there any basis to these allegations? Jesus Christ. These people were trying to hang him out to dry, Joe. They wanted him dead.'

'So – how did your friend deal with him?' I asked.

We had emerged on to one of the Bois's main axis routes. Steer stopped by a street light.

'He had him taken care of,' he said.

72

'How?'

'Doesn't matter how.' Steer's voice was harsh. 'He was going to bring my friend down with him, Joe. So he made sure he couldn't. He'd tried everything else, after all. What else could he do?'

'This friend of yours', I said carefully, 'sounds like he's someone I could do business with.'

'Good.'

'I mean, were he to trust me so much that he'd tell me what you've just told me, then I think I'd have no problem trusting him with my money.'

Steer was examining my face minutely, as if everything he wanted could be read there.

'It can be arranged,' he said softly. 'But it's a big, big call. The amount of trust involved is enormous.'

I said, 'But that's just it. That's what trust is all about. Your friend knows he can't ever screw me. I'm comfortable with that situation. So comfortable, in fact, that it's so much easier to make a major investment with this guy in something as subjective as horses. You understand my point?'

'Totally,' Steer said. 'Completely.'

The cars were at the kerbside behind us, throwing billows of exhaust up into the night.

He said, 'My friend is a very cautious man. But he would understand exactly where you're coming from. At the same time, he would need a very significant down payment of your total commitment to him before he would reveal himself in the way you suggest.'

'How much?'

'He would require $100 million of the $250 million upfront in US 3-month T-B, registered in my name for convenience.'

You have some neck, I thought.

'I'm pretty sure I want to meet your friend. But let me call you tomorrow,' I said.

He came in again for the hug.

'Keep safe, Joe.'

'I'll call you.'

I sat into the car and as we pulled away. Never before, ever, had I felt so spent.

73

It was after midnight when I walked into the foyer of the Crillon. My first thought was: I've been set up. Sam Landy was sitting there on a sofa. He stood up.

I said, 'What are you doing here?'

'Can we talk?'

The man looked as ill as I felt. I asked, 'How did you know where I was?'

Sam shook his head, not to deflect my question but in a gesture of despair. His mouth opened and for a moment he was unable to speak. I didn't understand.

Sam said, 'I made a mistake.'

I took him up to my suite on the first floor. Sam sat down heavily into an armchair.

'Do you want to tell me what's going on?' I asked.

'I have a confession to make.'

This was too much, I thought. 'What?'

'I wasn't straight with you.' Sam's voice wavered from its usual, assured tone. 'I could say I was afraid for your safety in this whole scheme, but although that would be true, it wouldn't be the whole truth. I suppose, to be completely honest, I wanted to keep tabs on you.' He took a deep breath. 'I had you followed.'

'You – *what*?'

Sam nodded. 'From the moment you left Mount Landy.'

'Jesus Christ.'

'I'm a fool, I know. But I wanted some insurance.'

I could not absorb this. 'Who the fuck did you have follow me?'

Sam closed his eyes. 'My manager. Sean Free.'

For a moment the images overwhelmed everything:

Leicester Square Underground, the coral reef off San Felipe, Dunty Rainway. And today in Saint-Cloud. The strength of madness.

I asked, 'Did Silken know?'

Sam shook his head.

I suddenly felt very angry. 'For God's sake! He knew my every move. It was him all the time.'

Sam appeared defeated. 'I've known Sean since he was a child. He grew up on Mount Landy. I could ask him to do anything. I don't know what I would have done without him when my wife was dying.' Sam's voice broke and he caught his breath sharply. 'Sean actually carried her from the helicopter into Mount Landy when she came home to die.'

I said, 'It's about Silken with him, isn't it?'

Sam nodded. 'He's obsessed with her. He's got a problem with women.'

'Go on.'

'There was an incident in Slow Creek, years ago. With a local girl. He beat her very badly, he would have done time if I hadn't intervened. He had to undergo a psychological assessment as part of the deal. They said he was emotionally unstable. That he needed treatment.' Sam looked at me forlornly. 'That was years ago. I put the report in a drawer, did nothing about it. I sent him on courses, including a five month *stage* here in Chantilly. Five years ago I put him in charge of security. He's been the most loyal employee anyone could wish for.'

'And then . . .' I said, although by then I knew.

'Then Silken came home. In the very first week of her arriving in Mount Landy, she went out with Sean and they had a brief affair. Silken is a sophisticated girl, she grew up in Hollywood. But now it seems that Sean could not accept that she didn't want to continue their relationship. The old emotional problems. Mount Landy is his home. He saw Silken and himself in charge there.' Sam shuddered. 'Then you arrived.'

'Oh, Jesus,' I said as I felt undiluted fear. 'Sam, where is he now?' I asked.

'He's right here in Paris,' Sam said. 'And he's got Silken.'

74

We sat in silence. The level of my exhaustion was over-whelming me.

I said at last, 'What does he want?'

'She just phoned. She says he wants to marry her,' Sam said. 'It's all crazy, but that's what she says he wants.'

I saw an old and beaten man sitting in front of me.

'If it's of any interest to you,' I said, 'I've just had dinner with Steer. He as good as told me that he had Tricky Dawson taken care of.'

Sam's mobile rang. He looked at me. His expression was that of the lost.

'Sean?'

Sam nodded.

'Tell him you'll meet him,' I whispered. 'Ask him to nominate a place. Do it!'

Sam put the phone to his ear. He said, 'Yes, Sean. Yes.' Then he held out the instrument between the two of us as a stream of invective flowed out into the room.

I nodded, urging the old man to do what I'd said.

'Sean, Sean, we must meet,' Sam said. 'I know, I know. No, there'll be no police. I give you my solemn word.' He winced as he listened. 'Very well, on my wife's memory I swear there'll be no police.' He began writing on a telephone pad. 'Very well. In an hour,' he said and disconnected.

'Well?'

'He's crazy,' he said. 'He'll kill her.' I saw sweat on his forehead and all of a sudden he went short of breath. 'My . . . pills . . .'

He was helpless. I found a card of pills in his pocket,

popped out two and cupped them to his mouth. Sam swallowed them. He sat back, ashen, but his breathing was steady. 'Oh my God, what have I created?' he asked in a whisper.

I took the pad and looked at the directions.

'Sam, we're going to do a deal', I said, 'and this one is going to stick.'

He looked at me emptily. Then he said, 'Very well. What do you want me to do?'

'I want you to put the original plan back on track. Steer will come to Ireland if he believes that by doing so he'll get me to invest with him as a co-partner in his bloodstock. You set that up.' I stood up. 'Meanwhile, I'll go and find Silken. Deal?'

Sam's eyes were somewhere else. Seeing what? Better days when money still seemed able to buy happiness, I imagined.

'I'll do it.' He stood up, but he was suddenly no taller than my shoulder. We shook hands. 'Good luck,' he said, tears standing in his eyes.

The taxi left the Périphérique by the Port d'Orléans and drove south on the A6 for Orly airport. Three a.m. We came to an intersection and followed the signs for Rungis. The road we had joined was busy with trucks, despite the hour.

'*Vous voulez le marché?*' enquired the driver. 'Do you want to go the market?'

'*Le Chat Noir*,' I said, looking to the pad. 'Another kilometre.'

Darkness clung resolutely, the yellow lights of the motorway and of vehicles accentuating the night. Strangely, I felt no personal antipathy towards Sean Free, unlike what I now felt about Steer. Sean needed help, but

Steer would scorn it. One was partly child, the other a devious manipulator. All at once a purple strip of neon broke from the night.

'*Le Chat Noir*,' the driver said and pulled in.

It was a truck stop, what the French call a *routier*, and although the time was now three-thirty a.m. the car park was almost full. The taxi pulled up between two trucks and I got out. What was Sean's reason for choosing here, I wondered? Or did reason come into it? I kept in shadow and made my way forward to get a view of the parking lot. Yellow arc lights caught a light mist in their ambit. I saw the hub caps first. The car was parked just outside the pool of yellow visibility, but not quite far enough to be completely hidden. A Volvo. Edging along by a row of trucks, conscious that I must be visible, I tried to get nearer. Then, as if in answer to my wish, slowly the car glided forward, into the glare, twenty metres from me.

I saw Silken at once, realizing as I did, that I had been meant to. She was sitting upright in the front seat. Her head was taped by the mouth and neck to the seat's headrest. Her arms were not visible. The driver's door opened slowly. Sean was dressed in a black anorak. His face, last seen in the sunlight of New South Wales, looked unhealthy in this light.

I said, 'Hello Sean.'

'Where's Mr Landy?'

'Mr Landy's not well, Sean. He asked me to come.'

'You.'

'I'm the only person he had to ask.' I took a step nearer. 'If it's any consolation to you, I've nothing against you. That's the truth.'

'You.' I was too far away to see his face in detail, but his voice quivered. 'I should have killed you the day I saw you with her. In the river.'

I remembered. He'd driven up on a quad, out of nowhere.

'Sean, this is not the way to do this.'

'You don't tell me what's right or wrong!' His voice rose.

I said, 'Let her go, Sean. Mr Landy wants to see her. He's waiting.'

'And if I do? Will you let her go? Will you leave her be? Leave her with me?'

It was hard, even then, hearing his words, looking at him standing there, to understand that sanity was playing no part in this.

He said, 'You want her, then follow me, but keep your distance.' Then he got back into the Volvo and started the engine.

I ran to the taxi and we hung behind the tail lights of the Volvo as it headed out of the lot and turned right. At that moment I had so much to regret, that now to add my impetuousness in coming out here alone seemed unnecessarily harsh. Instead I tried to figure how Sean's mind would work. What he would most like to achieve. A world without me seemed high on the agenda. The Volvo turned right and I saw lights on the horizon.

We had driven only a few kilometres. What looked like the outline of warehouses, or perhaps a shopping centre, came into view. There was a toll booth and we went through it after the Volvo.

'Where are we?' I asked the driver.

'*Marché du Rungis,*' he replied.

Free's car drove in a slow loop around a building as big as an aircraft hangar. At one end of it a door stood open. Inside, at waist-high benches, tall black men with mallets were smashing open the unattached heads of cattle. We drove on. The road dipped. Rose. Further buildings now appeared. All of a sudden my nostrils were overpowered by the stench of fish. Figures in long white rubber aprons, their hair in nets, hauled trolleys stacked high with ice-packed polystyrene boxes. The smell was as strong as chloroform. I heard the taxi driver gasp, then curse. The Volvo was going around the gable end of one huge building, past dozens of refrigerated trucks. We were in darkness again, around the very back of the fish market. Sean had pulled up and was standing beside his car, the engine running. He held a gun in his hand. The taxi stayed two dozen paces back and I got out.

'Send the cab home, Joe,' Sean called. 'And don't try anything silly or I'll kill her.'

He waited until the noise of the taxi's engine had vanished, then he walked around to the passenger door. I could see a livid line running down the left side of his face, from eye to mouth. Where my fingernails had scored him in Saint-Cloud.

'Sean, you can have anything you want – just as long as you let Silken go. You have Mr Landy's word on that.'

'Shut up!'

I could see her eyes. I thought of the first time I had really had those eyes to myself – or thought I had had. I looked around to see if anyone else was in the vicinity, but other than the sound of the Volvo all I could hear was the air-conditioning of the huge fish halls. The fish smell was nauseating.

'Walk over there, into the car lights,' Sean said.

I made my way in a cautious circuit around him. Suddenly I could make out the topography of the place: we were up one level, on a ramp designed for trucks to back up on. Signs with red no-go lines through their centre prohibited access. Then I saw where he was sending me.

Below the lip of the ramp, about two metres down, were tanks containing fish offal.

'Turn around when you reach the edge,' Sean said, his voice suddenly much nearer.

I turned to him. The car's lights were full in my face and I could see nothing. It was, I realized, the perfect place to dispose of a body – in hundreds of tons of decomposing fish. He wasn't completely mad.

'Sean – Mr Landy told me to bring you a message.'

'Mr Landy?'

'Yes. He told me to say that he loves you like a son. That he'll never forget the fact that it was you who carried Mrs Landy into the house when she came home to die.'

Although I was blinded, I could sense I had his attention.

'Are you going to throw all that away?' I asked. 'What's killing me going to achieve? You have a wonderful friend in Mr Landy. He'll forgive everything if you just stop now. But you must stop now, Sean. It's over.'

'Too right.'

I actually heard the knife blade whistle through the air. I jinked my head to one side and as I did so felt red-hot pain in my left shoulder. I grabbed out and caught fabric. Then I toppled back.

I did not expect to survive the fall, particularly with a man of over two hundred and fifty pounds falling on top of me. My first sensation was one of cold. Fighting to breathe, I realized there were layers of fish above me. I came up as something sharp lacerated my legs. The sensation that the other inhabitants of the tank were alive rather than dead, seemed to increase my sense of revulsion – to such an extent that for the moment I forgot Sean Free. I saw the rim of the tank and struck for it. Hauling myself up, trying with frenzy to lever myself out, I stopped as I saw a silhouette. Across the back of the tank ran a rigid pipe. His neck had met it on the way down. Somehow he had become lodged there, between the pipe and the far rim of the tank. His head was doubled back on his body. His dead eyes were staring at the ramp, as if expecting to see Silken.

75

Dawn was breaking over Paris as the Citroën Deux Chevaux van pulled up at the hotel. The driver was like a Frenchman from central casting, a black-bereted, Gauloise-smoking character with boxes of fish for shops in Paris. We'd sat amid *moules* and *huîtres* and shoals of white fish whose identities I would never learn. He refused my attempts to give him money.

I was numb. I'm not talking about a physical inability to feel external stimuli; I'm talking about a paralysis of the mind. Silken hadn't spoken since I'd untied her. Sam was sitting there at a table, a coffee in front of him. He got up when he saw us.

'I'm so sorry,' he said and put his arms around her. Then he sat down, face in his hands. 'Why?' he kept asking.

I had no answer. Nor did I need to be told that when it comes to life's main crossroads, that money can buy you nothing.

A waiter brought espressos and fresh croissants. My hand shook as I raised the cup.

'And now we go home', I said, 'and finish it.'

Part Five

76

I stood by the window of the private jet lounge in Dublin airport at nine-thirty am. The November day had begun grey and raining, but was now clearing to being simply grey and cold. There was a scream of engines and I saw the Falcon 900 touch down.

'Good luck,' said the Garda technician and touched my arm.

He left the room and moments later, on the other side of the building, I saw him get into a car. Fifteen minutes earlier he had fitted me with an Otis Tactical Throat Microphone, a lightweight elastic strap worn around my neck and now covered by my polo sweater. Sensitive enough to pick up a whisper, the mike would catch any conversation in the vicinity and transmit it to the miniature Sony tape recorder which was strapped to the small of my back. The gardai had considered using a transmitter instead of a tape, but the possibility that Bill Ruth might have a scanner to pick up such a device had ruled that out. The device was not going to work in the Bell 430 chopper to which Steer and I were due to travel down to Wicklow. I would activate it when we arrived.

The night before Mick had told me that some progress had been made in Amsterdam. Apparently a link had been established between the antiques dealer and a bank in the Isle of Man used by Steer. Not nearly enough yet to form a conclusive link between Steer and the contract killer, Crof, but a start. And enough for the Irish gardai to agree to go along with today's scam.

Now I saw the jet taxi in towards the building. Today when – if – Steer spoke, his words would be recorded. I had been given a palm-sized battery-operated transmitter to activate when I had him on tape. Mick and the Garda Special Response Unit would be waiting nearby, and when I gave them the signal they would move in.

The plane came to a halt and its steps dropped.

Although Sean Free's death had cleared most of the mystery about who had been trying to kill me these last weeks, the death of Stella, my housekeeper, and the attack on Hanny still remained to be accounted for. Maybe it had just been a grotesque coincidence. At this stage no better explanation existed.

Steer had seemed genuinely puzzled when I had called him in Paris with the invitation to Sam Landy's Wicklow pheasant shoot.

'You *know* Sam Landy?' he asked.

'Not from Adam,' I said, as rehearsed, 'but Tom Haines the trainer has asked me to do this. It's for a good cause – a kid's hospital someplace. Twenty-five thousand a man – I bought two.' I made a mental note that if we succeeded, for Sam and myself each to give twenty-five grand to the Crumlin Children's Hospital in Dublin. 'I understand it's one of the best shoots in the world. Your friend will like it.'

'My friend and Sam Landy don't see eye to eye on a few things,' Guy said with masterful understatement. 'I doubt Landy would want him there.'

'Haines has already told him I'm bringing your friend,' I said. 'Landy seemed fine with that. He just wants to raise money for charity.'

Over the phone line, Steer's doubt on the one side and his need for money on the other were palpable.

'I'm not sure my friend can make it. He's got to be in New York that day.'

'Then this will be on his way.'

'What about my friend's requirements?' he asked. 'Will

you be able to demonstrate a sufficient degree of trust to him? He has a lot going on, he has to go to New York. He needs to know now.'

'Tell him I am at this moment holding in my hand the hundred million dollars in T-Bills that he requires,' I said.

I could hear him suck in his breath.

I said, 'I'm having a contract drawn up, of course.'

'Of course.'

'I'm sure you'll find everything in order.'

I could hear his continuing hesitation. He didn't want to come to Ireland. He had retained all the instincts of the wilderness in which he had come of age. He felt uncomfortable at the thought of being even for a day in the country where he had had a man killed, and now his natural antennae were picking up something.

I said, 'Your friend can fly out to the States direct from Dublin. It'll be a fun day out.'

'OK,' he said slowly. 'I'll tell him. I'm sure he'll come.'

Now I watched him walk in from the tarmac, dressed in green tweed jacket and trousers and wearing a deerstalker hat. Two steps behind him came Cheetah with Tony Friar, then big Bill Ruth, carrying a gun case. The US Treasury bonds were in a fat envelope in my inside pocket. They had been arranged by Sam. But even with his financial muscle it had taken nearly forty-eight hours to put such an amount in place. We had considered using fake bonds, but I felt I knew Steer and that nothing short of the genuine article would work. Silken and Sam had agreed.

'What happens if he doesn't say what we want to hear?' I had asked.

'We can take him in anyway and question him for a few hours about Tricky's death,' Mick had replied, 'but I have a feeling that would be a waste of time.'

Now Steer came in for the hug. 'Joe!'

I winced, hoping he wouldn't feel the wire. 'Guy, I'm so glad you could make it.'

'Mr Joe,' said Bill Ruth.

'Heard any good jokes this morning, Bill?' I asked and Steer laughed, but Bill Ruth's face remained impassive.

Cheetah kissed me and we all went into the customs building in order that Steer could clear his shotguns – two 12-bore Purdeys with intricate scrolling on the metal of the stocks.

'Do you shoot?' I asked Friar as the customs official filled out a form. I had not expected Friar to be there.

'Nowadays I only fire blanks,' Friar grinned.

'Guy said we're going to a castle,' Cheetah said. 'I hope there's a fire. I've brought along a good thriller.'

I wondered what else she'd brought in her handbag. Whatever it was, I didn't envy her. Soon this sad woman's life of luxury would come crashing to dirt.

Steer signed the form, then we were all walking back out across the apron to the Bell. Steer's country clothes were expensive and looked as if they had been purchased that morning in Paris. The chopper, nose down, quivered for some moments a few feet above the apron. Then we roared up into the sky. It was all so easy. Too easy. Then I told myself that my pessimism was getting in the way of the facts. That's what I told myself.

We climbed over the south Dublin suburbs, over brown, bare-topped mountains and crossed into the green valleys and hills of Wicklow. The trip would take less than twenty minutes. Everyone wore a headset for communication, but Steer said little. Nor did he seem to take in much of the unfolding landscape, but stayed fixed on his own thoughts.

Mine were a jumble, starting with Lou and ending with Hanny, with Silken somewhere in between. The night before, Sam had called and told me that she would be at the shoot. I found myself counting the minutes until I saw her again. It was a primal feeling, something beyond my control. Maybe I needed counselling because, just at the point where I should have been sweeping Hanny off her feet and carrying her over a threshold, here I was longing for the sight of another woman. What set her apart to cause such longing in me? Her sense of danger, above all, I realized, the recklessness that had led us off the side of a cliff and into a river. Her look of wildness. This woman lived near death and danger and I found that irresistible.

The helicopter tilted slightly as the pilot realigned our flight path. I tried to concentrate on the task ahead and on the man sitting beside me in the helicopter.

'Two minutes,' the pilot's voice crackled in the headsets.

Sam's shoot was taking place on the Wicklow estate of an impoverished Irish earl, who reared pheasants in the tens of thousands to maximum plumpness on his otherwise barren acres, and who would that day provide beaters, loaders, drivers and pickers, and a picnic lunch by a gurgling winter stream, and afterwards, according to Sam, a slap-up supper and half-decent wine partaken in a stone-flagged, baronial hall before a massive fire. Today, if things went as planned, we'd not get to the supper and wine stage. I felt my ears pop. Gardens and a sprawling house came into view and we came in.

I saw Sam first. In a tweed peaked cap and a green padded jacket, he seemed to have shrunk even smaller than he had been in Paris. We hunched out from the helicopter and Sam came over – not to me but to Steer.

'Glad you could make it, Guy,' he said, the ever-genial host and they shook hands. 'Long time.'

'You look well, Sam,' Guy said.

Silken had been standing to one side, now she came over.

'Guy.'

'Here's my special girl.' As he kissed her she put her arms around his neck, drawing him close, and our eyes met. My longing for her was like a diving bell sinking through my guts.

'And you must be Mr Grace.' Sam turned to me, his aristocratic eyes empty of recognition. 'It's very kind of you to take the time.'

'My pleasure.'

Then Sam kissed Cheetah as if they met every other week and I shook hands with men in tweeds, among them Tom Haines, the Newmarket trainer and Sam's agent, George Scales. There were a few industrialists along too, people with whom Sam did business. The earl was called Johnnie. Further back stood about twenty men and youths, with dogs on leashes and stout sticks in their hands.

I asked to be excused and caught a knowing look from Sam as I was shown into a stone outbuilding with a toilet. A switch was located on the underside of the Sony. I turned it to on and flushed the toilet. When I emerged, Silken, Cheetah and Tony Friar had gone into the castle; it had begun to snow lightly. Sam was at the wheel of a Land Rover. The shooters, including Guy, were sitting up on straw bales on the back of a tractor trailer. I climbed up.

'Hang on!'

A man was running from the house, dragging one leg as he did so. He clambered aboard and I caught a delicate little spike of alcohol released on its maiden flight on the morning air.

'I'm really looking forward to this!' he chortled, extending his hand in my direction.

One of his eyes was half closed and his nose was skew ways.

'Dunty!' I exclaimed as we set out.

My shooting had all been done over the little, pocket-sized heather bogs of County Kildare. On winter days, before the light waned, my father and I would drive down boreens, put on boots and then walk two abreast across turf ground, heather to our knees. The snipe came in from the North Sea at the end of October. My old man had been a spectacular shot, his ratio of success on snipe had been over 75 per cent.

The snow had turned the Wicklow setting, already beautiful, into one of rich, almost theatrical embellishment. We trundled over an expanse of plough, all the tips crusted white. It was just eleven. I sat beside Steer on a straw bale. Bill Ruth sat on his other side. Dunty had produced a hip flask and it had already done one circuit of the trailer.

'You look well,' I said to the horse agent. He did, too, for a man I'd been told would never walk again.

'They said had I not been the clean-living type, I'd have been in real trouble,' Dunty chortled.

Down in the valleys each tree stood out, as if etched in silver. Sam had seen to it that Steer and I were put together for the first of the drives. The tractor, a big John Deere, stopped and several guns, including Sam, unloaded. The beaters had already gone ahead and were by now deep in the wood. We lurched off downhill and around the bottom end of the trees. Steer and I jumped down and the earl disembarked from his jeep and led the way to a wooden peg set back about thirty yards from the woodland.

'This is where you are, Mr Steer,' he said. 'Please only take birds with daylight behind them, not that you need to be told, I'm sure, but nowadays I spend my time stating the obvious.'

Bill Ruth unpacked Steer's guns, handed one to his employer, then put down a canvas bag and began removing boxes of cartridges. I was ushered further downhill by the earl, to the very lower extremity of the wood, and also given the safety talk. Then the earl scampered back uphill, leaped into his Land Rover and drove out of sight.

It was cold, but incredibly quiet. A mist lay between us and the valleys. I hoped Mick was in place.

78

Mick told me later about the scene. They were sitting in a VW Transporter: Mick, a Garda superintendent from Wicklow who was in charge of the operation, a technician from the Garda Technical Bureau and two police marksmen from the ERU, the Emergency Response Unit. Together with two armed detectives and two Garda officers in an unmarked police car from Arklow, and a four-wheel drive Mitsubishi jeep with a driver and two further ERU officers, the team had placed themselves on the side road running parallel to the estate and within five hundred yards of the first two drives.

The emerging Amsterdam connection had been crucial in persuading the Gardai to go ahead with this operation. They had also gone through copies of all the original Ito files I'd passed to Tricky and had concluded that Steer, whether or not he was guilty of murder, was certainly a high-class con artist. If they could now get him on tape admitting to Tricky Dawson's death, it would be enough to detain him in Ireland.

For the purposes of that morning's business, it had been considered involving the earl, but Sam had advised against it: the earl's excitable nature, not to mention his old-fashioned views on hospitality were not, in the end, thought auspicious for the type of co-operation needed.

Nevertheless, the fact that Steer would be armed, an unprecedented case of actually allowing the intended target to have a weapon, meant that Sam had been obliged to take with him, as a further guest, a member of the ERU. So a detective named Jeff May, equipped with an earpiece, dressed in immaculate tweeds and deerstalker and carrying

a 12-bore shotgun, not to mention a concealed Smith and
Wesson .45 automatic, had joined Sam's party at the
Wicklow estate to await our chopper.

Mick and the superintendent were drinking coffee in the
van. They could now see us in the distance through field
glasses from behind the one-way, blacked-out side-panel.
The gardai watched as a number of guns disembarked,
then the tractor headed downhill and out of sight. The
garda driver started the van and followed the downhill
camber of the boreen. The men in the van could hear the
cries of the beaters.

79

Steer stood less than fifty yards uphill of me, gun folded on the crook of his arm. I thought of Cheetah's story of the two young boys in the Canadian wild, and how there had been days when their meals had relied on his aim. He turned, looked at me, smiled. Bill Ruth was holding the second gun, loaded.

All at once there came the sound of shouts and clatter in the distance as the beaters moved into the top end of the wood. I'd worked that end of shoots myself as a boy and now the excitement came back, the primal sense of hunter and hunted, as the birds began to explode from bracken upwards through trees and the first guns spoke.

Steer and I were in the optimum position. I saw the first of the pheasants, as if miles away, sailing down towards us over all the tree tops. All at once, from right to left, I saw a pair of woodcock flit like thieves along the tree tips. Instinctively I brought up my gun, but there were two shots to my right and both birds fell. I looked around. Steer was already taking his loaded gun from Bill Ruth.

With the wind behind them, the pheasants were looming into range, clucking and squawking. I saw Steer take down a left and right, then smoothly take the once-more loaded gun from Ruth. A big cock pheasant barrelled over my head and I shot him. The bird folded in flight. I could hear him hit the field behind me as I turned to take another.

The numbers of birds increased; when I had shot six I stopped. But Steer was enjoying himself. I could see the way he fitted his guns, the way his cheek lay aligned along the stock, the way he led the bird with his barrels. This was his environment. Not the driven shoots of wealthy men, but the raw contest. Birds lay thick on the ground within a fifty-yard arc of him. He never missed.

Then there came a shrill whistle. The guns went silent. Out through the near trees broke the beaters and gillies with dogs.

'My word!' said the earl, as his eyes surveyed the dead birds.

The tractor chugged around the corner, Sam and his other guests already on it.

'How far is it to the next drive?' I enquired.

'Not far at all,' the earl said.

I said to Steer, 'Why don't we walk, just you and me?'

'Good idea,' he said. 'Why don't you let Bill carry your gun?'

Our eyes met. 'No problem,' I said.

80

We climbed a stile and walked across a green field on which the earlier snow had already begun to melt. Bill Ruth was carrying the guns in their sleeves and walking twenty yards behind us. There was a little stream with a stone bridge spanning it.

'Why don't we go over here?' Steer suggested.

We sat on the bridge. The icy water was choppy and very noisy.

'Did you bring my friend his bonds?' Steer asked.

'Sure, here they are.'

I took out the envelope. I wondered if the sound of the water was washing out our words. He took the envelope, slit it open, removed the bonds and fanned them with his thumb. Then very carefully he examined each bond in turn. He was smiling when he had finished.

'All here, Bill,' he called.

I frowned. Bill Ruth was now speaking into a mobile phone. I stood up.

'Over to you,' I said.

'Well, it's like this,' Steer said. 'My friend would have liked to take this further, Joe, he really would. But, unfortunately, it didn't work out like that.'

I heard a click and turned. I was looking down the barrels of my own shotgun. And then I heard the distinct sound of a helicopter.

'As much as twitch and he'll blow your head off,' Steer said.

Ruth moved in and rested the cold steel under my jawbone. Steer reached to my neck and yanked off the Otis. Flinging it into the water, he then rasped his fingers.

'The tape-recorder. Very gently. Please.'

I wondered if I could activate it, but then I saw Bill Ruth's eyes and I knew he was craving to waste me. I took out the Sony recorder. Steer snatched it from my hand and threw it over the bridge. The chopper was nearer.

'How did you find out?' I asked.

Steer laughed. 'I've known from day one,' he said and shrugged sympathetically. 'Sorry. I do regret what happened to your sister, by the way. But . . . sorry.'

'And Tricky?'

Steer frowned. 'Can you imagine the *damage* a bastard like Tricky Dawson can do? Can you? He had nothing – no responsibility, nothing. Yet he could destroy everything I've spent my life working to build up. For what? To sell a few hundred extra copies of a fucking newspaper.'

'So – you had him killed.'

Steer shook his head as if I were stupid, which was not an unreasonable proposition. 'Jesus no. Of course not! The little fuck died of natural causes, there was a post-mortem.'

A silver-coloured Sikorsky helicopter was suddenly and hugely over our heads.

I shouted, 'Did the same people who killed Tricky and Lou then come to my house on your instructions and kill the innocent woman they found working there? Before they tried to kill Hanny?'

Steer looked at me in genuine puzzlement. The chopper began to descend. I saw Bill Ruth thumb forward the safety of my gun.

81

I looked into Steer's empty eyes. The chopper's blades were churning up the grasses all around us. He nodded and Bill Ruth took two steps back, gun to his shoulder. And then utterly without warning, Dunty Rainway appeared behind him and was walking towards us, his face shining like an effervescent tomato. He was holding out a hip flask.

Bill Ruth's head turned minutely. I launched myself at him, the source of greatest danger. Ruth side-stepped daintily, took down Dunty with the right barrel, then swung back. I was dead, I knew. And then as I winced for the choke barrel, I saw – saw, not heard, because the helicopter meant I could hear nothing – Bill Ruth gasp. He flung his arms up. His eyes were already dead. A round, coin-sized wound had appeared in his throat. I looked uphill. A man in tweeds whom I had taken to be a beater was holding a pistol double-handed at arms' length, looking for his next target. The helicopter pilot had seen the trouble and had backed off. Steer ran to the chopper. I stared. A woman was at the door, stretching her hand to him. The eddies of air and the swirling blades made it difficult to see her. I just stared. At the upturned eyes. Silken. She was throwing Steer a machine-gun.

'Watch out!'

As Steer caught the gun and pivoted, I began to roll. A yellow burst of semi-automatic fire followed. It cut into the man holding the pistol and made him cough a red cloud. I was still rolling, trying to find cover. I reached for my shotgun, which lay beside Bill Ruth, caught it up in both hands and, rolling all the time, squeezed off the choke barrel at the chopper. The windscreen fell in and the machine seemed to rear. I'd done it on auto-pilot, without thinking of who was in it. I saw Steer fall back on the grass. Up went the helicopter on its tail, as if performing a trick. It climbed vertically for maybe fifty feet. I saw the woman's face. She was calm. And very beautiful, I thought. Then ever so slowly the chopper eased over, belly up, and thrashing deafeningly it plummeted into the wood a hundred yards away. I buried my head. The explosion of high-octane aviation fuel sucked all the oxygen from the immediate environment. My hair went on fire. I rolled into the stream.

82

I climbed from the water as if into another world. To one side trees were burning merrily. There was a strong smell of flesh. Across the bridge were parked a number of vehicles, including the tractor and trailer. At least a dozen men, some of then gardai in uniform, had appeared. One of them was giving Bill Ruth mouth-to-mouth resuscitation – a waste of time since the man was dead as mutton. Another guard was bent over Dunty.

'Is he—?'

'Got him in the leg,' the policeman said.

'Dunty?'

Dunty's eyes flickered open.

'Flesh wound,' he said and winced. 'Often got into far worse trouble at a horse sale.'

I had to grin.

'Go and catch the fucker,' Dunty said.

It was only then I realized that Steer wasn't there.

'Where does that track lead?' asked a big man in an anorak, who I later learned was the superintendent. He was addressing the earl. Stunned at events, the earl could not speak. One of the beaters told the policeman that the track led back up to the public road.

I asked, 'Where is Sam Landy?'

No one had seen him or the Land Rover.

'Perhaps he's gone back to the castle,' the earl suggested, although it sounded unlikely.

It was snowing thickly now. A four-wheel-drive Mitsubishi with Mick and the other members of the ERU team slewed down the hill. The super ran over and jumped on board. I was behind him. He got in.

'This is operational,' he said to me. 'Stay here.'

'Operational my bollocks,' I said, 'what have I been doing for the last three months?'

But Mick just shrugged as the super shut the Mitsubishi's door in my face. They left in a huge spray of mud and when it had cleared they were halfway to the wood. I looked around. The morning seemed to oscillate between frantic activity and, as now, utter calm.

I said to the numb-faced earl, 'What way will he try to get back to the other helicopter?'

The earl seemed, however dimly, to be tuning in. 'He could try and come out the bottom of the wood and come around by the lake.'

I said, 'Unhitch the trailer.'

The earl nodded and two of the gillies came forward and took out the holding pin and then uncoupled the heavy trailer from the John Deere. The earl climbed up beside me in the cab. He slammed the door.

'There are some people I shan't be inviting back,' he murmured.

I had not been in a tractor in quite a while, but then this was not a day for regular activities. I hit the revs, stuck her into gear and we were halfway towards the bottom of the wood before I realized I had forgotten my shotgun.

83

A gate below the fringe of the wood led into a long, down-hill field, at whose further extremity the land flattened out into snipe grass and bogland. I could hear little now above the tractor engine. I blotted out the facts as they had unravelled. My concern for Sam was the only thing on my mind, for it was no longer possible that Steer was going to escape. And yet the vastness of the bleak landscape was not reassuring. We roared downhill, the earl bracing his legs against the dashboard. I stopped, opened the door of the cab and stood out on the footplate. I could see no move-ment or life.

'You drive,' I said, and the earl eased over behind the wheel. The sight of a man being killed, although not my first, had happened with such brutal simplicity. This was the world Steer had created. A casino where people played for the very highest stakes. Bill Ruth had just lost all his chips. So had an Irish detective. Nothing made sense – except the fact that Guy had the T-Bills.

Then I saw the Land Rover. It had driven much further than I could have imagined and was making its way across the bottom fields, hoping to escape by the longest route. The earl powered the throttle and launched the John Deere. The jeep was on the headland and travelling at its maximum speed, bouncing up and down at every rut and indentation. A closed gate appeared and we burst through it. Now at the base of the land trees appeared to our right and I lost sight of Steer. We kept going, but the terrain was marshy and the tractor needed a lower gear. There was a gap. A flock of pigeons, hungry in the weather, flew up in a slate-grey cloud. This field rose slightly and we made for

the crown of it to get a view. The day had clouded further
and there was a persistent mist, which added to the sense
of desolation. I wondered where the ERU team was. No
sight or sound of another vehicle. The earl switched off the
engine and we both got out to listen. I could hear nothing.
My sense of location told me that the jeep still had to be in
front of us, that Steer would still have to drive further
along the right-to-left axis of the estate in order to try and
regain the house. If that was his plan, of course, for there
was nothing guaranteed about my hunch, he could have
seen us and be heading directly away from our position.

'He must have gone for the road,' the earl said.

I wasn't convinced. I walked fifteen yards towards the
ditch, to try and hear better. There was an engine sound.
I turned. The jeep was hurtling for me.

84

I threw myself to one side and felt agony in my leg. The jeep screamed past. I knew what would happen next. I stayed down and crawled for the tractor. Lead pinged from the chassis as Steer, one-handed, fired a shotgun from the window. I looked around for the earl, then saw him face down about twenty yards out. Abruptly, the jeep did a U-turn and tore down the field to the left in the direction of the house.

I could put no weight on my left foot. I rolled the earl over on his back. His sightless eyes confirmed that he had just hosted his last shoot. Using my arms, I levered myself back up into the cab. I could see the tail lights of the jeep as it negotiated the stone piers of a gateway at speed, slamming off one pier as it went through and out of sight. I put the throttle to maximum and pointed the tractor.

I was possessed by something between hopeless rage and desperation. I just wanted to end it. I took a fence of sheep wire at the boundary and kept going. The jeep was in heavy ground to my right, fifty yards ahead. The John Deere rode the sloppy ground like a big ship. Small birch trees and pieces of exposed bog oak were swept aside. I aimed for the jeep. I was on its passenger side, but could not see Sam. Neither, at this angle, could Steer see me to get a shot. I slammed the throttle for the absolute limit. We were going so fast that suddenly the jeep seemed stationary. I hit it broadside and it flipped over, rolling, two entire revolutions, until it came to a rest, upright, in a gripe.

My leg was hot with pain as I slid down. About twenty yards from the jeep, blood all over his face, Steer was standing, holding a shotgun. His chest rose and fell.

'Why?' he asked. 'Why?'

'It was just how it worked out,' I said.

He shook his head, as if still coming to terms with my part in events. 'He was nothing.'

'He was a man.'

'We could have had a lot of fun.'

I said, my own voice a stranger to me, 'Look, you can't get out of here, the place is surrounded.'

He said, 'Well, Joe, that may well be, but if there's no way out for me, there's certainly not one for you.' He brought up the gun. 'No way at all.'

I heard the shot. I was confused because I had always been told that one heard the shot after one felt it, not before. And, so far as I could tell, I felt nothing. And then I saw Steer's upper body flower into bright red as he fell. Sam was standing behind the jeep. He lowered his gun.

'That was for Elizabeth,' he said.

Epilogue

They say that in Ireland spring begins on the first day of February – and they may well be right. In February we Irish have already begun to talk about what we call 'the stretch in the evenings'. The countryside has begun to stir, ever so slightly. Snowdrops are up and on bright mornings you can smell the hope that has re-entered the world.

It was the second week of February, fifteen months after it had all taken place, and I was driving down into County Westmeath. Although the sun was still low, it flung generous yellow spars across the little fields and illuminated the headlands. My car was a refurbished E-Type Jaguar, the model most often said to be driven by men obsessed with their penis size. I reckoned I'd got beyond that – just about. I reckoned I'd got to the point where I could drive what kind of a car I wanted without it leading to a psychological assessment.

I was happy, for a change. I was, in fact, happy enough to be togged out in riding breeches and a tweed jacket, with a white hunting stock wrapped around my neck secured by a gold pin and riding boots encasing my lower legs. If I'd come out of the Guy Steer affair with nothing but a bundle of singed T-Bills and my love for horses and riding rekindled, then I was happy. I was happy too that Hanny was coming down to Westmeath to meet me after the hunt had concluded. We were staying that night in a small, local hotel, a find we'd made six months before, where the owner served roasted snipe and woodcock and bottles of Hermitage La Chapelle that he had hoarded away under his stairs. Life wasn't all bad.

A Garda inquiry had been held into the events in

Wicklow – and into those in Ringsend. A lot of hard
questions had been asked. In the end, it was decided that
everyone had acted properly. Tony Friar was arrested, but
denied he knew anything about the murders of Tricky or
Lou. He was released without charge. The trail from
Amsterdam to Steer's Isle of Man bank account was
established and a second person, the man who had helped
Anton Crof murder Tricky, was identified. He was a
criminal from London, but when the gardai went
enquiring after him, they found he had disappeared a year
before and was now presumed dead.

For a few days after Wicklow the Steer story was
headline news all over the world. Six people had died,
including Silken; the helicopter had disintegrated into
fragments, none bigger than six inches in length. The
bodies had likewise been cremated beyond all recognition.
The Steer organization was wound up and all the horses
were dispersed in a special sale. The banks took the biggest
hit. Alan Steer was put into a state mental institution in Los
Angeles. As for the others: Davey Delgado, the Doc and the
Piranha were still there, as far as I knew, on the fringes of
the horse business. It was really reassuring to think that if
I ever wanted to buy another horse, that such expertise
awaited me.

Cheetah had managed to sideline $5 million into
accounts in her own name and, although the banks had
tried to get it back, it looked as if they would fail to do so.
I was glad. Without that stash, I don't think she could have
survived – she could never make the climb back up again,
as she had out of Baton Rouge. It would be too hard. She
lived somewhere near Houston, Texas, I had last heard. I
hoped she had found happiness.

The little, cold fields and villages of Westmeath slid by.
I turned the car's heater off so that when I arrived at the

meet and got out I would not be perished. There was one development which no one expected: of the three horses I had purchased in Newmarket, two, the Rainbow Quest and the Kingmambo, both of them outstanding physical specimens that had cost Sam and myself nearly £15 million, were useless. One of them never even got to a race course and the other was slower than a wet week. But the third animal, the colt by Royal Academy whose fate had been decided by a tossed coin over breakfast in Claridge's, was turning out to be a star. He had triumphed in the important two-year-old races the previous autumn and was now winter, ante-post favourite for the Derby at Epsom. This had made Sam Landy the happiest man alive. Sam had needed some happiness after Silken.

I had never asked him too much – I never had to. Sam didn't have to give me chapter and verse in order that I understand how the daughter of his jilted mistress, of the woman who had expected to marry him and who had borne him his only child, had been raised in California in an atmosphere of naked hatred towards him. Silken had seen Guy Steer as her ticket to get even. She had helped him initially to swindle Sam as Mrs Landy lay dying, and then she had walked us into a trap of Steer's making. He had known from the start what we were up to. He had mirrored our own actions, duping us into thinking he had bought the sting. And in the end he had nearly succeeded in getting the one thing he lacked: cash. I often thought of Steer. The truth was that part of me had liked him. Despised him for what he had done, of course, but still admired him. Or perhaps I recognized that he had certain qualities which, if only they could have been separated from the bad in him, would have redeemed the whole man. A fanciful notion, perhaps.

The events I'd been through now played more quietly in

my mind than they had in the immediate aftermath. I
pulled up beside the village pub. It was a Sunday. No more
than twenty horses ever followed these rag-taggle harriers.
The farmer who looked after my horse was standing
cheery faced to one side. I got out of the car.

Most of the other people I had encountered during the
Steer business were still in the same positions as they were
then: Tom Haines, Diana Bigge. Fizzy Wilson. Steer had
simply been someone passing through. They, on the other
hand, were part of a system that had endured for hundreds
of years and seemed likely to keep going in the same
fashion into the future. As for Dunty, he'd made a full
recovery and become a top agent. Last I heard, he'd cut
down on the booze. Not cut out, of course, just cut down.
But still . . .

The one loose end that had never been tied up was still
a loose end: Stella, my cleaning lady, had been killed and
Hanny attacked by someone unknown. Hanny had
described her assailant as a human frog. Mick, I knew, had
taken a close interest in the case, which was being pursued
by the Murder Squad. I thought his interest had gone on
permanent hold until two months before when Sam Landy
had died.

He must have been very lonely back in Mount Landy:
the daughter he had loved and Sean Free, the manager he
had trusted, were both dead. At dawn one beautiful
morning in Mount Landy, Sam had apparently gone out
riding alone, insisting that Jacquimo stay behind. They
found his horse six hours later, grazing at the river beside
his body at the spot where Silken and I had had our picnic
what now seemed like a century ago. Sam's neck was
broken. No one could say for certain what had happened.
It was assumed the horse had stumbled and thrown the
master of Mount Landy.

Mick called me a week later. 'I want to talk to you about Sam Landy,' he said.

So we met over pints and talked. Landy's empire was being dissolved and dispersed – the word was that the new master of Mount Landy would be the Sultan of Tamil.

'Who gets the money?' I asked.

'Some nephew in San Francisco he hardly knew,' Mick said. 'But that's what I want to talk about – Sam's relationships.'

I told him the little I had picked up from Silken and from Sam. After half an hour I was none the wiser. 'Why are you interested?' I asked.

'His neck was broken,' Mick said thoughtfully. 'They've emailed me over the post-mortem report.'

'And?'

'Stella's neck was broken', Mick said, 'in almost exactly the same way.'

Hanny and I had been out to dinner in Howth the night before and I'd slept late. Now the other hunt followers had drunk their half-ones and were coming out of the pub, laughing and bantering with each other. I put on my hard hat, locked the car and walked over to my horse. He was a big, rangy half-bred, well over seventeen hands high. I called him Blackie. I took a carrot from my pocket. Blackie knew the routine. His upper lip curled back in anticipation. I felt his soft muzzle in my palm.

'Good man, Blackie.'

I mounted.

After Wicklow it had taken me weeks to stop seeing Silken at every corner, in every shop window. All deaths reduced mankind and hers had reduced me. I had wanted her, I would always remember – wanted her, even when I knew what she was. Seen through the chopper's blades, the image of her face, slightly blurred, had remained powerfully in my memory.

We clip-clopped out of the village, down past a row of houses, up a lane and into a field. The harriers spread out like a tan cloak ahead of us, immediately giving tongue as they picked up the scent of a hare on the soft morning. I felt my excitement surge. I gave Blackie his head. We were off.

Hanny and I had spent the Christmas after Wicklow with friends in Beaver Creek, Colorado. We skied most days. The mountain air brought molecules of sanity into my blood. When we got home she gave up her flat in Jervis Street and moved in with me to Howth. We didn't talk of marriage. It seemed safer not to. We still had not got to that point – and perhaps never would.

The hounds cast in circles for ten minutes, then found the scent of a fox and headed due west. Blackie loved it when we were hunting. As he warmed up he began to stand back from his ditches and give me the sort of airborne thrill that sticks your stomach to the roof of your mouth. We came to a gorse cover and the hounds ran into it, howling. The hunt followers stood over to one side, the horses' flanks heaving. Something made me turn my head. Alone on a little rise fifty yards away stood a solitary white horse ridden by a woman.

I had not seen her at the meet, but then I had been late. What I now noticed most was how well she sat her horse, her inherent athleticism, the length of her leg and the fact that she wore a veil. That was sexy. Anachronistic, yes, but sex is not something that goes out of date. The hounds' cries suddenly rose an octave and the chase resumed, arrow straight across some of the most unspoiled landscape left in Europe.

The veiled woman was superbly mounted. I found myself watching the line she was taking: a little to the right of the other horses as she correctly anticipated the direction. We met a series of ditches into which immense white boulders had been incorporated. Rapidly, the field thinned. One moment the woman and I were on the fringe of half a dozen horses; the next it was just the two of us, wither to wither, our horses rising to the fences, the sense of competition and the resolve not to quit like zest in the air.

We hunted like this for nearly fifteen minutes. The ground had become steep and the hounds were halfway up a hill, panting, sniffing around the mouth of a deep earth. We pulled up and I looked back and down. We had left the others so far behind that it seemed we were the only living creatures in that immense landscape.

'That was amazing!' I said and as I did so caught an airborne block of her scented perfume. My mind rushed back. The scent was sandalwood.

'I'm glad you think so.'

I stared. The woman, still astride, was calmly pointing a palm-sized pistol at my face.

'What the—'

Very slowly she lifted the veil.

'Silken—?'

'Get down, Joe.'

I was shaking as I did what she said.

'How—?'

I felt a hammer in my chest as my lungs battled to overcome the shock. I thought of Sam, of Stella. Of a lithe but murderous green frog.

'Kneel down.'

I did that too. I heard a footfall and realized she had dismounted. She stood, the reins of her horse looped over her arm. Blackie was grazing to one side, unconcerned at what was about to happen.

'Look at me.'

I turned and saw the unwavering snout of the gun. Again, her face, too beautiful ever to forget. And then it dawned on me. 'In Wicklow – that was your mother, wasn't it?'

She smiled. 'At last he understands.'

I said, 'It must have really rankled when Sam refused to marry her. At least when his wife was alive there was a reason. But when she died your mother must have seen herself as the rightful mistress of Mount Landy.'

In a motion too quick to follow, she swung her heel and kicked me in the side of the head. I went down.

'Sam Landy was pathetic,' Silken said, standing back. 'He exploited people. He didn't deserve happiness.'

'It takes some doing to poison a child against her father the way your mother poisoned you. It cost her her life.'

'No, you did,' she said, 'and now I'm going to do what I've been dreaming of ever since my mother died.'

'You made Sam's death look like an accident – but a corpse with a bullet is hardly usual at an Irish hunt,' I said.

She said, 'It doesn't matter any more. You're the last.'

She held the gun straight armed. As she did so her horse took a step back and pulled her slightly off-balance. I sprang. The gun roared and I felt heat across the top of my shoulder. The pistol spun from her hand and rolled down the hill. I spun around and felt something like a log hit the side of my head. Reeling back I saw her coming, hands flattened and out in front of her. She came in for me now, the air whistling. She could rotate her legs like cudgels. Again she caught me, this time where the bullet had gouged, and I cried out. Going down, I scooped gravel and flung it at her. She grunted. Her heel caught my jaw. I heard the bone click. The full force of her boot sank into my ribcage. She was making for the gun. I lunged for her, but

in this competition I was always going to be runner-up.
The horses were spooking at the fuss. I came up from the
ground and rammed into her, pushing her back up the hill.
She was wiry beyond my experience. And very strong.
Nonetheless I got her ten yards back up and away from the
gun before she chopped me viciously to the neck with both
her hands. Lights exploded in my eyes. Reflexively I swung
up with my head and caught her on the bridge of the nose.
She cried out. I tried to punch her, but she came in flat-
handed again for my throat as if she were trying to sever
my head. I fell back. And as I did, she too took a step back
in order to launch herself. I then saw the white horse.
White-eyed in terror, it pulled back. Silken's heels skidded.
She had stood on her horse's reins. The animal reared,
neighing. Silken fell under the hooves. Both her ankles
were bound together by the leather rein straps. The horse
turned, kicking out. I saw its hind hoof strike the side of
her head. Then it bolted, down the hill and Silken's inert
body was dragged along, pummelled with each stride by
the flying hooves.

I sat there for a very long time. The sun was going down,
as if conceding that everything was finally over. At last. I
was weak as a kitten. My biggest quandary was what to
tell Hanny when I got back to the village.

Blackie ambled around the side of a gorse bush and
made his way over to me. He was a magnificent hunter, an
animal capable of crossing country anywhere. I reached to
my pocket for a carrot and he came and nuzzled up for it.
Then he sauntered off, flicking his tail, cropping the grass.

I thought then of the man who had known the days
when thousands had cheered him home, when there was a
conduit of perfect understanding between him and the
horse beneath him. And I thought of Lou who had loved

him. Then I thought too of another hunter, at that moment at the other end of the world, chomping the grass in Mount Landy. The Hunter's sons and daughters and grandsons and granddaughters – and their progeny too – would continue to run and win on every continent of the world. As long as they did so, I thought, Tricky would never be dead. He had made it all possible. His presence on the great horse's back had been the difference between success and failure. And so The Hunter's progeny were Tricky's legacy. They would go on for hundreds of years – ever year another one of them became a stallion in his own right. They would be like stars in the sky.

Blackie knew I was still there, he was keeping one eye on me. I called him and he pricked his ears, just for a moment. I decided I'd tell him my story while I sat and waited for my energy to return. The full story. With nothing left out.

That's the good thing about horses. You can share secrets with them and no one will ever know.